UNDER HANDICAP

A NOVEL

JACKSON GREGORY

1st WORLD
LIBRARY
Literary Society

Under Handicap

Jackson Gregory

© 1st World Library, 2007
PO Box 2211
Fairfield, IA 52556
www.1stworldlibrary.com
First Edition

LCCN: 2007927836

Softcover ISBN: 978-1-4218-4550-0
Hardcover ISBN: 978-1-4218-4466-4
eBook ISBN: 978-1-4218-4634-7

Purchase *"Under Handicap"*
as a traditional bound book at:
www.1stWorldLibrary.com/purchase.asp?ISBN= 978-1-4218-4550-0

1st World Library is a literary, educational organization dedicated to:

- Creating a free internet library of downloadable ebooks

- Hosting writing competitions and offering book publishing scholarships.

Interested in more 1st World Library books?
contact: literacy@1stworldlibrary.com
Check us out at: www.1stworldlibrary.com

1st World Library Literary Society

Giving Back to the World

"If you want to work on the core problem, it's early school literacy."

- James Barksdale, former CEO of Netscape

"No skill is more crucial to the future of a child, or to a democratic and prosperous society, than literacy."

- Los Angeles Times

"Literacy... means far more than learning how to read and write... The aim is to transmit... knowledge and promote social participation."

- UNESCO

"Literacy is not a luxury, it is a right and a responsibility. If our world is to meet the challenges of the twenty-first century we must harness the energy and creativity of all our citizens."

- President Bill Clinton

"Parents should be encouraged to read to their children, and teachers should be equipped with all available techniques for teaching literacy, so the varying needs and capacities of individual kids can be taken into account."

- Hugh Mackay

TO

"MY LADY"

LOTUS McGLASHAN GREGORY

THIS BOOK IS DEDICATED

CHAPTER I

Outside there was shimmering heat and dry, thirsty sand, miles upon miles of it flashing by in a gray, barren blur. A flat, arid, monotonous land, vast, threatening, waterless, treeless. Its immensity awed, its bleakness depressed. Man's work here seemed but to accentuate the puny insignificance of man. Man had come upon the desert and had gone, leaving only a line of telegraph-poles with their glistening wires, two gleaming parallel rails of burning steel to mark his passing.

The thundering Overland Limited, rushing onward like a frightened thing, screamed its terror over the desert whose majesty did not even permit of its catching up the shriek of the panting engine to fling it back in echoes. The desert ignored, and before and behind the onrushing train the deep serenity of the waste places was undisturbed.

Within the train the desert was nothing. Man's work defied the heat and the sand and the sullen frown outside. Here in the Pullman smoking-car were luxury, comfort, and companionship. Behind drawn shades were the whir of electric fans, an ebon-faced porter in snowy linen, the clink of ice in long, misted glasses, the cool fragrance of crushed mint. Even the fat man in shirt-sleeves reading the Denver *Times*, alternately drawing upon his fat cigar and sipping the glass of beer at his elbow, was not distressing to look upon.

The four men busy over their daily game of solo might have been at ease in their own club.

At one end of the long car two young men dawdled in languid comfort, their bodies sprawling loosely in two big, soft arm-chairs, a tray with a couple of half-emptied high-ball glasses upon the table between them. They had created an atmosphere of their own about them, an atmosphere constituted of the blue haze from cigarettes mingled with trivial talk. The immensity outside might have bored them, so their shade was drawn low. For a moment one of the two men lifted a corner of it. He peered out, only to drop it with a disgusted sigh and return to his high-ball.

He was slender, young, pale-eyed, pale-haired, white-handed, anemic-looking. He was patently of the sort which considers such a thing as carelessness in the matter of a crease in one's trousers a crime of crimes. His tie, adjusted with a precision which was a science, was of a pale lavender. His socks were silk and of the same color. His eyes were as near a pale lavender as they were near any color.

"The devilish stupid sameness of this country gets on a man's nerves." He put his disgust into drawling words. "Suppose it's like this all the way to 'Frisco?"

His companion, stretching his legs a bit farther under the table, made no answer.

"I said something then," the lavender young gentleman said, peevishly. "What's the matter with you, Greek?"

Greek took his arms down from the back of his chair where he had clasped his hands behind his head, and finished his own high-ball. Nature in the beginning of things for him had been more kind than to his petulant friend. He was scarcely more than a boy—twenty-five, perhaps, from the looks of him—but physically a big man. He might have weighed a hundred and eighty pounds, and he was maybe an inch over six feet. But evidently where nature had left off there had been nobody to go on save the tailor. His gray suit was faultlessly correct, his linen immaculate, his hose silken and of a brilliant, dazzling blue. His face was fine, even handsome, but indicating about as much purpose as did his faultlessly correct shoes. There was an extreme, unruffled good humor in his eyes and about his mouth, and with it all as much determination of character as is commonly put into the rosy face of a wax doll.

"Seeing that you have made the same remark seventeen times since breakfast," Greek replied, when he had set his empty glass back upon the tray, "I didn't know that an answer was needed."

"Well, it's so," the pale youth maintained, irritably.

Greek nodded wearily and selected a cigarette from a silver monogrammed case. The cigarettes themselves were mono-grammed, each one bearing a delicately executed *W. C.* His companion reached out a shapely hand for the case, at the same time regarding his empty glass.

"Suppose we have another, eh?"

Again Greek nodded. The lavender young man reached the button, and a bell tinkled in the little buffet at the far end of the car. The negro lazily polishing a glass put it down, glanced at the indicator, and hastened to put glasses and bottles upon a tray.

"The same, suh?" he asked, coming to the table and addressing Greek.

It was the pale young man who assured him that it was to be

the same, but it was Greek who threw a dollar bill upon the tray.

"Thank you, suh. Thank you." The negro bobbed as he made the proper change—and returned it to his own pocket.

Greek appeared not to have seen him or heard. He poured his own drink and shoved the bottles toward his friend, who helped himself with skilful celerity.

"Suppose the old gent will hold out long this time, Greek?" came the query, after a swallow of the whisky and seltzer, a shrewd look in the pale eyes.

Greek laughed carelessly.

"I guess we'll have time to see a good deal of San Francisco before he caves in. The old man put what he had to say in words of one syllable. But we won't worry about that until we get there."

"Did he shell out at all?"

"He didn't quite give me carte blanche," retorted Greek, grinning. "A ticket to ride as far as I wanted to, and five hundred in the long green. And it's going rather fast, Roger, my boy."

"And my tickets came out of the five hundred?"

Greek nodded.

"It's devilish the way my luck's gone lately," grumbled Roger. "I don't know when I can ever pay—"

Greek put up his hand swiftly.

"You don't pay at all," he said, emphatically. "This is my treat. It was mighty decent of you to drop everything and come along with me into this d——d exile. And," he finished, easily, "I'll have more money than I'll know what to do with when the old man gets soft-hearted again."

"He's d——d hard on you, Greek. He's got more——"

"Oh, I don't know." Greek laughed again. "He's a good sort, and we get along first rate together. Only he's got some infernally uncomfortable ideas about a man going to work and doing something for himself in this little old vale of tears. He shaves himself five times out of six, and I've seen him black his own boots!" He chuckled amusedly. "Just to show people he can, you know."

Roger shook his head and applied himself to his glass, failing to see the humor of the thing. And while the bigger man continued to muse with twinkling eyes over the idiosyncrasies of an enormously wealthy but at the same time enormously hard-headed father, with old-fashioned ideas of the dignity of labor, Roger sat frowning into his glass.

The silence, into which the click of the rails below had entered so persistently as to become a part of it rather than to disturb it, was broken at last by the clamorous screaming of the engine. The train was slackening its speed. Greek flipped up the shade and looked out.

"Another one of those toy villages," he called over his shoulder. "Who in the devil would want to get off here?"

Roger sank a trifle deeper into his chair, indicating no interest. The fat man had dropped his newspaper to the floor and was leaning out the window.

"Great country, ain't it?" he called to Greek.

"Yes, it certainly *ain't!* What gets me is, why do people live in a place like this? Are they all crazy?"

The train now was jerking and bumping to a standstill. Sixty yards away was a little, bluish-gray frame building, by far the most pretentious of the clutter of shacks, flaunting the legend, "Prairie City." Beyond the station was the to-be-expected general store and post-office. A bit farther on a saloon. Beyond that another, and then straggling at intervals a dozen rough, rambling, one-storied board houses. For miles in all directions the desert stretched dry and barren. The faces of women and children peered out of windows, the forms of roughly garbed men lounged in the doorways of the store and the saloons. All the denizens of Prairie City manifested a mild interest in the arrival of Number 1.

"I guess you called the turn," sputtered the fat man. "Here come the crazy folks now!"

A cloud of dust swirling higher and higher in the still air, the clatter of hoofs, and two horses swept around the farthest house, carrying their riders at breakneck speed into the one and only street. At first Greek took it to be a race, and then he thought it a runaway. As it was the first interesting incident since Grand Central Station had dropped out of sight four days ago, he craned his neck to watch.

The two riders were half-way down the street now, a tall bay forging steadily ahead of a little Mexican mustang until ten feet or more intervened between the two horses. The train jerked; the Wells Fargo man, with his truck alongside the express-car far ahead, yelled something to the man who had taken his packages aboard.

"The bay wins," grinned the fat man. "It looks—Gad! It's a woman!"

Greek saw that it was a woman in khaki riding-habit, and that the spurs she wore were gnawing into her horse's flanks. He began to take a sudden, stronger interest. He leaned farther out, hardly realizing that he had called to the conductor to hold the train a moment. For it was at last clear that these were not mad people, but merely a couple of the dwellers of the desert anxious to catch Number 1. But the conductor had waved his orders and was swinging upon the slowly moving steps. From the windows of the train a score of heads were thrust out, a score of voices raised in shouting encouragement. And down to the tracks the woman and the man behind her rushed, their horses' feet seeming never to touch the ground.

A bump, a jar, a jerk, and the Limited was drawing slowly away from the station. The woman was barely fifty yards away. As she lifted her head Greek saw her face for the first time. And, having seen her ride, he pursed his lips into a low whistle of amazement.

"Why, she's only a kid of a girl!" gasped the fat man. "And, say, ain't she sure a peach!"

Greek didn't answer. He was busy inwardly cursing the conductor for not waiting a second longer. For it was obvious to him that the girl was going to miss the train by hardly more than that.

But she had not given up. She had dropped her head again and was rushing straight toward the side of the string of cars. Greek held his breath, a swift alarm for her making his heart beat trippingly. He did not see how she could stop in time.

Again a clamor of voices from the heads thrust out of car windows, warning, calling, cheering. And then suddenly Greek sat back limply. The thing had been so impossible and in the end so amazingly simple.

Not ten feet away from the train she had drawn in her horse's reins, "setting up" the half-broken animal upon his four feet, bunched together so that with the momentum he had acquired he slid almost to the cars. As he stopped the girl swung lightly from the saddle and, seeming scarcely to have put foot upon the sandy soil, caught the hand-rail as the car came by and swung on to the lowest step. The man behind her caught up her horse's reins, whirled, sweeping his hat off to her, and turned back.

"Which is some riding, huh?" chuckled the fat man, his own head withdrawn as he reached for his beer-glass.

"What's the excitement?" Roger's interest had not been great enough to send him to the window.

"Some people trying to catch the train," Greek told him, shortly. For some reason, not clear to himself, he did not care to be more definite.

"I don't blame the poor devils. Think of waiting there until another came by!" Roger washed the dryness out of his mouth with a generous sip of his whisky and seltzer.

The fat man finished his glass of beer and rang for another. Greek sat gazing out over the wide wastes of the desert. He had never before been in a land like this. Now that more than two thousand miles lengthened out between him and New York, he had felt himself more than ever an exile. Heretofore he had given no thought to the people dwelling here beyond the last reaches of those things for which civilization stood to him. He was not in the habit of

Jackson Gregory

thinking deeply. That part of the day's work could be left to William Conniston, Senior, while William Conniston, Junior, more familiarly known to his intimates as "Greek" Conniston, found that he could dispense with thinking every bit as easily as he could spend the money which flowed into his pockets. But now, as unexpectedly as a flash from a dead fire, a girl's face had startled him, and he found himself almost thinking—wondering—

Conniston turned swiftly. The girl was passing down the long narrow hallway leading by the smoking-car, evidently seeking the observation-car. Through the windows he could see her shoulders and face as she walked by him. He could see that there was the same confidence in her carriage now that there had been when she had jerked her horse to a standstill and had thrown herself to the ground. Even Roger, turning idly, uttered an exclamation of surprised interest.

She was dressed in a plain, close-fitting riding-habit which hid nothing of the undulating grace of her active young body. In her hand she carried the riding-quirt and the spurs which she had not had time to leave behind. Her wide, soft gray hat was pushed back so that her face was unhidden. And as she walked by her eyes rested for a fleeting second upon the eyes of Greek Conniston.

Her cheeks were flushed rosily from her race, the warm, rich blood creeping up to the untanned whiteness of her brow. But he did not realize these details until she had gone by; not, in fact, until he began to think of her. For in that quick flash he saw only her eyes. And to this man who had known the prettiest women who drive on Fifth Avenue and dine at Sherry's and wear wonderful gowns to the Metropolitan these were different eyes. Their color was elusive, as elusive as the vague tints upon the desert as dusk drifts over it; like that calm tone of the desert resolved into a deep, unfathomable gray, wonderfully soft, transcendently serene. And through the indescribable color as through untroubled skies at dawn there shone the light which made her, in some way which he could not entirely grasp, different from the women he had known. He merely felt that their light was softly eloquent of frankness and health and cleanness. Their gaze was as steady and confident as her hand had been upon her horse's reins.

"She must have been born in this wilderness, raised in it!" he mused, when she had passed. "Her eyes are the eyes of a glorious young animal, bred to the freedom of outdoors, a part of the wild, untamable desert! And her manner is like the manner of a great lady born in a palace!"

"Hey, Greek," Roger was saying, his droning voice coming unpleasantly into the other's musings, "did you pipe that? Did you ever see anything like her?"

Conniston lighted a fresh cigarette and turned again to look out across the level gray miles. Ignoring his friend, Greek thought on, idly telling himself that the Dream Girl should be born out here, after all. Here she would have a soul; a soul as far-reaching, as infinite, as free from shackles of convention as the wide bigness of her cradle. And she would have eyes like that, drawing their very shade from the vague grayness which seemed to him to spread over everything.

"I say, Greek," Roger was insisting, sufficiently interested to sit up straight, his cigarette dangling from his lip, "that little country girl, dressed like a wild Indian, is pretty enough to be the belle of the season! What do you think?"

Conniston laughed carelessly.

"You're an impressionable young thing, Hapgood."

"Am I?" grunted Roger. "Just the same, I know a fine-looking woman when I clap my bright eyes on her. And I'd like to camp on her trail as long as the sun shines! Say"—his voice half losing its eternal drawl—"who do you suppose she is? Her old man might own about a million acres of this God-forsaken country. If she goes on through to 'Frisco—"

"You wouldn't be strong for stopping off out here?" the fat man put in genially. Hapgood shuddered.

And to Greek Conniston there came a sudden inspiration.

"Anyway," Roger Hapgood went on in his customary drawl, "I'm going to find out. It's little Roger to learn something about the prairie flower. I'll soon tell you who she is," he added, rising from his seat.

But he never did. For one thing, young Conniston was not there when Roger returned five minutes later, and it is extremely doubtful if Roger Hapgood would have told how his venture had fared. Being duly impressed with the fascination of his own debonair little person, and having the imagination of a cow, he had smirked his way to the girl, who now sat in the observation-car, and had begun on the weather.

"Dreadfully warm in this desert country, isn't it?" he said, with over-politeness and the smile which he knew to be irresistible.

The girl turned from gazing out the window, and her eyes met his, very clear and very much amused.

"Very warm," she smiled back at him. Even then he had a faint fear that she was not so much smiling as laughing. "The surprising thing is how well things keep, is it not?"

"Ah—yes," he murmured, not entirely confident, and still dropping into a chair at her side. "You mean—"

"How fresh some things keep!"

Roger Hapgood's pink little face went violently red.

"I say!" he began. "I didn't mean any offense. I thought—"

"Oh, that's all right," she laughed, gaily. "No offense whatever. Will you please open that window for me?"

His face became normally pink again as he hastened to throw up the window in front of her. His eyelid fluttered downward as he met the regard of a couple of men facing them. Then he came back to her side.

"Thank you," she smiled sweetly up at him. And she held out her hand.

He didn't know what she wanted to do that for, but had a confused idea that in the free and easy spirit of the West she was going to shake hands. The next thing which he realized clearly was that she had dropped a shining ten-cent piece into his palm.

"Oh, look here," he stammered, only to be interrupted by her voice, a gurgle of suppressed mirth in it.

"I'm sorry that that's all I have in change! And now, if you will hand me that magazine—I want to read!"

Roger Hapgood fumbled with the dime and dropped it. He swept up the magazine from a near-by chair and held it out to her. As he did so he caught a glimpse of the faces of the two men at whom he had winked so knowingly, heard one of them break into loud, hearty laughter. Dropping the magazine to her lap, the lavender young man, with what dignity he could command, marched back to the smoking-car.

A few minutes later Greek Conniston, returning to the smoking-car, found his friend pinching his smooth cheek thoughtfully and frowning out the window. He dropped into his chair, deep in thought. In the brief interval he had taken his resolution, plunging, as was his careless nature, after the first impulse. The girl had interested him; he did not yet realize how much. She came aboard the train without bag or baggage. Certainly she could not be going far. And he—it didn't matter in the least where he went. All that he had to do was to keep out of his father's way until the old man cooled down, and then to wire for money. His ticket read to San Francisco, but he had no desire to go there rather than to any other place. And he told himself that he had a sort of curiosity about this bleak, monotonous desert land.

An hour later the train ran into another little clutter of buildings and drew up, puffing, at the station. Conniston's eyes were alert, fixed upon the passageway from the observation-car rather than on the view from his window. Mail-bags were tossed on and off, a few packages handled by the Wells Fargo man, and the train pulled out. Conniston leaned back with a sigh.

"Roger," he said, at last, "I've got a proposition to make."

"Well?"

"Let's drop off at one of these dinky towns and see what it's like. I've a notion we might find something new."

"That's a real joke, I suppose?"

"Not at all," maintained Conniston. "I'm going to do it. Are you with me?"

Hapgood sat bolt upright.

"Are you crazy, man!" he cried, sharply.

Conniston shrugged. "Why not? You've never seen anything but city life and the summer-resort sort of thing any more than I have. It would be a lark."

"Excuse me! I guess I'm something of a fool for having chased clean across the continent, but I'm not the kind of fool that's going to pick a place like this sand-pile to drop off in!"

"All right, old man. Nobody's asking you to if you feel that way."

Hapgood waited as long as he could for Conniston to go on, and when there came no further information he asked, incredulously:

"You don't mean that, do you, Greek? You don't intend to stop off all alone out here in this rotten wilderness?"

"Yes, I do. If you won't stop with me."

"But how about me? What am I to do? Here I am—busted! What do you think I'm going to do?"

"You can go on to San Francisco if you like. You can have half of what I've got left—or you can drop off with me."

Hapgood argued and exploded and sulked by turns. In the end, seeing the futility of trying to reason with a man who only laughed, and seeing further the disadvantage of being cut off from his source of easy money, Roger gave in, growling. So when the train drew into Indian Creek that afternoon there were three people who got down from it.

CHAPTER II

Indian Creek stood lonely and isolated in the flat, treeless, sun-smitten desert. Only in the south was the unbroken flatness relieved by a low-lying ridge of barren brown hills, their sides cut as by erosion into steep, stratified cliffs. Even these bleak hills looked to be twenty miles away, and were in reality fifty. Beyond them, softened and blurred by the distance, was a blue-gray line where the mountains were.

"Of all the wretched holes in the world!" fumed Hapgood.

But Conniston didn't hear him. The girl had stepped down from the train, and, without casting a glance behind her, walked swiftly across the wriggling thing which stood for a street in Indian Creek. There was a saloon with a long hitching-pole in front of it, to which a couple of saddle-horses were tied, and a buckboard with two fretting two-year-olds in dust-covered harness. A man, a swarthy half-breed, with hair and eyes and long, pointed mustaches of inky blackness, was on the seat, handling the jerking reins. He called a soft "*Adios, compadre*" to the man lounging in the doorway, and swung his colts out into the road, making a sweeping half-circle, bringing them to a restless halt, pawing and fighting their bits, at the girl's side. While with one brown hand he held them back, with the other he swept off his wide, black hat.

Jackson Gregory

"How do, Mess!" he cried, softly, his teeth flashing a white greeting.

She answered him with a "Hello, Joe!" as she climbed to his side.

Joe loosened his reins a very little, called sharply to his horses, and in a whirlwind of dust the buckboard made an amazingly sharp turn and shot rattling down the road and out toward the mountains in the south.

"And now what?" grinned Hapgood, maliciously. "Even your country girl has gone!"

Greek Conniston gazed a moment after the flying buckboard, a vague, wavering, unreal thing, through the dust of its own making, and, hiding his disappointment under a shrug, turned to Hapgood.

"Now for a hotel somewhere, if the place has one. Come on, Roger. We're in for it now, so let's make the best of it."

Carrying his suit-case, he strode off toward the saloon, Roger following silently. The lanky, sunburned individual in the doorway watched their approach idly for a moment and then turned his lazy eyes to a cow and calf trudging past toward the watering-trough.

"Hello, friend!" called Conniston.

The lanky individual drew his eyes from the cow and calf, bestowed a long look and a fleeting nod upon the two strangers, and turned again toward the trough, little impressed, little interested in the Easterners.

"I say!" went on Conniston, brusquely. "Where'll a man get a room here?"

"Down to the hotel."

"So you do have a hotel? Where is it?"

The lazy individual ducked his head toward the east end of the street, cast a last look at the cow and calf, and, turning, went back into the saloon.

"Nice sort of people," grunted Hapgood.

Conniston laughed. "Buck up, Roger," he grinned, his own spurt of irritation lost in his enjoyment of Hapgood's greater bitterness. "It's different, anyhow, isn't it? Come on. Let's see what the hotel looks like."

The hotel was a saloon with a long bar at the front, a little room just off, containing a couple of tables covered with red oil-cloth. Beyond were half a dozen six-by-six rooms separated from one another by partitions rising to within two feet of the unceiled roof. The proprietor, busy with some local friends in the card-room, saw the two young men come in and yelled, lustily:

"Mary!"

Mary, a stout and comfortable-looking woman, appeared from the kitchen, wiping her hands upon her blue apron, and with a sharp glance at the newcomers bobbed her head at them and said, briefly, "Howdy."

Conniston took off his hat and came into the bar-room. Roger, with a careless glance at the woman, came in without taking off his hat and dropped into one of the rickety chairs against the wall. And there he sat until Conniston had negotiated for two rooms for the night. Then he got jerkily to his feet and stalked after his friend and their hostess to the back of the house. A moment later he and Conniston, left alone, sat upon their two beds and stared at each other through the doorway connecting their rooms. Conniston studied the bare floors, the bare walls of rough, unplaned twelve-inch boards set upright with cracks between them ranging from a quarter of an inch to an inch in width, and, rumpling up his hair, sat back and grinned into Hapgood's woebegone face. And Hapgood after the same examination and a sight of the rough beds covered with patchwork comforters, groaned aloud.

"Maybe it's funny," he muttered. "But if it is, I don't see it."

"What are you going to do about it?" chuckled Conniston. "You can't fling out and go to the rival hotel, because there isn't any! You can't sleep outdoors very well. And you can't catch a train until a train comes. Which, I believe, will be sometime to-morrow morning."

It was already late afternoon. That day Roger Hapgood got no farther than the bar-room at the front of the house. There he sat in one of the rickety chairs, brooding, sullen, and silent, smoking cigarettes, drinking high-balls, and cursing the whole God-forsaken West. And there Conniston left him.

In spite of his naturally buoyant spirits, in spite of the fact that he knew he had only to swing upon the next train which came through, Conniston felt suddenly depressed. The silence was a tangible thing almost, and he felt shut out from the world, lost to his kind, marooned upon a bleak, inhospitable island in an ocean of sand. The few men whom he met upon the sun-baked street eyed him with an indifference which was worse than actual hostility. When he spoke they nodded briefly and passed on. It was clear that if he looked upon them as aliens, they looked upon him as a being with whom and whose class they had nothing in common, no desire to have anything in common. For a moment his good nature died down before a flash of anger that these beings, with little, circumscribed existences, should feel and manifest toward him the same degree of contempt that he, a visitor from a higher plane of life, experienced toward them. But in Greek Conniston good humor was a habit, and it returned as he assured himself that what these desert-dwellers felt was worth only his amusement.

At the store he bought some tobacco for his pipe and engaged the storekeeper in trifling conversation. The talk was desultory and for the most part led nowhere. But the little, brown, wizened old man, contemplatively chewing his tobacco like a gentle cow ruminating over her cud, answered what scattering questions Conniston put to him. The young man learned that the town took its name from the stream which crept rather than ran through it to spread out on the thirsty sands a few miles to the north, where it was absorbed by them. That the creek came from the hills to the south, and from the mountains beyond them. When one crossed the brown hills he came to the Half Moon country and into a land of many wide-reaching cattle-ranges.

"I saw a team drive out that way after the train came in," said Conniston, carelessly. "Headed for one of the cattle-ranges, I suppose?"

The old man spat and nodded, wiping his scanty gray beard with his hand.

"That was Joe from the Half Moon. Took the ol' man's girl out."

"I did see a young lady with him. She lives out there?"

"Uh-uh." The old man got up to wait upon a customer, a cowboy, from the loose, shaggy black "chaps," the knotted neck handkerchief, the clanking spurs and heavy, black-handled Colt revolver at his hip. He bought large quantities of smoking-tobacco and brown cigarette-papers, "swapped the news" with the storekeeper, and clanked his way across to the saloon. He did not appear to have seen Conniston.

"The girl's father run a cattle-range out there?"

"Uh-uh. The Half Moon an' three or four smaller ranges. He's old man Crawford—p'r'aps you've heard on him?"

Conniston shook his head, suppressing a smile.

"I don't think I have. Far out to his place?"

"Oh, it ain't bad. Let's see. It's fifty mile to the hills, an' he's about forty mile fu'ther on." He stopped for a brief mental calculation. "That makes it about ninety mile, huh?"

"How does a man get out there? A narrow-gauge running from somewhere along the main line?"

"Darn narrow, stranger. You can walk if you're strong for that kind of exercise. Mos' folks rides. Goin' out?"

"It's rather a long walk," Conniston evaded. And shortly afterward, hearing a clanging bell up the street in the direction of the hotel, he strolled away to his dinner.

He found Hapgood scowling into his high-ball glass and dragged him away to the little dining-room. Both the tables were set. At one of them the cowboy whom he had seen at the store was already eating with two of his companions. Conniston and Hapgood were shown to the other table by the stout Mary. Hapgood cast one glance at the stew and coarse-looking bread put before him, and pushed his plate away. Conniston, who had had fewer high-balls and more fresh air, actually enjoyed his meal. The men at the other table glanced across at them once and seemed to take no further interest.

Hapgood waited, bored and conventional, until Conniston had finished, and then the two went back into the bar-room. The sun had gone down, leaving in the west flaring banners of brilliant, changing colors. The heat of the day had gone with the setting of the sun, a little lost, wandering breeze springing up and telling of the fresh coolness of the coming night. And it was still day, a day softened into a gray twilight which hung like a misty veil over the desert.

From the card-room came the voices of the proprietor and the men with whom he was still playing. They had not stopped for their supper, would not think of eating for hours to come.

"If you feel like excitement—" began Conniston, jerking his head in the direction of the card-room.

Hapgood interrupted shortly. "No, thanks. I've got a magazine in my suit-case. I suppose I'll sit up reading it until morning, for I certainly am not going to crawl into that cursed bed! And in the morning—"

"Well? In the morning?"

"Thank God there's a train due then!"

Conniston left him and went out into the twilight. He passed by the store, by the saloon, along the short, dusty street, and out into the dry fields beyond. He followed the road for perhaps a half-mile and then turned away to a little mound of earth rising gently from the flatness about it. And there he threw himself upon the ground and let his eyes wander to the south and the faint, dark line which showed him where the hills were being drawn into the embrace of the night shadows.

The utter loneliness of this barren world rested heavy upon his gregarious spirit. Sitting with his back to Indian Creek, he could see no moving, living thing in all the monotony of wide-reaching landscape. He was enjoying a new sensation, feeling vague, restless thoughts surge up within him which were so vague, so elusive as to be hardly grasped. At first it was only the loneliness, the isolation and desolation of the thing which appalled him. Then slowly into that feeling there entered something which was a kind of awe, almost an actual fear. A man, a man like young Greek Conniston, was a small matter out here; the desert a great, unmerciful, unrelenting God.

First loneliness, then awe tinged with a vague fear, and then something which Conniston had never felt before in his life. A great, deep admiration, a respect, a soul-troubling yearning toward the very thing from which his city-trained senses shrank. He was experiencing what the men who live upon its rim or deep in its heart are never free from feeling. For all men fear the desert; and when they know it they hate it, and even then the magic of it, brewed in the eternal stillness, falls upon them, and though they draw back and curse it, they love it! The desert calls, and he who hears must heed the call. It calls with a voice which talks to his soul. It calls with the dim lure of half-dreamed things. It beckons with the wavering streamers of gold and crimson light thrown across the low horizon at sunrise and sunset.

Greek Conniston was not an introspective man. His life, the life of a rich man's son, had left little room for self-examination of mood and purpose and character. He had done well enough during his four years in the university, not because he was ambitious, but simply because he was not a fool and found a mild satisfaction in passing his examinations. Nature had cast him in a generous physical mold, and he had aided nature on diamond and gridiron. He had taken his place in society, had driven his car and ridden his horses. He had through it all spent the money which came in a steady stream from the ample coffers of William Conniston, Senior. His had been a busy life, a life filled with dinners and dances and theaters and races. He had not had time to think. And certainly he had not had need to think.

But now, under the calm gaze of the desert, he found himself turning his thoughts inward. He had been driven out of his father's house. He had been called a dawdler and a trifler and a do-nothing. He had been told by a stern old man who was a *man* that he was a disgrace to his name. He had never done anything but dance and smoke and drink and make pretty speeches which were polite lies and which were accepted as such. And now a minor note, as thin as a low-toned human voice heard faintly through the deep music of a cathedral organ, something seemed to call to him telling him again of these things.

The darkening line where the far-away hills in the south were dragged deeper and deeper into the night drew his wandering thoughts away from himself and sent them skimming after the girl he had seen that day. Somewhere out there she was moving across the desert, plunged into the innermost circle of the grim solitude. He remembered her eyes and the look he had seen in them. He could see her again as she jerked in her plunging horse, as she caught the step of the swiftly moving train. The desert had called her; and she, purposeful, strong, as clean of soul, he felt, as she was of body, had answered the call. With the compelling desire to know her springing full-grown from his first swift interest in her, his fancies, touched by the subtle magic of the desert, showed her to him out yonder with the dusk and the silence about her. He got to his feet and stood staring into the gathering gloom as though he would make out across the flat miles the flying buckboard.

"After all," he told himself, with a restless, half-reckless little laugh, "why not?"

He turned and went back toward the town. On his way he overtook a boy, a little fellow of eight or nine, driving a milk-cow ahead of him. He found him the shy, wordless child he had expected, but chatted with him none the less, and by the time they had reached the first of the scattered buildings the boy had thawed a little and responded to Conniston's talk. After the brief, somewhat uncomfortable lonesomeness of a moment ago Conniston found himself glad of any company. And upon leaving the boy at a tumbled-down house a bit farther on he found a half-dollar in his pocket and proffered it.

"Here, Johnny," he said, smiling. "This is for some candy."

The boy put his hands behind his back. "My name's William," he said, with a quiet, odd dignity. "An' I don't take money off'n no one 'less I work for it!"

"My name's William, too, my boy," Conniston answered, much amused; "but you and I have very different ideas about taking money!"

"Proud little cuss," he told himself, as he strode on along the street. "Wonder who taught him that?"

Here and there in the dull dome above him the stars were beginning to come out. On either hand the pale-yellow rays from kerosene-lamps straggled through windows and doors, making restless shadows underfoot. From the door of the saloon the brightest light crept out into the night. And with it came men's voices. Having a desire for companionship, and not craving that of Hapgood in his present mood, Conniston stepped in at the low door, and, going to the bar, called for a glass of beer. There were half a dozen men, among whom he recognized the proprietor of the "hotel" and the men with whom he had been playing cards, and also the cowboys who had eaten at the other table. In the center of the room, under a big nickeled swinging-lamp, a man was dealing faro while the others standing or sitting about him made their bets. A glance told Conniston that the hotel man was playing heavily, his chips and gold stacked high in front of him.

"The strange part of it," he thought, as he watched the bartender open his bottle of beer, "is where they get so much money! Do they make it out of sand?"

He invited the bartender to drink with him, chatted a moment, and then strolled over to the table. The dealer, a thick-set, fat-fingered, grave-eyed man who moved like a piece of machinery, glanced up at him and back to his game. There was no "lookout." A man whom he had not seen before, deft-fingered and alert, was keeping cases. The proprietor of the hotel, the three cowboys, and one other man were playing.

Familiar with the greater number of common ways of separating oneself from his money, Conniston was no stranger to the ways of faro. He watched the fat fingers of the banker as they slipped card after card from the box, and smiled to himself at the fellow's slowness. And before half a dozen plays were made his smile was succeeded by a little shock of surprise. It certainly did not do to judge people out here in a flash and by external signs. What seemed awkwardness a moment ago was now perfected, automatic skill.

The hotel man won and lost, his face always inscrutable, tilted sidewise as he closed one eye against the up-curling smoke from the cigar which he turned round and round between his pursed lips. He had in front of him a stack of ten or twelve twenty-dollar gold pieces which his fingers continually moved and shifted, breaking them into several smaller stacks, bringing them together again, slipping one over another, gathering them into one stack, breaking them down again, so that the golden disks gave out the low musical clink which rose at all times faint and clear through the few short-spoken words. And meanwhile his eyes never left the table and the box.

At the end of the sixth deal he coppered his bet and leaned back to light a fresh cigar. He stood already a hundred dollars to the good. One of the cowboys was winning, having taken in something like twenty or thirty dollars since Conniston came in. The other two were playing recklessly and with little skill, and were losing steadily. The fifth man contented himself with small bets.

Presently the younger of the two cowboys, the fellow whom Conniston had seen at the store in the afternoon, shoved his last two dollars and a half onto the table, lost, and got to his feet, shrugging his shoulders.

"Cleaned," he grunted, laconically. "Gimme a drink, Smiley."

He went to the bar with one lingering look behind him. And in another play or two his companion followed him.

"No kind of luck, Jimmie," he said to the first to be "cleaned." "Ain't it sure enough hell how steady a man can lose?"

"Bein' as my luck took a day off six months ago an' ain't showed up yet," retorted Jimmie, "I guess I'd ought to had sense to leave inves'ments like the bank alone. Only I ain't got the gumption. An' I'm always figgerin' it's about time for my luck to git over her vacation an' come back to work. How much did you drop, Bart?"

"Forty bucks," returned Bart, reaching for the whisky-bottle. "Which same forty was all I had. Here's how."

"How," repeated his companion.

"I'm laying you a bet," said Conniston, quietly, coming toward them from the table.

Jimmie put down his glass, stared reminiscently at it for a moment, and then, lifting his eyebrows, turned to Conniston. "Evenin', stranger. You might have made a remark?"

"If your luck has been working for other people for six months it's my bet that it's on the way home to you right now! I don't mean any offense, and I am not sure of your customs out here. But I'll stake you to five dollars and take half what you win."

Jimmie grinned and put out his hand. "Which I call darn good custom, East *or* West!"

For a few minutes it looked as though Conniston's money were going to retrieve the cowboy's losses. Jimmie had already twenty dollars in front of him. And then a gambler's "hunch," a staking of everything on one play, and Jimmie sat back with nothing to do but roll a cigarette.

"I might have giv' back your fiver a minute ago, but now—"

He ended by licking his brown cigarette-paper together. But his credit was good with the bartender, and Conniston and Bart joined him in having a drink.

"It looks like my luck had started back toward the home corrals all right," said Jimmie, with a meditative smile. "Only she wasn't strong enough to make it all the way. She got weak in the knees an' went to sleep on the road. Now, if I had a fist full of money—" He sighed the rest into his glass.

"If the stranger," put in Bart, studying his own brown paper and tobacco-sack, "has got any more money he wants to—"

Conniston laughed. "Much obliged. I think I'll quit with five to-night."

Suddenly Jimmie got another of his "hunches." He cast a swift, apprising glance at Conniston, and then, tugging Bart's sleeve, drew him to the door. Conniston could hear their voices outside, and, although he could not catch their words, he knew from the tone that Jimmie was urging, while Bart demurred. They came back and had another drink at the bartender's invitation, after which they stepped to the table and watched the play for five minutes.

"I'd 'a' won twice runnin'," grunted Jimmie. "We ought to make a try."

Bart hesitated, watched another play, and said, shortly: "Go to it. If you can put it across I'm with you."

Whereupon Jimmie returned to Conniston and made him a proposition. And ten minutes later, when Conniston went smiling back to the hotel, Jimmie and Bart were playing again, each with a hundred dollars in front of him.

CHAPTER III

Roger Hapgood lifted his pale, heavy-lidded eyes from the pages of his magazine and regarded Conniston with a look from which not all reproach had yet gone.

"I hope you've been enjoying yourself in this Eden of yours," he said, sourly.

Conniston sent his hat spinning across the room, to lodge behind the bed, and laughed.

"You've called the turn, Sobersides! I've been having the time of my young life. And now all I have to do is sit tight to see—"

"See—what?" drawled Roger.

"I've laid a bet, and it's wedged so and hedged so that I win both ways!" Greek chuckled gleefully at the memory of it.

"What sort of a bet?"

"Two hundred dollars!"

Hapgood put down his magazine and got to his feet, plainly concerned. "You don't mean that, Greek?"

"I mean exactly that." Conniston tossed to the bed a small handful of greenbacks and silver. "This is all that's left to the firm of Conniston and Hapgood."

With quick, nervous fingers Hapgood swept up the money and counted it. His eyes showing the uneasiness within him, he turned to the jubilant Conniston.

"There are just twenty-seven dollars and sixty cents. Are you drunk?"

Conniston giggled, his amusement swelling in pace with Hapgood's dawning discomfiture.

"I told you I had made a bet. I have laid a wager with the Fates. And right now, my dear Roger, while we sit comfortably and smoke and wait, the Fates are deciding things for us!"

Roger paused, regarding him. "Yes, you're drunk. If you are not, is it asking too much to suggest that you explain?"

"No. I'll explain. At the sign of the local Whisky Barrel there is a game of faro now in progress. Two very charming young gentlemen, named Jimmie and Bart, punchers of cattle, whatever that may be, are deciding things for Roger Hapgood and William Conniston, Junior, of New York. Each of the amateur gamblers—and they actually do play very badly, Roger!—has before him a hundred dollars of my money. If they win to-night I get back two hundred dollars plus half their winnings, and you and I take the train for San Francisco!"

"If they win. And if they lose?"

"We'll take it as a sign that the Fates have decreed that we're not to go on to the city by the Golden Gate, but tarry here!

Both Jimmie and Bart are provided with saddle-horses, with chaps—chaps, my dear Roger, are wide, baggy, shaggy, ill-fitting riding-breeches, made, I believe, out of goat's hide with the hairy side out!—spurs and quirts—in short, all the necessary paraphernalia and accoutrements of a couple of knights of the cattle country. If they lose the two hundred dollars we win the two outfits! And to-morrow, instead of riding in a Pullman toward San Francisco, we straddle what they call a hay-burner for the blue rim of mountains in the south!"

Hapgood stared incredulously, a sort of horror dawning in his pale little eyes.

"I suppose this is another of your purposeless jokes," he said, stiffly, after a moment.

"Nothing of the kind! Don't you see we win either way? Frankly, I am persuaded that the two hundred dollars are now winging their way into the pockets of an apparently awkward dealer with slow fingers, and into the pockets of our friend the hotel man. But we will get the horses, and think of the lark—"

"Lark!" shrilled Hapgood. "A lark—to go wandering off into the desert—"

"Not wandering! *Pirutin'* is the word you want, the real vernacular of the West. Or *skallyhutin*! I'm strong for the sound of the latter myself—"

"Oh, rot!" broke in Hapgood. "I was a fool to come out here with a fool like you."

He turned his back squarely upon Conniston and stood staring out the little window, biting his thin lips. Conniston stood eying him, and slowly the smile passed from his face,

Jackson Gregory

to be followed by a serious frown.

"I thought you'd kick in for the sport of it," he said, after a moment, his voice quiet and a trifle cold. "You don't have to if you feel like that about it. You still have your ticket to San Francisco. You can have half of that twenty-seven dollars. You can sell your horse if we win the brutes."

Hapgood had been thinking about that before Conniston spoke. And his thoughts had gone further. It would not be long, he told himself shrewdly, before Conniston Senior softened. And then there would be much money to help spend, many dinners to help eat, much wine to help drink, a string of glittering functions to attend. And if he broke with Greek now—

"See here, Greek," he said, affably, forcing a smile. "What's the use of this nonsense? Why not slip your father a wire now. He'll come across. And then we can go on as we had intended and—"

"Nothing doing." For once Conniston was stubborn. "I'm going on with this thing. If those horses come to us I am going to start early in the morning for the mountains to see what I can see. You can do as you please."

Hapgood glanced at him quickly, and, despite the wrath boiling up within him, the shrewder side of his nature prompted a peaceful answer.

"Then I'll go with you. You didn't think that I was the sort of a fellow to go back on you now, did you? We'll see this thing through together."

Conniston put out his hand impulsively, ashamed of having misjudged his friend.

Long before midnight Jimmie left the saloon and crept away to the stable to stroke the soft nose of a restive cow-pony, and to swear soft, endearing curses of eternal farewell. Not long afterward he had the satisfaction of seeing his fellow-cowboy steal through the darkness to whisper good-by to his own horse. And in the early dawn both Jimmie and Bart stood peering out from behind the corner of the barn at two figures riding rapidly southward into the morning mists.

That day's ride was a matter never to be forgotten by the two men. Their muscles were soft from dissipation and long years of idleness. In particular did Hapgood suffer. He was a slight man to whom nature had given none of the bigness of body which she had bestowed upon Conniston. His luxury-loving disposition had made him abjure the sports which the other at one time and another had enjoyed. He was, besides, a very poor horseman, while Conniston had ridden a great deal. To-day his horse—a spirited colt newly broken—was not content to go straight ahead as Hapgood would have had him, but danced back and forth across the road, shied at every conceivable opportunity, threatening constantly to unseat his rider, and jerked at the restraining, tight-gathered reins until Hapgood's arms ached.

The sun soon drove away the early mists and beat down upon the two men mercilessly from a blazingly hot sky. Nowhere was there any shade except the tiny pools of shadow at the roots of the scrub brush. The heat, the dry air shimmering over the glowing sands, abetted by the many high-balls of yesterday, soon engendered a scorching thirst, and as mile after mile of the treeless desert slipped behind they found no water. Over and over Hapgood was tempted to turn back. He felt that his shoulders, from which he had removed his coat, were blistering under the sharp rays of the sun. At every swinging stride his horse made he felt the skin being rubbed off of his legs where they rubbed against the saddle leather. His soft hands were cut by the reins, he was

Jackson Gregory

sore from the tips of his fingers to the soles of his feet. But as each fresh temptation assailed him a glance at Conniston, riding a few paces ahead, made him pull himself together. For some day the old man would relent, and then Roger Hapgood would see that for every agonized mile now he would be amply repaid.

And no water would they find until Indian Creek was thirty miles behind them unless they turned from their way and rode a couple of miles to the westward where the straggling stream crawled through the sand. It was as well that they did not know, for the stream, like many of its kind in the dry parts of the West, ran for the greater part of its course underground, showing only here and there in a pool, where, beneath the sand, there was the hard-pan through which the water could not seep.

They had left the town behind them at a lope. Now they rode at a walk, curbing their horses' impatience with tight-drawn reins. They had thought to have reached the brown hills and shade before the day's heat was upon them. But now it was already intense, stifling, awaking from its light doze almost as the sun rolled upward across the low horizon.

And now the temptation upon Roger Hapgood, urging him to turn back—back toward the little town, hateful yesterday, but spelling now at least the courtyard to comfort—was so strong that he would not have had strength to resist had he not realized that the ride back would be longer than the ride on to water. He made no answer to Conniston's sallies, but, sullenly silent, clung to his reins with one hand, to the horn of his saddle with the other, lifting his head now and again to gaze with red-rimmed eyes ahead along the dusty, flat stretch of the desert, for the most part head down, the picture of misery.

Conniston, feeling the heat riotous in his own veins, feeling the ache of fatigued muscles, felt a sudden pity for Hapgood. And still, even through his own discomfort, there laughed always a certain something in his buoyant nature which saw the humorous in the adventure.

It was late in the forenoon when they saw a clump of green willows, and ten minutes later came to a roadside spring and watering-trough. Hapgood threw an aching leg over the horn of his saddle and slipped stiffly to the ground. Conniston dismounted after him, holding the two horses' reins as they thrust their dry muzzles deep into the clear water. Hapgood, applying his mouth to the pipe from which the water ran into the trough, drank long and thirstily, and then, dragging his feet heavily, went to the clump of willows and dropped to the ground in their shade.

"We've done thirty miles, anyway," said Conniston, cheerily, when he, too, had drunk. "Twenty miles farther to the hills, and—"

Hapgood, his head between his hands, groaned.

"Twenty miles farther and I'll be dead. I couldn't eat any of that infernal mess last night, and I couldn't eat beefsteak and mashed potatoes this morning. And I've got pains through me now in a dozen places. I wish—"

He broke off suddenly. There was little use to tell what he wished: a cool club-room on Broadway; a deep, soft leather chair; a waiter to bring him delicate dishes and cool drinks.

For an hour they sat in the shade resting. Then Conniston got to his feet and threw his reins over his horse's head.

"Come on, Roger," he said, quietly, the unusual gentleness of his tone showing the pity he felt. "We can't stay here all day."

Hapgood rose wordlessly and walked stiffly to his horse. He cursed it roundly when it jerked back from him, and for five minutes he strove to mount. The animal, high strung and restless, was frightened, first at his lunging gait, then at his loud, angry voice, and jerked away from him each time that he tried to get his foot into the stirrup. But at last, with the aid of Conniston, who rode his own horse close to the other, preventing its turning, Hapgood climbed into the saddle. And again in silence they pushed on toward the hills.

It took them five hours to do the twenty miles lying between the watering-trough and the edge of the hills. A large part of the last ten miles Hapgood did on foot, leading his astonished horse. And often he stopped to rest, squatting or lying full length on the ground. It was nearly five o'clock in the afternoon when at last they came to the second spring by the roadside. And here Hapgood sank down wearily, muttering colorlessly that he could not and would not go a step farther. And they were still forty miles to the nearest cabin and bed.

Conniston unsaddled the two horses, watered them, and staked them out to crop the short, dry grass. And then he stood by the spring, smoking and frowning at the barren brown hills. They had had nothing to eat since early morning; they had not thought to bring any lunch with them. And now if they spent the night here it would be close upon noon on the next day before they could hope to find food. He looked covertly at his friend, only to see him sprawled on the ground, his head laid across his arm.

"Poor old Roger," he muttered to himself. "This is pretty hard lines. And a night out here on the ground—"

He determined to wait until the cool of the evening and then to persuade Hapgood to ride with him across the hills. It would be hard, but it seemed not only best, but almost the only way. So Conniston filled his pipe, thought longingly of the cigarettes he had left in his suit-case at the hotel, and, lying down near Hapgood, smoked and dozed in the warm stillness.

An hour passed. The shadow of the scrub-oak under which they had thrown themselves was a long blot across the sand. About them everything was drowsy and sleepy and still. Conniston, turning upon his side, his pipe dropping dead from between his teeth, saw that Hapgood was asleep. He lay back, looking upward through the still branches of the oak, his spirit heavy with the heaviness of nature about him. And musing idly upon the new scenes his exile had already brought him, musing on a pair of gray eyes, Conniston himself went to sleep.

The sun was low down in the western sky, dropping swiftly to the clear-cut line of the horizon, the air growing misty with the coming night, the sunset sky glowing gold and flaming crimson, when Conniston awoke. He sat up rubbing his eyes, at first at a loss to account for his surroundings. Then he saw Hapgood sprawled at his side and remembered. And then, too, he saw what it was that had awakened him.

A man in a buckboard drawn by two sweating horses was looking curiously at him while his horses drank noisily at the trough. He was an unmistakable son of the West, bronzed and lean and quick-eyed. The long hair escaping from under his battered gray hat vied with his long drooping mustache in color, and they both challenged the flaming crimson of the sunset. Conniston told himself that he had never seen hair one-half so fiery or eyes approaching the brilliant blueness of this man's. And he told himself, too, that he had never been gladder to see a fellow human being. For the horses were headed toward the hills in the south.

"How are you?" Conniston cried, scrambling to his feet and striding with heavy feet to the buckboard.

"Howdy, stranger?" answered the red-headed man, his voice strangely low-toned and gentle.

"My name's Conniston," went on the young man, putting out a hand which the other took after eying him keenly.

"Real nice name," replied the red-headed man. And dropping Conniston's hand and turning to his horses, "Hey there, Lady! Quit that blowin' bubbles an' drink, or I'll pull your ol' head off'n you!"

Lady seemed to have understood, and thrust her nose deeper into the water. And the new-comer, catching his reins between his knees, took papers and tobacco from the pocket of a sagging, unbuttoned vest and made a cigarette. Licking the paper as a final touch, his eyes went to Hapgood.

"Pardner sick or something?"

"No. Just fagged out. We came all the way from Indian Creek since morning."

"That's real far, ain't it?" remarked the man in the buckboard, with a little twitch to the corner of his mouth, but much deep gravity in his eye. "Which way you goin', stranger?"

"We're going across the hills into the Half Moon country. It's forty miles farther, they tell me."

"Uh-uh. That's what they call it. An' a darn long forty mile, or I'll put in with you."

"And," Conniston hurried on, "if you are going—You are

going the same way, aren't you?"

"Sure. I'm goin' right straight to the Half Moon corrals."

"Then would you mind if my friend rode with you? I'll pay whatever is right."

The other eyed him strangely. "I reckon you're from the East, maybe? Huh?"

"Yes. From New York."

"Uh-uh. I thought so. Well, stranger, we won't quarrel none over the payin', an' your frien' can pile in with me."

Conniston turned, murmuring his thanks, to where Hapgood now was sitting up. And the red-headed man climbed down from his seat and began to unhitch his horses.

"You needn't git your frien' up jest now in case he ain't finished his siesta. We won't move on until mornin'."

"Where are you going to sleep?" Hapgood wanted to know.

"I had sorta planned some on sleepin' right here."

"Right here! You don't sleep on the ground?"

The red-headed man, drawing serenely at his cigarette, went about unharnessing his horses.

"Bein' as how I ain't et for some right smart time," he was saying as he came back from staking out his horses, "I'm goin' to chaw real soon. Has you gents et yet?"

They assured him that they had not.

"Then if you've got any chuck you want to warm up you can sling it in my fryin'-pan." He dragged a soap-box to the tail end of the buckboard and began taking out several packages.

"We didn't bring anything with us," Conniston told him. "We didn't think—"

The new-comer dropped his frying-pan, put his two hands on his hips, and stared at them. "You ain't sayin' you started out for the Half Moon, which is close on a hundred mile, an' never took nothin' along to chaw!"

Conniston nodded. The red-headed man stared at them a minute, scratched his head, removing his hat to do so, and then burst out:

"Which I go on record sayin' folks all the way from Noo York has got some funny ways of doin' business. Bein' as you've slipped me your name, frien'ly like, stranger, I don't min' swappin' with you. It's Pete, an' folks calls me Lonesome Pete, mos'ly. An' you can tell anybody you see that Lonesome Pete, cow-puncher from the Half Moon, has made up his min' at las' as how he ain't never goin' any nearer Noo York than the devil drives him."

He scratched his head again, put on his hat, and reached once more for his frying-pan.

CHAPTER IV

Lonesome Pete dragged from the buckboard a couple of much-worn quilts, a careful examination of which hinted that they had once upon a time been gay and gaudy with brilliant red and green patterns. Now they were an astonishing congregation of lumps where the cotton had succeeded in getting itself rolled into balls and of depressions where the cotton had fled. Light and air had little difficulty in passing through. Lonesome Pete jerked off the piece of rope which had held them in a roll and flung them to the ground, directing toward Hapgood a glance which was an invitation. And Hapgood, the fastidious, lay down.

The red-headed man dumped a strange mess out of a square pasteboard box into his frying-pan and set it upon some coals which he had scraped out of his little fire. There was dried beef in that mess, and onions and carrots and potatoes, and they had all been cooked up together, needing only to be warmed over now. The odor of them went abroad over the land and assailed Hapgood's nostrils. And Hapgood did not frown, nor yet did he sneer. He lifted himself upon an elbow and watched with something of real interest in his eyes. And when black coffee was made in a blacker, spoutless, battered, dirty-looking coffee-pot Roger Hapgood put out a hand, uninvited, for the tin cup.

Conniston, his appetite being a shade further removed from

starvation than his friend's, divided his interest equally between the meal and the man preparing it. He found his host an anomaly. In spite of the fiery coloring of mustache and hair he was one of the meekest-looking individuals Conniston had ever seen, and certainly the most soft-spoken. His eyes had a way of losing their brightness as he fell to staring away into vacancy, his lips working as though he were repeating a prayer over and over to himself. The growth upon his upper lip had at first given him the air of a man of thirty, and now when one looked at him it was certain he could not be a day over twenty. And about his hips, dragging so low and fitting so loosely that Conniston had always the uncomfortable sensation that it was going to slip down about his feet, he wore a cartridge-belt and two heavy forty-five revolvers. He gave one the feeling of a cherub with a war-club.

During the scanty meal Lonesome Pete ate noisily and rapidly and spoke little, contenting himself with short answers to the few questions which were put to him, for the most part staring away into the gathering night with an expression of great mildness upon his face. Finishing some little time before his guests, he rolled a cigarette, left them to polish out the frying-pan with the last morsels of bread, and, going back to the buckboard, fumbled a moment in a second soap-box under the seat. It was growing so dark now that, while they could see him take two or three articles from his box and thrust them under his arm, they could not make out what the things were. But in another moment he had lighted the lantern which had swung under the buckboard and was squatting cross-legged in the sand, the lantern on the ground at his side. And then, as he bent low over the things in his hand, they saw that they were three books and that Lonesome Pete was applying himself diligently to them.

He opened them all, one after the other, turned many pages,

stopping now and then to bend closer to look at a picture and decipher painstakingly the legend inscribed under it. Finally, after perhaps ten minutes of this kind of examination, he laid two of them beside him, grasped the other firmly with both awkward hands and began to read. They knew that he was reading, for now and again his droning voice came to them as he struggled with a word of some difficulty.

Hapgood smoked his last cigarette; Conniston puffed at his pipe. At the end of ten minutes Lonesome Pete had turned a page, the rustling of the leaves accompanied by a deep sigh. Then he laid his book, open, across his knee, made another cigarette, lighted it, and, after a glance toward Conniston and Hapgood, spoke softly.

"You gents reads, I reckon? Huh?"

"Yes. A little," Conniston told him; while Hapgood, being somewhat strengthened by his rest and his meal, grunted.

"After a man gets the swing of it, sorta, it ain't always such hard work?"

"No, it isn't such hard work after a while."

Lonesome Pete nodded slowly and many times.

"It's jest like anything else, ain't it, when you get used to it? Jest as easy as ropin' a cow brute or ridin' a bronco hoss?"

Conniston told him that he was right.

"But what gits me," Lonesome Pete went on, closing his book and marking the place with a big thumb, "is knowin' words that comes stampedin' in on you onexpected like. When a man sees a cow brute or a hoss or a mule as he ain't never clapped his peepers on he knows the brute right away. He says, 'That's a Half Moon,' or, 'It's a Bar Circle,' or 'It's a U Seven.' 'Cause why? 'Cause she's got a bran' as a man can make out. But these here words"—he shook his head as he opened his book and peered into it—"they ain't got no bran'. Ain't it hell, stranger?"

"What's the word, Pete," smiled Conniston.

"She ain't so big an' long as bothers me," Lonesome Pete answered. "It's jest she's so darn peculiar-lookin'. It soun's like it might be *izzles*, but what's *izzles*? You spell it i-s-l-e-s. Did you ever happen to run acrost that there word, stranger?"

Conniston told him what the word was, and Lonesome Pete's softly breathed curse was eloquent of gratitude, amazement, and a certain deep admiration that those five letters could spell a little island.

"The nex' line is clean over my head, though," he went on, after a moment of frowning concentration.

Conniston got to his feet and went to where the reader sat, stooping to look over his shoulder. The book was "Macbeth." He picked up the two volumes upon the ground. They were old, much worn, much torn, their backs long ago lost in some second-hand book-store. One of them was a copy of Lamb's *Essays*, the other a state series second reader.

"Quite an assortment," was the only thing he could think to say.

Lonesome Pete nodded complacently. "I got 'em off'n ol' Sam Bristow. You don't happen to know Sam, do you, stranger?"

Conniston shook his head. Lonesome Pete went on to enlighten him.

"Sam Bristow is about the eddicatedest man this side San Francisco, I reckon. He's got a store over to Rocky Bend. Ever been there?"

Again Conniston shook his head, and again Lonesome Pete explained:

"Rocky Bend is a right smart city, more'n four times as big as Injun Creek. It's a hundred mile t'other side Injun Creek, makin' it a hundred an' fifty mile from here. In his store he's got a lot of books. I went over there to make my buy, an' I don't mind tellin' you, stranger, I sure hit a bargain. I got them three books an nine more as is in that box under the seat, makin' an even dozen, an' ol' Sam let the bunch go for fourteen dollars. I reckon he was short of cash, huh?"

Since the books at a second-hand store should have been worth about ninety cents, Conniston made no answer. Instead he picked up the dog-eared volume of "Macbeth."

"How did you happen to pick out this?" he asked, curiously.

"I knowed the jasper as wrote it."

Conniston gasped. Lonesome Pete evidently taking the gasp as prompted by a deep awe that he should know a man who wrote books, smiled broadly and went on:

"Yes, suh. I'm real sure I knowed him. You see, I was workin' a couple er years ago for the Triangle Bar outfit. Young Jeff Comstock, the ol' man's son, he used to hang out in the East. An' he had a feller visitin' him. That feller's name was Bill, an' he was out here to git the dope so's he could write books about the cattle country. I reckon his las' name was the same as the Bill as wrote this. I don't know no other Bills as writes books, do you, stranger?"

Conniston evaded. "Are you sure it's about the cattle country?"

"It sorta sounds like it, an' then it don't. You see it begins in a desert place. That goes all right. But I ain't sure I git jest what this here firs' page is drivin' at. It's about three witches, an' they don't say much as a man can tie to. I jest got to where there's something about a fight, an' I guess he jest throwed the witches in, extry. Here it says as they wear chaps. That oughta settle it, huh?"

There was the line, half hidden by Lonesome Pete's horny forefinger. "*He unseamed him from the nave to the chaps!*" That certainly settled it as far as Lonesome Pete was concerned. Macbeth was a cattle-king, and Bill Shakespeare was the young fellow who had visited the Triangle Bar.

Thoughtfully he put his books away in the box, which he covered with a sack and which he pushed back under the seat. Then he looked to his horses, saw that they had plenty of grass within the radius of tie-rope, and after that came back to where Hapgood lay.

"I reckon you can git along with one of them blankets, stranger. You two fellers can have it, an' I'll make out with the other."

Hapgood moved and groaned as he put his weight on a sore muscle.

"The ground will be d—d hard with just one blanket," he growled.

Lonesome Pete, his two hands upon his hips, stood looking

down at him, the far-away look stealing back into his eyes.

"I hadn't thought of that. But I reckon I can make one do, all right."

Whereupon without more ado and with the same abstracted gleam in his eyes he stooped swiftly and jerked one of the quilts out from under the astonished Hapgood.

The man who had traveled from the Half Moon one hundred and ninety miles to spend fourteen dollars for a soap-box half full of books was awake the next morning before sunrise. Conniston and Hapgood didn't open an eye until he called to them. Then they looked up from their quilt to see him standing over them pulling thoughtfully at the ends of his red mustache, his face devoid of expression.

"I'll have some chuck ready in about three minutes," he told them, quietly. "An' we'll be gittin' a start."

"In the middle of the night!" expostulated Hapgood, his words all but lost in a yawn.

"I ain't got my clock along this trip, stranger. But I reckon if we want to git across them hills before it gits hot we'll be travelin' real soon. Leastways," as he turned and went back to squat over the little fire he had blazing merrily near the watering-trough, "I'm goin' to dig out in about twenty minutes."

Hapgood, remembering the ride of yesterday, scrambled to his feet even before Conniston. And the two young men, having washed their faces and hands at the pipe which discharged its cold stream into the trough, joined the Half Moon man.

He had already fried bacon, and now was cooking some

flapjacks in the grease which he had carefully saved. The coffee was bubbling away gaily, sending its aroma far and wide upon the whispering morning breeze. The skies were still dark, their stars not yet gone from them. Only the faintest of dim, uncertain lights in the horizon told where the east was and where before long the sun would roll up above the floor of the desert. The horses, already hitched to the buckboard, were vague blots in the darkness about them.

They ate in silence, the two Easterners too tired and sleepy to talk, Lonesome Pete evidently too abstracted. And when the short meal was over it was Lonesome Pete who cleaned out the few cooking-utensils and stored them away in the buckboard while Conniston and Hapgood smoked their pipes. It was Lonesome Pete who got his two quilts, rolled, tied, and put them with the box of utensils. And then, making a cigarette, he climbed to his seat.

"An' now if one of you gents figgers on ridin' along with me—"

"I do!" cried Hapgood, quickly. And he hastened to the buckboard, taking his seat at the other's side.

"I thought you had a hoss somewheres! An' your saddle?" continued Lonesome Pete.

"I thought that while you were getting your horses—Didn't you saddle him?"

For a moment Lonesome Pete made no answer. He drew a deep breath as he gathered in his reins tightly. And then he spoke very softly.

"Now, ain't I sure a forgetful ol' son of a gun! I did manage to rec'lec' to make a fire an' git breakfas' an' hitch up my hosses an' clean up after breakfas' an' put the beddin' in—but would you believe I clean forgot to saddle up for you!"

He laughed as softly as he had spoken. Hapgood glanced at him quickly, but the cowboy's face was lost in the black shadow of his low-drawn hat. Hapgood got down and saddled his own horse, and it was Hapgood who, riding with Lonesome Pete, led a stubborn animal that jerked back until both of Hapgood's arms were sore in their sockets. Lonesome Pete, the forgetful, remembered after an hour or two of quiet enjoyment to tell the tenderfoot that he could tie the rope to the buckboard instead of holding it. For the first hour Hapgood was, consequently, altogether too busy even to try to see the country about him, and Conniston, riding behind, could make out little in the darkness. The one thing of which he could be sure was that they were leaving the floor of the desert behind, that they were climbing a steep, narrow road which wound ever higher and higher in the hills. Then finally the day broke, and he could see that they were already deep in the brown hills which he had seen from Indian Creek. There was scant vegetation, a few scattered, twisted, dwarfed trees, with patches of brush in the ravines and hollows. Nowhere water, nowhere a sprig of green grass. As in the flat land below here, there was only barrenness and desolation and solitude.

As had been the case yesterday, so now to-day when the sun shot suddenly into the sky the heat came with it. But already the three travelers had climbed to the top of the hills where Pocket Pass led across the uplands and were once more dropping down toward a gray level floor. On a narrow bit of bench land, where for a space the country road ran level, lined with ruts, gouged with uncomfortable frequency into dust-concealed chuck-holes, Lonesome Pete pulled in his horses and waited for Conniston to ride up to his side.

"In case you've got a sorta interest in the country we're goin' to drop down in," he said, as he took advantage of the stop to roll a cigarette, "you might jest take a look from here. This is what they call Pocket Pass as we jest rode through. An' from this en' you can see purty much everything as is worth seein' in this country an' a whole hell of a lot as ain't." He made a wide sweep with his arm, pointing south-ward and downward. "That there's where we're headed for."

"And that's the Half Moon!" Conniston was eager, as he saw at a glance how the range got its name.

The hills fell away even more abruptly here than they did in the north, cut so often into straight, stratified brown cliffs of crumbling dirt that Conniston wondered how and where the road could find a way out and down into the lower land. They swept away, both east and west, in a wide curve, roughly resembling a half moon. Toward the east, perhaps twenty-five miles from where Conniston sat upon his horse, the distant mountains sent out two far-reaching spurs of pine-clad ridges between which lay Rattlesnake Valley. Due south, as Lonesome Pete's outstretched finger indicated, lay the road which they were to follow and the headquarters of the Half Moon. There again a thickly timbered spur of the mountains ran down into the plain on each side of a deeply cleft canon from which Lonesome Pete told them that Indian Creek issued, and in which were the main corrals and the range house of the Half Moon.

"Which is sure the finest up-an'-down cow-country I ever see," he added, by way of rounding off his information. "Bein' well watered by that same crick, an' havin' good feed both in the Big Flat, as folks calls that country down below us, an' in the foothills. Rattlesnake Valley, over yonder, ain't never been good for much exceptin' the finest breed of serpents an' horn-toads a man ever see outside a circus or the jimjams. There ain't nothin' as 'll grow there outside them animals. The ol' man's workin' over there now, tryin' to throw water on it an' make things grow. The ol' man," he ended, shaking his head dubiously, "has put acrost some big jobs, but I reckon he's sorta up against it this trip."

"Reclamation work," nodded Conniston.

"That's what some folks calls it. Others calls it plumb foolishness. Git up, there, Lady! Stan' aroun', you pinto hoss!"

An hour more of winding in and out, back and forth, along the narrow grade cut into the sides of the hills, just wide enough for one team at the time, with here and there a wider place where wagons might meet and pass, and they were down in the Half Moon country. The cowboy let his horses out into a swinging trot; Conniston followed just far enough behind to escape their dust; and the miles slipped swiftly behind them.

They had crossed the floor of the lower Half Moon and were moving up a gentle slope leading along the spur of the mountains to the right of Indian Creek when they met one of the Half Moon cowboys driving a small band of saddle-horses ahead of him. Lonesome Pete stopped for a word with him, and Conniston, seeing the road plain ahead, rode on alone. A mile farther and he had entered the forest of pines through which the road lay, winding and twisting to avoid the boles of the larger trees or the big scattered boulders which were many upon the steepening slope. Now he could seldom see more than a hundred yards in front of him, and now he had left the stifling heat behind him for the cool shadows which made a dim twilight of midday.

Two miles of this pleasant shade, fragrant with the spicy balsam of the forest, and the road began to turn to the left, across the spine of the ridge and into the deep ravine. Presently he heard the bawling of the stream somewhere through the undergrowth below him, its gurgle and clatter making merry music with the swish of the stirring pine-tops. And suddenly, as he made a sharp turn, he drew in his horse with a little exclamation of surprise.

Here the road plunged abruptly downward and across the rocky bed of Indian Creek. Just above the crossing, so near that a passing vehicle must be sprinkled with the spray of its headlong leaping waters, was a waterfall flashing in white and crystal down a cliff of black rock ten feet high. On either side the stately pine-trees, their lowest limbs forty feet above the ground, marched in patriarchal dignity to the edge of the stream. And above the waterfall, farther back between the jaws of the ravine, Conniston could see the red-tiled roofing and snow-white towers of such a house as he had never dreamed of finding lost in the Western wilderness.

He rode on down into the stream and across. Upon the other side the road again ran on into the canon, climbing twenty feet up a gradual slope. And here upon the top of the bank Conniston again drew in his reins with a jerk, again surprised at what he saw before him.

Here was a long, wide bench of land which had been carefully leveled. Through the middle of it ran the creek. Feeding the waterfall was a dam, its banks steep, its floor, seen through the clear water, white sand. And it was more than a dam; it was a tiny mountain lake. A drifting armada of spotlessly white ducks turned their round, yellow eyes upon the trespasser. Over yonder a wide flight of stone steps led to the water's edge. And the flat table-land, bordered with a dense wall of pines and firs, was a great lawn, brilliantly green, thick strewn with roses and geraniums and a riot of bright-hued flowers Conniston did not know.

He turned his eyes to the house itself. It was a great,

two-storied, wide-verandaed building, with spacious doors, deep-curtained windows, a tower rising above the red tiles of the roof at each corner, everywhere the gleam of white columns. Each tower had its balconies, and each balcony was guessed more than seen through the green and red and white of clambering roses.

Midway between the broad front steps and the edge of the little toy lake was a summer-house grown over with vines, its broad doorway opening toward Conniston. And sitting within its shade, a book in her lap, her gray eyes raised gravely to meet his, was the girl he had seen on the Overland Limited. Conniston rode along a graveled walk toward her, his hat in his hand.

"Good morning," she said, as he drew in his horse near her. "Won't you get down?"

"Good morning."

He swung to the ground with no further invitation, his horse's reins over his arm.

His eyes were as grave as hers, and he was glad, glad that he had ridden here through the desert.

"You came to see my father?"

Conniston colored slightly. Why had he come? What was he going to do now that he was here? How should he seek to explain? He hesitated a moment, and then answered, slowly:

"I am afraid that my reasons for coming at all are too complicated to be told. You see, we just got off the train in Indian Creek out of idle curiosity to see what the desert country was like. We're from New York. And then we rode out toward the hills. One of your father's men overtook us there, and, as he was coming this way and as we were anxious to see the cattle-country and—" he broke off, smiling. "You see, it is hard to make it sound sensible. We just came!"

She looked up at him, a little puzzled frown in her eyes.

"You have friends with you?"

"One friend. He was pretty well tuckered out, and the red-headed gentleman who calls himself Lonesome Pete is bringing him along in his buckboard."

"And you have no business at all out here?"

"I *had* none," he retorted.

"You don't know father?"

"I am sorry that I don't."

"You are going on to Crawfordsville?"

"I don't know where Crawfordsville is. Is it the nearest town?"

"Yes."

"Since I don't see how we can stay here, I suppose we'll go on to Crawfordsville, then. That would be the best way, wouldn't it?"

"Really," she replied, quietly, "I don't see that I am in a position to advise. If you haven't any business with my father—"

Then the buckboard drove up, and Greek Conniston

devoutly wished that he had left Roger Hapgood behind. And when he saw the radiant smile which lightened the girl's gray eyes as they rested upon Lonesome Pete and took notice of the wide, sweeping flourish with which the cowboy's hat was lifted to her, he wished that the red-headed student of Shakespeare was with Hapgood on Broadway.

CHAPTER V

Roger Hapgood, the stiff soreness of yesterday only aggravated by the cramp which had stolen into his legs during the ride of to-day, climbed down from the buckboard and limped across the lawn to where Conniston stood.

"I say, Greek," he was growling, as he trudged forward, "what fool thing are you going to do next?" He stopped suddenly, in his surprise forgetting to shut his mouth. The same eyes which had laughed up into his when she offered him ten cents as a tip were laughing into them now. He dragged his hat from his head, stammering.

"Miss Crawford—for you are Miss Crawford, aren't you?" began Conniston.

She nodded.

"I should have introduced myself. I am William Conniston, Junior, son of William Conniston, Senior, as one might guess. This is my friend, Mr. Hapgood."

The girl inclined her head very slightly and turned toward Conniston.

"If you have come all the way from the hills this morning,"

she was saying, "and if you plan to go on to Crawfordsville, you will want to rest until the cool of the evening. We have eleven-o'clock luncheon in summer, and have already eaten. But if you will come in I think that we can find something. And, anyway, you can rest until evening. If you are not in a hurry to go right on?"

"We have all the time in the world!" Conniston hastened to assure her. And Hapgood of the aching muscles added fervently, "If it's more than a mile to Crawfordsville, I've got to rest awhile!"

"It is something more than that." She rose and moved toward the house. "Through the short cut straight back into the mountains it's twenty."

Lonesome Pete was turning to drive toward a gap in the encircling trees when the girl called to him to take Conniston's horse. And then the three went to the house.

The flight of steps led them to a wide veranda, eloquent of comfort with its deep wicker rockers and hammocks piled temptingly with cushions. Then came the wide double doors, and, within, a long, high-ceilinged room whose appointment in every detail spoke of wealth and taste and the hand of a lavish spender. And into this background the slender form of the girl in the close-fitting, becoming gown entered as harmoniously as it had the other day when clad in khaki and against a background of limitless desert.

The floor here was of hard wood, polished until it shone dully like a mirror in a shaded room. No rugs save the two great bear-skins, one black, the other white; no pictures beyond the one great painting against the farther wall. There was a fire-place, wide and deep and rock-bound. And yonder, a dull gleam as of ebony, a grand piano. Leather chairs, all elegant, soft, luxurious.

Jackson Gregory

She would leave them here, she said, smiling, and see if there was anything left to eat. And while they marveled at finding the splendid comfort of Fifth Avenue here on the far rim of the desert, a little Japanese boy in snowy linen bowed himself in to them and invited them to follow. They went down a long hallway after his softly pattering footsteps and were shown into a large airy bath-room, with a glimpse beyond of a cozy sitting-room.

"You wish prepare for luncheon, honorable sirs," said the boy, his teeth and eyes shining in one flash. "You find rest-room there. I call for you. Anything?"

Conniston told him that there was nothing further required, and he withdrew, stepping backward as from royalty, bowing deeply.

"Here's where I lose about half of the desert I've been carrying around with me," muttered Hapgood. "The Lord knows when we'll see another tub!"

Luxury of luxuries! The bath-room was immaculate in white tiling, the tub shone resplendently white, and there was steaming-hot water! Conniston, having strolled into the "rest-room," where he found a deep leather chair with a table close to its elbow decorated simply but none the less effectively with a decanter of whisky and a silver box containing cigarettes, leaned back, enjoying himself and the sound of the splashing in the bath-room.

Once more in familiar and comfortable environment, even Hapgood for the moment forgot to be miserable, and as he smoked a good cigarette and watched the water running into the tub now and then hummed a Broadway air. As for Conniston, his serene good nature under most circumstances, his greatest asset in the small frays he had had with the world, was untroubled by a spot.

"How do you like the West, Roger?" he called, banteringly.

"Something like, eh, Greek?" Hapgood laughed back. "Do you know, I believe I'll stay! And the dame, isn't she some class, eh?"

He finished his bath finally, and at last emerged, half dressed, to lounge in the big chair while his friend took his plunge. He heard Conniston singing to the obligato of the running water, and, with eyes half closed, leaned back and watched his smoke swirl ceilingward. Presently the bath-room door opened again, and he saw Conniston, his trousers in his hand, standing in the doorway, grinning as though at some rare laughter-provoking thought.

"Well, old man," Hapgood smiled back at him, "whence the mirth?"

Conniston chuckled gleefully.

"Another joke, Roger, my boy! I wonder when the Fates are going to drop us in order to give their undivided attention to some other lucky mortals? You know that twenty-seven dollars and sixty cents?"

"Well?"

"I've lost it!" Conniston laughed outright as his ready imagination depicted amusing complications ahead. "Every blamed cent of it!"

"What!" Hapgood was upon his feet, staring. Hapgood's complacency was a thing of the past.

Conniston nodded, his grin still with him.

"Every cent of it! And here we are the Lord knows how far

from home—"

"Have you looked through all your pockets?"

"Every one. And I found—"

"What?"

"A hole," chuckled Conniston. "Just a hole, and nothing more."

Hapgood jerked the trousers from the shaking hand of the man whom such a catastrophe could move to laughter, and made a hurried search.

"What the devil are we going to do?" he gasped, when there was at last no doubting the truth.

Conniston shrugged. "I haven't had time to figure out that part of it. Haven't you any money?"

"About seven dollars," snapped Hapgood. "And a long time that will keep the two of us. It's up to you, Greek!"

"Meaning?"

"Meaning that you've got to wire your dad for money. There's nothing left to do. Dang it!" he finished, bitterly, throwing the empty trousers back to Conniston, "I was a fool to ever come with you."

"You've said that before. But"—his good humor still tickled by his loss, which he refused to take seriously in spite of the drawn face staring into his—"I haven't even the money to wire the old gent!"

"Oh, I'll pay for it."

"I didn't want to do it so soon," Conniston hesitated. "But it begins to look as though—"

"There's nothing to it. You've got to do it! Why, man, do you realize what a confounded mess you've got us into?"

Conniston went back into the bath-room rather seriously. But a moment later Hapgood heard him chuckling again.

The Japanese boy came to summon them, and they followed him, once more clean and feeling respectable, into a cozy little breakfast-room where their hostess was waiting for them. And over their cold meat, tinned fruits and vegetables, and fresh milk Conniston told her of their misfortune. She laughed with him at his account of the winning of the two horses and seemed disposed to indorse his careless view of the whole episode rather than Hapgood's pessimistic outlook.

"It's all right, I suppose, since Conniston has a rich father," Roger admitted, with a sigh.

She regarded him curiously for a moment.

"Some men," she said, quietly, "have been known to go to work and make money for themselves when they needed it."

Conniston told her of his little friend William, of Indian Creek, adding, carelessly, "I'm glad I don't have to feel like that."

"You mean that you had rather have money given to you than to feel that you had earned it yourself?"

"Quite naturally, Miss Crawford. My father is William Conniston, Senior. Maybe you have heard of him?"

He was proud to be his father's son, to have his own name so intimately connected with that of a man who was not only a millionaire many times over, but who was a power in Wall Street and known as such to the four ends of the earth.

"Yes. I have heard of him. He made his own money, didn't he? In the West, too."

"Yes. A mining expert in the beginning, I believe, and a mine-owner in the end. Oh, the governor knows how to make the dollars grow, all right!"

Again she made no answer. But after a little she said: "If you wish to wire to your father for money"—and there was just the faintest note of scorn in her voice—"you needn't wait until you get to Crawfordsville. We have a telephone, and you can telephone your message from here."

"Good!" cried Hapgood, eagerly. "Better do that—and right away, Greek. There's no use losing time."

Conniston thanked her, and a moment later, they rose from the table and stepped to the telephone, which she showed to him in a little library. When he got Central in Crawfordsville Miss Crawford told the girl for him to charge all costs to her father and that Mr. Conniston would pay here for the service. So she took his message and telephoned it to the Western Union office.

"You will rush it, will you, please?" asked Conniston.

"Certainly. And the answer? Shall we telephone it out to you?"

"No. We'll be in Crawfordsville, and—Wait a moment." To Miss Crawford: "We may stay here until evening?"

"Oh, you must. It is too hot now to think of riding."

"Thank you." And then into the receiver: "If you should get an answer before seven o'clock, please telephone it to me here."

Then the three went out to the front porch. They found chairs in the shade where a welcome little breeze made for cool comfort. Miss Crawford sat with the men, answering their questions about that wild country, chatting with them. And there, at her invitation, they sat and smoked when she left them and went into the house.

"A charming girl," Hapgood was moved to say enthusiastically. "Really a charming girl! Who would have thought to find her out here? And say, Greek"—being confidentially nearer—"her old man must be tremendously rich, eh? You don't need to think of such things, of course, but take me—" He paused, and then continued, thoughtfully: "Sooner or later, old man, it's got to come to one end for Roger Hapgood. And, do you know, I'm half in love with her already?"

His verbal enthusiasm in no way imparted itself to young Conniston. So Roger puffed complacently at his cigarette in thoughtful silence, rather more than usually well pleased with himself.

The late afternoon drew on, and the girl had not returned to them. Conniston looked at his watch and saw that it was half-past five. They would have to leave within an hour and a half; they could not impose longer than that. He was hoping that she would spend at least the last half-hour with them when he heard the door open and looked up quickly, thinking she was coming. It was the Japanese boy, bowing and smiling.

"Most honorable sir," looking doubtfully from one of them to the other, "the telephone would speak with you."

Conniston sprang to his feet. Hapgood smiled his satisfaction. "The old gent is as prompt as the very deuce, God bless him!"

Conniston hurried after the boy into the house, leaving Hapgood beaming.

"Mr. Conniston?" the telephone-girl was asking.

"Yes, I'm Conniston. You have the answer?"

"Yes. Shall I read it to you?"

"Please."

"It's rather long," she laughed into the telephone. "But it's paid. It runs:

"MY DEAR SON,—Your wire received. Sorry you misunderstood me. So that you may make no mistakes in the future I shall be more explicit now. I shall not send you one single dollar for at least one year from date. If at the end of that time you have done something for yourself I may help you. I leave for Europe to-morrow to be gone for a year on my first vacation. It will do no good for you to telegraph again. I cannot help you beyond wishing you luck. You are on your own feet. Walk if you can.

"Yours,

"WILLIAM CONNISTON, Senior."

Conniston leaned limply against the wall, staring into

the telephone.

"Look here!" he cried, after a moment. "There's a mistake somewhere."

"No mistake. The wire was just brought in from the Western Union office."

"But I don't understand—"

"I'm sorry. Is there anything else?"

"No. That's all."

Even Conniston's sanguine temperament was not proof to the shock of his father's message. He knew his father too well to hope that he would change his mind now. His eyes showed a troubled anxiety when he went slowly back to confront Hapgood.

"Well, what's the good news?" cried Hapgood. And then, when he had seen Conniston's face, "Gad, man! What's wrong?"

Conniston shook his head as he sank into a chair.

"I—I'm a bit upset," he answered, unsteadily. "I made a mistake; that's all."

"It wasn't your father?"

"That's the trouble. It was! He refuses to send a dollar. And he's leaving to-morrow for a year in Europe."

"What!" yelled Hapgood, leaping to his feet in entire forgetfulness of his sore muscles.

"That's it. And when the old man says he'll do a thing he'll do it."

Hapgood stared at him speechless. And then, his hands driven deep into his pockets, he began an agitated pacing up and down the porch, his brows drawn, his eyes squinting as they had the habit of doing when he was excited.

"What are we going to do?" he demanded, stopping before Conniston.

"I wish that somebody would tell me! We have a couple of horses. You have seven dollars. Maybe," with a faint, forced smile, "we can ride back to New York!"

With a disgusted sniff Hapgood left him again to pace restlessly up and down. And finally, when he again stopped in front of Conniston's chair, his face was white, his thin lips set bloodlessly.

"I guess there's only one thing left to us. We'll go on into Crawfordsville and put up for a day or two while we try to raise some money. Your seven dollars ought to keep us from starving—"

"Will you wire your father again?"

"No. There would be no use. I tell you that when he says he is going to do a thing that settles it. If I broke both arms and legs now he wouldn't pay the doctor's bill."

"Then I'll tell you something, my friend!" The pale little eyes were glowing, malevolently red. "You've played me for a sucker long enough. You towed me along out into this cursed West of yours, making me think all the time that when you got ready to call on your father he'd come through like a flash. And you knew that he had turned you out for good. Now I am through with you. Get that? I mean it! And if I have seven dollars I guess I'll need it myself before I get out of this pickle you've got me into!"

Conniston stared at him incredulously. "Come, now, Roger. You don't mean—"

"But I do, Mr. William Conniston, fraud! I'm through with you."

Conniston got to his feet, his own face as white as Hapgood's.

"You mean what you are saying?"

"I most certainly and positively do!"

"And the wire I sent to dad—"

"You can pay for it if you want to! You don't get a cent out of me."

Conniston took one stride to him, putting a heavy hand upon Hapgood's narrow shoulder.

"You infernal little shrimp!" he cried, hoarsely. "If we weren't guests here I'd take a holy glee in slapping your face! By the Lord, I've a mind to do it anyhow!"

Hapgood jerked back, his arm lifted to shelter his face. And Conniston, with a short laugh, dropped his hand to his side. As he did so he saw Miss Crawford was coming toward them through the yard from the corner of the house. A middle-aged man, heavy and broad-shouldered and white-haired, was with her. He turned to meet her.

"Mr. Conniston," she was saying, "this is my father. And,

papa, this is Mr. Hapgood."

Mr. Crawford came up the steps, giving his hand in a hearty grip to the two men who came forward to meet him, his voice, deep and grave, assuring them that he was glad that they had stayed over at his home. His face was stern, grave like his voice, clean-shaven, and handsome in a way of manly, independent strength.

"Argyl tells me," he said, to Conniston, as they all sat down, "that you are expecting some money by wire. You are leaving us, then, right away?"

"I did expect some money," Conniston laughed, his good humor with him again. "I wired to my father for it. And I just had his answer. There is nothing doing."

Mr. Crawford lifted his eyebrows. Argyl leaned forward.

"He said," went on Conniston, lightly, "that he would not send me a dollar. You see, he wants me to do something for myself. And," with a rueful grin, "I am in debt to you for a dollar to pay for my message—and I haven't ten cents!"

Mr. Crawford laughed with him. "We won't worry about the dollar just now, Mr. Conniston. What are you going to do?"

Conniston scratched his head. "I don't know. I—" And then Argyl's words came back to him, and he surprised himself by saying: "Most men go to work when they're strapped, don't they? I guess I'll go to work."

"I don't mean to be too personal, but—are you used to working?"

"I never did a day's work in my life."

"Then what can you do?"

"I don't know. I—you see, I never figured on this. I—I—Do you happen to know anybody who wants a man?"

A little flicker of a smile shot across Crawford's face.

"We're all looking for men—good men—all the time. I can use a half-dozen more cow-punchers right now. Do you want to try it?"

Conniston's one glance of the girl's eager face decided him.

"I've always had a curiosity to know what they did when they punched the poor brutes," he grinned back. "And I can work out that dollar I owe you too, can't I?"

"You're engaged," returned Mr. Crawford, crisply. "Thirty dollars a month and found. I'll have one of the boys show you where the bunk-house is. You'll begin work in the morning."

CHAPTER VI

As the significance of his change of fortunes began slowly to dawn on him, Conniston was at first merely amused. One of the men employed by John W. Crawford, a man whom Conniston came to know later as Rawhide Jones, conducted him at the Old Man's orders to the bunk-house. The man was lean, tall, sunburned, and the *tout ensemble* of his attire—his flapping, soiled vest, his turned-up, dingy-blue overalls, his torn neck-handkerchief, and, above all, the two-weeks' growth upon his spare face—gave him an unbelievable air of untidiness. He cast one slow, measuring glance at the young fellow who Mr. Crawford had said briefly was to go to work in the morning, and then without a word, without a further look or waiting to see if he was followed, slouched on ahead toward the gap in the encircling trees into which Lonesome Pete had disappeared earlier in the afternoon.

Conniston saw that Argyl Crawford was standing at her father's side and that she was smiling; he saw that Hapgood was laughing openly. And then he turned and strode on after his guide, conscious that the blood was creeping up into his face and at the same time that he could not "back down."

The graveled road wound through the pines for an eighth of a mile, leaving the bench land and finding its way into a hollow cleared of trees. Here was a long, low, rambling building—a stable, no doubt. At each end of the stable was a stock-corral. And at the edge of the clearing was another building, long and very low, with one single door and several little square windows. A stove-pipe protruded from the far end of this house, and from it rose a thin spiral of smoke.

"The Ol' Man said I was to show you your bunk," Rawhide Jones muttered under his breath. "You're to have the one as was Benny's. Benny got kilt some time back."

He flung the door open and entered. Conniston, at his heels, paused a moment, staring about him. A man in dingy-blue undershirt, the sleeves rolled back upon forearms remarkable for their knotting, swelling muscles, was frying great thick steaks upon the top of the stove, enveloped in the smoke and odor of his own cooking. In the middle of the room was a long table, covered with worn oil-cloth, set out with plates and cups of heavy white ware and with black wooden-handled knives and forks. Running up and down each side of the one unpartitioned room were narrow bunks, a row close to the floor, another row three feet higher, arranged roughly like berths on board a steamer.

Sitting on chairs, or on the edges of the bunks with their legs a-dangle, their eyes interestedly upon the cook's operations, were half a dozen men, rough of garb, rough of hands, big, brawny, uncouth. As Conniston came into the room every pair of eyes left the cook to examine him swiftly, frankly. He paused a moment for the introduction Rawhide Jones would make. But Rawhide Jones had no idea of doing anything more than enough to fulfil his orders. He strode on through the men until he stopped at one of the upper bunks, about the middle of the room, from which a worn, soiled red quilt trailed half-way to the floor.

"This here was Benny's. It's yourn now."

He had turned away, and, standing with his big hands resting upon his hips, was watching the cook. And Conniston saw that all of the other men, seemingly forgetful of his entrance, were again doing the same thing. He felt suddenly a deep lonesomeness, greater a thousand times than when he had been actually alone under the spell of the desert. For here there were men about him who, having seen him, turned away, shutting him out from them, with no one word of greeting, not so much as a nod. He was not in the habit of being received this way. It was, his sensitive nature told him, as though he had been examined by them, had been recognized as an alien, and had had the doors of their fraternity clicked in his face.

He felt a sudden bitterness, a sudden anger. And with it he felt a deep contempt for them, for their petty, unenlightened lives, their coarseness, their blackened hands and unshaved faces. He was a gentleman and a Conniston! He was the son of William Conniston, of Wall Street! He told himself that when they came to know who he was, who his father was, their incivility would change fast enough into servility.

And still he had as much as he could do to keep the little hurt, the sting of his reception, from showing in his face. He glanced as disgustedly as Hapgood could have done into the rude bunk with its tangled pile of coarse blankets, and turned away from it. For one fleeting second the temptation was strong upon him to turn his back upon the lot of them, to stalk proudly to the door, to go to Mr. Crawford and tell him that he was not used to this sort of thing and did not intend to try to grow accustomed to it. One thing only restrained him. He knew that even as he closed the door behind him he would hear their voices in rude laughter, and Greek Conniston did not like being laughed at. Instead he left the bunk and walked quietly to one of the farther chairs. The air of the bunk-house was already thick with smoke from the stove and from cigarettes and pipes. Conniston took out his own pipe, filled it, and, sitting back, added his smoke to the rest.

The cook had turned to say something to Rawhide Jones, and, carelessly putting his hand behind him, blistered it against the red-hot top of the stove, whereupon he burst into such a volley of curses as Conniston had never heard. The words which streamed from the big man's mouth actually made Conniston shiver. He turned questioning eyes to the other men in the room. They were again talking to one another, no man of them seeming to have so much as heard. Rawhide Jones laughed at the cook's discomfiture and went back to the door, where he washed his face and hands at a little basin, plastered his wet hair down as his companions had already done, and dropped into easy conversation with the heavy, round-shouldered, yellow-haired man sitting across the room from Conniston.

"Looks like the Ol' Man means real business, huh, Spud?"

Spud answered with a joyous oath that it certainly looked like it.

"He's puttin' Brayley in on this en' an' takin' ol' Bat Truxton clean off'n it to throw him onto the Rattlesnake," Spud went on. "Bat 'll have nigh on a hundred men down there workin' overtime before the week's up, he says. I guess he'll have his paws full without tryin' to run the cow en', too."

"An' I reckon," continued Jones, thoughtfully, "as how Brayley won't sleep all the time up here. He's got to swing the whole Half Moon an' the Lone Dog an' the Five Hills an' the Sunk Hole outfit." He shook his head and spat before he concluded. "What with the Ol' Man buyin' the Sunk Hole, an' figgerin' on marketin' in Injun Creek, an' crowdin' work down in the Rattlesnake, Brayley 'll be some busy if he don't take on another big bunch of punchers. Huh?"

Spud made no answer, for at this juncture the cook put a big platter of steak, piled high, upon the table, and the men, dragging their chairs after them, waited no other invitation "to set in." Conniston for a moment held back. Then, as he saw that there were several vacant places, he took up his own chair and sat down at the end of the table nearest him. The man at his left helped himself to meat by harpooning the largest piece in sight and dragging it, dripping, over the edge of the platter and to his own plate. Then he shoved the platter toward Conniston without looking to see whether or not it arrived at its proper destination, and gave his undivided attention to the dish of boiled potatoes which the man upon his left had shoved at him. Conniston, helping himself slowly, found soon that the potatoes, the rice, and a tray of biscuits were all lodged at his elbow, waiting to be ferried on around the end of the table.

For a few moments all conversation died utterly. These men had done a day's work, a day's work calling upon straining muscles and unslacking energy, and their hunger was an active thing. They plied their knives and forks, took great draughts of their hot tea and coffee, with little attention to aught else. But presently, as their hunger began to be appeased, they broke into conversation again, talking of a hundred range matters of which Conniston understood almost nothing. He drew from the fragments which reached him above the general clatter the same thing that he had got from the few words which had passed between Rawhide Jones and Spud. Evidently, the cowboys were pressed with work both on the Half Moon and on the other ranges, and the new foreman, Brayley, was putting on more men and sparing no one in carrying out the orders which came from headquarters. Equally apparently, the man whom they called Bat Truxton was in command of the reclamation work in Rattlesnake Valley, and now with a force of a hundred men was working with an activity even more feverish than Brayley's.

During the meal five more men came in, and with a word of rough greeting to their fellows dropped into their chairs and helped themselves deftly. Conniston recognized one of the men as the half-breed, Joe, whom he had seen meet Miss Crawford in Indian Creek. Another was Lonesome Pete. Conniston was more gratified than he knew when the red-headed reader of "Macbeth" nodded to him and said a quiet "Howdy." The last man to come in was Brayley.

He was a big man, a trifle shorter than Conniston, but heavier, with broader shoulders, rounded from years in the saddle, with great, deep chest, and thick, powerful arms. He lurched lightly as he walked, his left shoulder thrust forward as though he were constantly about to fling open a door with its solid impact. He was a man of forty, perhaps, and as active of foot as a boy. His heavy, belligerent jaw, the sharp, beady blackness of his eyes, the whole alert, confident air of him bespoke the born foreman.

Conniston was conscious of the piercing black eyes as they swept the table and rested on him. He noticed that Brayley alone of the men who had entered late had no word of greeting for the others, received no single word from them. And he saw further, wondering vaguely what it meant, that as the big foreman came in the eyes of all the others went first to him and then to Conniston.

Brayley stopped a moment at the door, washing his face and hands swiftly, carelessly, satisfied in rubbing a good part of the evidence of the day's toil upon the towel hanging upon a nail close at hand. Three strokes with the community comb, dangling from a bit of string, and jerking his neck-hand-kerchief into place, he lurched toward the table. Five feet away he stopped suddenly, his eyes burning into Conniston's.

"Who might you be, stranger?" he snapped, his words coming with unpleasant, almost metallic sharpness.

There fell a sudden silence in the bunk-house. Knives and forks ceased their clatter while the cowboys turned inter-ested eyes upon the Easterner.

Conniston caught the unveiled threat in the foreman's tones, saw that he had come in in the mood of a man ready to find fault, and took an instinctive disliking for the man he was being paid a dollar a day to take orders from. He returned Brayley's glance steadily, angered more at knowing that the blood was again creeping up into his cheeks than because of the curt question. And, staring at him steadily, he made no further answer.

"Can't you talk?" cried Brayley, angrily. "Are you deef an' dumb? I said, who might you be?"

"I heard you," replied Conniston, quietly. And to the man upon his left, "Will you kindly pass me the bread?"

The man grinned in rare enjoyment, and, since he kept his eyes upon Brayley's glowering face, it was hardly strange that he handed Conniston a plate of stewed prunes instead.

"Thank you," Conniston said to him, still ignoring Brayley. "But it was bread I said."

"An' I said something!" cut in Brayley, his voice crisp and incisive. "Did you get me?"

"I got you, friend." Conniston put out his hand for the bread and caught a gleam of sparkling amusement in Lonesome Pete's eyes from across the table. "And maybe after you tell me who you are I might answer you."

"Me!" thundered the big man, lurching one step nearer, his under jaw thrust still farther out. "Me! I'm Brayley, that's who I am! An' I'm the foreman of this here outfit."

"Thank you, Brayley." Conniston's anger was pounding in his temples, but he strove to keep it back. "I'm Conniston. I was told to report here by Mr. Crawford to go to work in the morning. I suppose I report to you?"

"Conniston are you, huh? All right, Conniston. Now who happened to tell you to slap yourself down in that there chair, huh?"

"Nobody," returned Conniston, calmly. "I didn't suppose that I was to stand up and eat."

Lonesome Pete's grin overran his eyes, and the ends of his fiery mustache curved upward. Two or three men laughed outright. Brayley's brows twitched into a scowling frown.

"Nobody's askin' you to git funny, little rooster! You git out 'n that chair an' git out 'n it fas'. *Sabe?*"

Calm-blooded by nature and by long habit, Conniston had mastered the flood of blood to his brain and grown perfectly cool. Brayley, on the other hand, had come in in a seething rage from a tussle with a colt in which his stirrup leather had broken and he had rolled in the dust of the corral, to the boundless glee of two or three of his men who had seen it, and now there was nothing to restrain his anger. Conniston was laughing into his face.

"I hear you," he said, lightly. "My ears are good, and your voice is not bad by any means. Only I'd really like to know why you want me to get up. Is it custom here for a new man to remain standing until the foreman is seated? If I am violating any customs—"

Again Brayley took one lurching step forward. Conniston pushed his chair back so that his feet were clear of the table leg.

"I say, Brayley"—Lonesome Pete had half risen from his chair and was speaking softly—"Conniston here didn't know. Nobody put him wise as how you sat in that particular chair. An'," even more softly, "he's a frien' of Mr. Crawford."

"Who's askin' you to chip in?" challenged Brayley, his eyes flashing for the moment from Conniston to Lonesome Pete. "An' if he's a frien' of Crawford's, why ain't he up to the house instead of down here? Huh?"

Lonesome Pete shrugged his shoulders and settled back into his chair.

"Slip me a sinker, Rawhide," he said, quietly, to the man next to him as though he had lost all interest in the conversation.

"Frien' of the Ol' Man's or no frien'," blustered Brayley, his eyes again on Conniston's, "if you're goin' to work I guess you're goin' to take orders from me like the rest of the boys. An' the first order is, *git out'n that there chair!*"

"Look here," Conniston replied, quietly, "I didn't know that I was taking a seat reserved for you, and I didn't mean any offense. You can take that as a sort of an apology if you like. But at the same time, even if I am to take orders from you, I am not going to be bulldozed by you or anybody like you. If you will ask me decently—"

"Ask you!" bellowed Brayley. "Ask you! By the Lord, I don't *ask* my men! I *make* 'em!"

He had leaped forward with his last word, his two big hands outstretched with clawing fingers. Before Conniston could spring from his chair to meet the attack the iron hands were upon his shoulders. He felt himself being lifted bodily from his seat. His weight was scarcely less than the irate foreman's, and he employed every pound of it as he staggered to his feet and flung himself against his burly antagonist. The men about the table sat still, watching, saying no word.

Conniston's strength was less than the other's, and he knew it, knew that his endurance would be nothing against the muscles seasoned by daily physical work until they were like steel. He knew that in two minutes of battling struggle he would be like a kitten in the big, powerful hands. And he was of no mind to have Brayley manhandle him before such an audience as was now sitting quietly watching, listening to his panting breaths. In one straining effort he jerked his right shoulder free, swung his clenched fist back, and drove it smashing into Brayley's face.

Brayley's head snapped back, and the blood from his cut mouth ran across his white, bared teeth. Conniston sprang forward to follow up the blow. But Brayley had caught his balance and was leaping to meet him, snarling. His hard, toil-blackened fist drove through Conniston's guard, striking him full upon the jaw. Conniston reeled, and before he could catch himself a second blow caught him under the ear, and with outflung arms he pitched backward and fell, striking the back of his head upon the rough boards of the floor.

For one dizzy moment the world went black for him. And then it went red, flaming, flaring red, as he heard a man's laugh. An anger the like of which he had never known in the placid days of his easy life was upon him, an anger which made him forget all things under the arch of heaven excepting the one man with bloody fists glaring into his eyes, an anger blind and hot and primitive. Again he knew that he was on his feet; again he was rushing at the man who stood waiting for him.

"Stan' back!" roared Brayley. "I ain't goin' to play with you all day."

Conniston laughed and did not know that he had done so. He only saw that Brayley had stepped back a pace, and that he had something, black but glistening in the pale light, tight clenched in his hand. Crying out hoarsely, inarticulately, he threw himself forward.

Again Brayley met him, this time the revolver in his hand thrust before him. It was almost in Conniston's face now. Somebody cried out sharply. Several of the men jumped from their seats and leaped out from behind Conniston. Two or three of them slipped under the table to crawl out on the other side. Then Conniston saw what the something was in Brayley's hand.

"Shoot, you dirty coward!" he yelled, as he swung his arm out toward the big six-shooter.

For one moment Brayley seemed to hesitate. And then as the two men came together the barrel of the gun rose and fell swiftly, striking Conniston full upon the forehead. His arms dropped like lead; the dizzy blackness came back upon him, growing blacker, blacker; and he fell silently, unconsciously.

It was very quiet in the bunk-house when he opened his eyes. A sudden pain through the temples, a rising nausea, blackness and dizziness again, made him close them, frowning. He knew that he was lying in his bunk and that he was very weak. There was a cold, wet towel tied tight about his forehead.

The table had been cleared away, and the cook was finishing his dish-washing by the stove. A lantern swinging from the beam which ran across the middle of the room showed him that all the men were in their bunks with the exception of two who were playing cribbage at the table. They were Lonesome Pete and Rawhide Jones. When they saw him leaning out from his bunk Lonesome Pete put down his cards and came to him.

"How're they comin', stranger?" he asked, with no great expression in either eyes or voice.

"Where's Brayley?" demanded Conniston, quickly.

"He ain't here none jest now. No, he ain't exac'ly ran away, nuther. Brayley ain't the kind as runs away. He was sent for to come to the Lone Dog, where there's some kind of trouble on. Seein' as that's thirty mile or worse, the chances is he'll ride mos' all night an' won't be back for a day or two."

Conniston sank back upon his straw pillow. "What I have to say to him will keep," he said, quietly.

The red-headed man looked at him curiously. "Brayley's the boss on this outfit, pardner. What he says goes as she lays. It's sure bad business buckin' your foreman. If you can't hit it up agreeable like, you better quit."

For a moment Conniston lay silent, plucking with nervous

fingers at the worn red quilt.

"What did he do to me?" he asked, presently. "Hit me over the head with a revolver?"

Lonesome Pete nodded.

"That's what you call fair play out in the West?"

"What fooled me, Conniston, is that he didn't drill a couple er holes through you! He ain't used to bein' so careful an' tender-hearted-like, Brayley ain't."

"Just because I'm to work under him, does that mean that in the eye of you men he had a right—"

An uplifted hand stopped him. "When two men has onpleasant words it ain't up to anybody else to say who's right. Us fellers has jest got to creep lively out'n the line of bullets an' let the two men most interested settle that theirselves. Only I don't mind sayin', jest frien'ly like, as it is considered powerful foolish for a man to prance skallyhutin' into a mixup as is apt to smash things considerable onless he's heeled."

"Heeled? You mean—"

Lonesome Pete whipped one of the guns from his sagging belt and laid it close to Conniston's pillow.

"That when a man's got one of them where he can find it easy he ain't got to take nothin' off'n nobody! An' one man's jest as good as another, whether he's foreman or a thirty-dollar puncher! An' bein' as we got to go to work early in the mornin', I reckon you better roll over an' hit the hay!"

He turned abruptly and went back to his discarded hand. And Greek Conniston, the son of William Conniston, of Wall Street, lay back upon his bunk and thought deeply of many things.

CHAPTER VII

The next day the gates of a new world opened for Greek Conniston. And it was a world which he liked little enough. The cook, rattling his pots and pans and stove-lids, woke him long before it was four o'clock. One by one the men tumbled out, dressed swiftly, washed and combed their hair at the low bench by the door, and then sat about smoking or wandered away to the stable to attend to their horses. At four o'clock the table was set, coffee and biscuits and steaks sending out their odors to float together upon the morning air. Conniston got up with the others and washed at the common basin, contenting himself with running his fingers through his hair rather than to use the one broken-toothed comb. One or two of the boys said a short "Mornin'" to him, but the most of them seemed to see him no more than they had when he had entered the bunk-house last evening. Lonesome Pete nodded to him and, when they all sat down, indicated a chair at his side for him to sit in.

There was a great bruise upon his forehead and a cut where the muzzle of Brayley's gun had struck him, but he was surprised to find that both dizziness and faintness had passed entirely and that he was feeling little inconvenience from the blow which last night had stretched him out unconscious.

He ate with the others in silence, making no reference to

Brayley, noting that they gave no evidence of remembering the trouble of last night. The fare was coarse, and he was not used to such dishes for breakfast any more than he was used to getting up at four o'clock to eat them. But he was hungry, and the coffee and the biscuits were good. After breakfast he found himself outside of the bunk-house with Lonesome Pete.

"When Brayley's away," the cowboy was saying, over his cigarette-making, "Rawhide Jones takes his place. An' Rawhide says you're to come with me an' give me a hand over to the cross-fence. I guess we'd better be makin' a start, huh?"

Conniston went with him to the stable. "We ain't brought in any extry hosses," Pete was explaining, as they came into one of the corrals. "You'll ride your own to-day?"

In one of the stalls Conniston found the horse he had ridden from Indian Creek, with his saddle, bridle, spurs, and chaps hanging upon wooden pegs. And in the next stall he saw the horse Hapgood had ridden.

"Hasn't Hapgood gone yet?" he asked of Pete.

"I don't reckon he has. He had supper with the Ol' Man up to the house las' night. An' I guess he's stayed over to res' up."

They swung to their horses' backs and rode through the trees and on eastward across a long grassy slope from which the shadows of the night were just beginning to lift. As day came on Conniston saw that ahead of them for miles ran a barren-looking, treeless country, rising on the one hand to the foot of the mountains, falling away gradually on the other to the Big Flat. They rode swiftly, side by side, for five miles, passing through many grazing herds of cattle, many smaller bands of horses. And finally, when they came to a wire fence running north and south, Lonesome Pete swung down from his saddle.

On the ground near the fence were hammers, a pick, a shovel, and a crowbar. The old barley-sack at the foot of one of the posts gave out the jingle of nails as Pete's boot struck against it. And Conniston, dismounting and tying his horse, began his first lesson in fence-repairing.

The loose wires they tightened with the short iron bar, in the end of which a V-shaped cut had been made. While Pete caught the slack wire with this bar, and, using the post as a fulcrum, the bar as a lever, drew it taut, Conniston with hammer and staples made it secure. Now and again they found a rotten post which must be taken out, while a new one from a row which had been dumped from a wagon yesterday was put into its place.

It was easy work, and Conniston found, that he rather enjoyed the novelty of it. But as hour after hour dragged by with the same unceasing monotony, as the sun crept burning into the hot sky, and the wires, the crowbar, even the pick-handle blistered his hands, he began to feel the cramp of fatigue in his stooping shoulders and in his forearms and back. Noon came at last, and he and Lonesome Pete ate the cold lunch which the latter had brought, drank from the bottle of water, and lay down for a smoke. Conniston had left his pipe at the bunk-house, and accepted from his fellow-worker his coarse, cheap tobacco and brown papers.

The morning had been endlessly long. The afternoon was an eternity. It was hotter now that the sun had rolled past the zenith, now that the sand had drunk deep of its fiery rays. The air shimmered and danced above the gray mono-tone of flat country, Conniston's eyeballs were burning with it. And back and arms and shoulders ached together. He had hoped that they would quit work at five o'clock. Five o'clock came and went, and the red-headed man said no word of stopping. Half-past five, six o'clock. And still they tightened wires, hammered burning staples, dug endless post-holes. Conniston's hands were torn with the sharp staples, blistered with the work. Half-past six, and he was ready to throw down his tools and quit. But a glance at his companion's face, sweat-covered but showing nothing of the fatigue of the day, and Conniston held doggedly to his work, ashamed to stop.

And, together with the breathless heat of the still afternoon, the ache and dizziness returned to his head where Brayley's gun had struck him; a new and growing nausea told him that a man is not knocked unconscious one day to forget all about it the next. As he straightened up from bending over the lowest wire, nausea and faintness together threatened to make him throw up his hands and acknowledge himself unfit for the new sort of existence into which he had rushed carelessly. He was not certain why, in spite of all that he felt, he held on. He knew only that as the son of William Conniston he must be the superior in all things to the man who worked at his side like a machine; he knew that in spite of his liking for Lonesome Pete he held the cowboy in a mild contempt, and that he must not be outdone by him.

When at length the sun had sunk out of sight through the flaming colors of its own weaving in the flat lands to the west, and Lonesome Pete threw down his tools at the foot of the last post which they had planted in the sandy soil, Conniston was too tired to greatly care that the day was done. He refused the proffered cigarette, and slowly walked away to where his horse was waiting for him. He did not know that the other man was looking at him curiously, that there was much amusement and a hint of surprise in the bright-blue eyes. He knew only that he had toiled from before sunrise until after sunset; that the waking hours to which he had been long accustomed had been turned topsy-turvy; that instead of spending money he had been making money; that he had earned his board and lodging and one dollar! And even while he ached and throbbed throughout his whole weary body he was vaguely amused at that.

When finally they came again into the Half Moon corrals Lonesome Pete carelessly offered to unsaddle for Conniston and water and feed his horse. And Conniston, while not ungrateful, answered with short doggedness that he could do his own part of the work.

They came to the bunk-house to find that several of the boys had eaten before them, that two or three of them were already in bed. The cook, however, had supper waiting for them, kept hot in the oven of his big stove. Conniston knew that he was hungry; during the ride in he had thought longingly of a hot meal and bed. But now he learned what it was to be hungry and at the same time too tired to eat. He drank some coffee, ate a little bread and butter, and, pushing his plate away, climbed into his bunk.

He thought longingly of silk pajamas and a hot bath—and started up finding himself half asleep, dreaming of miles of wire fence, of hammering staples and tightening wires, of laboring with breaking back over holes which, as fast as he dug them, filled with the shifting sand. And then—it seemed to him that he had been in bed ten minutes—he heard the cook rattling his pots and pans and stove-lids, and knew that the night had gone and that the second day of his new life had come.

The first day had been purgatory. The second was hell. His raw, blistered fingers shrank from his hammer-handle, from the sun-heated iron bar. The muscles which through long idleness had grown soft, and which had been taxed all day yesterday, cried out with sharp pains as to-day they were called upon. He had thought that the night would have rested him; instead it had but made his arms and hands and back stiff and unfit. When ten o'clock came he felt as tired as he had been last night at quitting-time. The heat was more intense, the day sultry, with a thin film of clouds across the gray sky allowing the sun's rays to scorch the earth, refusing to let the sand radiate the heat which clung to it like a bank of heavy steam. Their water-bottle, although they kept it always in the shade of some scorched tree or bush, grew as warm as the air about it. Still Conniston drank great quantities of the warm water until even it warred against him and made him sick. All morning long he fought against a dull, throbbing headache. At noontime he ate little, but sat still, with his bursting temples between his hands.

Again the afternoon dragged on, unbearably long, each tortuous second a slow period of agony. Lonesome Pete's stories of the range country he heard, while he did not attempt to grasp their significance. They no longer amused him. His own position, his own condition, no longer amused him. He felt that he could not laugh; he knew that he would not. He told himself over and over that he was a fool for attempting drudgery like this. He vowed that when at last the day's work was done he would go to Mr. Crawford and say, "I have worked off what I owe you. I am going to quit." They could think what they chose. They could laugh if it pleased them. His was a finer nature than theirs; he was a gentleman, thank God, and no day-laborer.

And night came, and he ate what he could and dragged himself into his bunk in silence. He saw the glances which were directed toward him when he came into the bunk-house; he knew what the men were thinking. He knew what they would say. And while it had been pride until now, now it was nothing in the world but lack of moral courage which made him stick to the thing which he hated.

This day again he had seen Roger Hapgood's horse in the stable. He had heard one of the men say that Hapgood was still resting up at the house as a guest. He himself had not had a fleeting glimpse of Argyl Crawford, and he knew that Hapgood was seeing her constantly. A quick bitterness made up of resentment and a kind of jealousy sprang up within him. He knew that at least the girl was blameless, and yet he blamed her. He told himself, knowing that he was wrong, that she was unfair, unjust, even unkind.

The third day came. It was longer, drearier, wearier than the other two had been. He began to fear that soon he should have to give up. His body, instead of becoming gradually inured to the long hours of toil, seemed to be gradually succumbing to them. He felt that he was wearing out, breaking down. He did not know if Hapgood were still on the Half Moon or if he had gone. He did not greatly care.

Brayley was back from the Lone Dog. He saw him at night when he came into the bunk-house. He and Brayley looked at each other, saying no word. Brayley turned with a casual remark to one of the men; Conniston took his place at the table. Still they said nothing to each other, each man knowing without words that what had passed between them was passed until some new incident should arise to settle matters for them. Brayley, being quick of eye, saw that Conniston had adopted at least one of the customs of the range, and that he carried a revolver at his belt.

The third day was Friday. Conniston determined to work Saturday. Then he would have Sunday for rest. And when Sunday afternoon came he could quit if he felt that his aching body had not recuperated enough to make the following week bearable. But he had yet to learn that in the rush of busy days on the range there is no Sunday. For

Sunday morning came and brought no opportunity to sleep until noon. Breakfast was ready at the usual dim hour, and the men went to work as they had on every day since he came to the Half Moon. They knew what he did not, that for many weeks to come they might have no single day off. And they understood, and did not complain.

Brayley stopped him that morning as he was going out of the bunk-house door with Lonesome Pete.

"We got something else to do besides tinker with ol' fences," he said, roughly. "Pete, you got to git along alone to-day. I'll give you a man to-morrow if I can spare one. Conniston, you git your hoss an' go with Rawhide an' Toothy."

Not stopping for an answer, Brayley lurched away toward the range-house. Lonesome Pete, nodding his red head to show that he had heard, filled his water-bottle and got the lunch the cook had ready for him. And Conniston, wondering vaguely what work the Sunday was to bring for him, turned silently and followed Rawhide and the man whom they called Toothy to the stables.

Toothy was a little man, so stubborn, they said, that he even refused to let the sun brown his skin. Instead of being the coppery hue of his companions, the parchment-like stuff drawn tight over his high cheek-bones was a dirty yellow. His eyes were small, set close together, and squinted eternally in a sort of mirthless grin. His teeth, which had given him his name, were the most conspicuous of his odd features. The two front incisors of his upper jaw protruded outward so as to close when his mouth was shut—and generally it wasn't—over his lower lip. He was the smallest man on the range and by long odds the ugliest. But he could ride!

Conniston was sorry to be separated from Lonesome Pete,

the only man of the outfit with whom he spoke a dozen words a day, the only man who did not treat him as a rank outsider and an alien. But, on the other hand, he was glad that he was to be given a respite from the blistering wires of the cross-fence, that he was to be given change of work. And when he learned what the work was he was doubly glad. The three men were to ride twenty miles from the bunk-house to the lower corrals of the Lone Dog to gather up a herd of steers there and drive them across to the Sunk Hole. It would mean long hours in the saddle, but Conniston told himself that riding, urging on lagging cattle, would be almost rest after the drudgery of the last four days. And in some elusive way, not clear to himself, he felt that this work carried with it a bit less humiliation than the sort of "hired man's work" which he had been doing with Lonesome Pete.

Like many men who know of the range only what they have read in books, only what they have seen in breezy pictures, it seemed to Conniston that there could be no life so lazy as that of the cowboy who has nothing to do but ride a spirited horse, day in and day out to drive sluggish-blooded cows from one pasture to another or to a market-place, to watch over them as they grazed, or to ride along the outskirts of a scattering herd to see that they did not stray beyond a set boundary-line. That life, as he saw it, was an existence without responsibility, without fatigue, even tinged with something of exhilaration as one galloped up and down over wide grassy meadows. To-day he began to learn that a gay-colored picture may hide quite as much as it shows.

They left the Half Moon corrals at a gentle canter, Conniston swinging along beside the other men, actually enjoying himself. He wondered at the deliberate slowness with which Rawhide Jones and Toothy began their errand. For he had heard the few short orders which Brayley had given, and he knew that to-day was a day of haste, with much to be done. But before they had cantered more than a mile across the rolling country to the west he saw that there was going to be no loitering. They had ridden slowly only until their horses had "warmed up," and now, shaking out their reins loosely, they swept on at a pace which allowed of little conversation. They drew away from the Half Moon corrals at four o'clock. It was not yet six when they pulled in their panting, sweat-covered horses at the corrals of the Lone Dog.

These corrals were at the lower, eastern end of the Lone Dog, and some ten miles from the Lone Dog bunk-house. To reach them the three men had ridden across three spurs of the mountains, across much rough country, and always at a swinging gallop. Conniston's legs, where they rubbed against the sweat leathers of his saddle, were already chafed and raw. With the day's work still ahead of him he was tired and sore. He was more glad than he was willing to confess even to himself when he saw the corrals ahead. For now, he assured himself, there could be little to do but jog along after a slow-moving body of cattle.

The three big corrals were crowded with a bellowing, churning, restless mass of cattle, big, long-horned steers for the most part, and vicious-looking. In a much smaller inclosure were a few saddle-horses—half-broken colts, to look at them—thrusting their long noses above their fence to stare at the seething jam of cattle, or, with tails and manes flying, to run here and there snorting. Two men on horse-back were sitting idly near the corrals, seeming to have nothing in all the world to do but smoke cigarettes and watch the milling cattle.

Conniston drew rein with his companions as they stopped for a word with the two men from the Lone Dog. And then he followed them when they turned and rode to the little corral. The horses in it bunched up, quick-eyed, alert, at the far side of the inclosure. Rawhide Jones and Toothy as they rode were taking down the ropes coiled upon their saddles.

"We're goin' to change hosses here," Rawhide said, shortly. "Pick out one for yourse'f, Conniston."

They had ridden into the corral, their ropes in their hands, each man dragging a wide loop at his right side. Toothy rode swiftly into the knot of horses, scattered them, and, as they shot across the corral, sent his rope flying out over their heads. The long loop widened into a circle, hissed through the air, and settled about the neck of a little pinto mare, tightening as it fell. A quick turn about the horn of his saddle, and Toothy set up his own horse. The pinto mare, checked in her headlong flight, swung about, confronting her captor with quivering nostrils and belligerent, flashing eyes. Almost at the same instant Rawhide's rope obeyed Rawhide's hand as Toothy's had done, settling unerringly about the neck of a second horse. And Conniston, with grave misdoubtings and a thumping heart, took his own rope into his hand and rode among the untamed brutes, one of which he was to ride.

Here was another thing which seemed, upon the face of it, so simple and which was simple—to the range born and bred. He knew that there were four men watching him as he fumbled awkwardly with his rope. He knew that in spite of their grave faces they were laughing inwardly. He found that to hold the coil of rope in his left hand while that same hand must keep a tight rein upon his mount, to whirl the widening loop with his right, throwing it at just the right second with just the right force, was one of the things which in pictures looked to be so easy and which were not at all easy to accomplish. He grew hot and red as he became entangled in his own rope.

At last he selected a big roan and threw his rope. He threw awkwardly and a second too late. The loop fell fifteen paces behind the horse, who had seen, understood, and shot by in a flash. Again he coiled his rope, drawing it in to him as he had seen the others do; again he threw, and again he missed. He heard Rawhide Jones curse softly, contemptuously.

Now the horse which he was riding began to plunge and rear, frightened at the rope which now fell upon its back, now struck its flanks in the unskilled hands of the man who was growing the more awkward as his anger surged higher within him.

"You blame fool!" yelled Rawhide Jones. "What in hell are you tryin' to do? Want to throw your own cayuse?"

Conniston glared at him and again coiled his rope. The big roan was once more surrounded by a crowd of his fellows, his ears erect, his long neck outstretched, his eyes watchful and distrustful. The man who was beginning to look upon lassoing as a sheer matter of sleight of hand made his loop again carefully, slowly, trying to convince himself that here was an easy matter, and that the next time he should succeed. And even as he began whirling it above his head, one half of both mind and muscle given over to restrain his nervous mount, he saw another rope shoot out from behind him and settle, tightening, about the roan's neck.

"Bein' as we ain't got all summer to practise up lass'in' bosses," Toothy murmured, apologetically.

Conniston tied his rope to his saddle-strings in silence. After all, there was something to do beyond sit in a saddle. And he soon found that even that was not always play. For the roan which he had selected fought at having the saddle thrown upon his back, so that Toothy had to lend a helping hand. And when the cinch was drawn tight he fought at being mounted. He had been broken, at least—and at most—as much broken as the rest of the three and four year olds in the corral. But he had not been ridden above a dozen times, and certainly had not known the feel of rope or bridle or saddle for months. When at last Conniston got his foot into the stirrup and swung up, violating all range ethics by "pulling leather," the colt shot through the gate of the corral which Rawhide Jones had thrown open, and across the uneven plain, determined, since he could not run away from his enemy, to run away with him.

At home Conniston was accounted an excellent horseman. That meant that he was used to horses, that he rode gracefully, that he was not afraid of them. Horses like the maddened, terrified brutes in the corral, like the quivering, frantic thing he precariously bestrode, he had never even seen. And still, because he was doggedly determined not to fail in everything, because he knew that the men who were watching were enjoying themselves hugely and that they would be greatly delighted to see him thrown, he at last stopped his horse, and with spur and quirt urged him back to the corrals. The roan still fought, still half bucked. But he had not entirely forgotten his past defeats in encounters like this, and finally allowed himself to be mastered.

Then began the real day's work. There were perhaps fifty cows and young heifers in the corrals which were to be left behind, as only the steers were to be driven across country to the Sunk Hole. While Rawhide Jones and Toothy rode into one of the corrals Conniston was to sit his horse at the open gate, allowing the steers to run by him into the open, but heading off any of the smaller cattle. The two Lone Dog men were together working another corral.

Steer after steer passed by Conniston as he held his horse aside, keeping a watchful eye for the cows. Rawhide and Toothy were "cutting them out" as best they could, urging the steers toward the gate, trying to keep the cows to the far side of the inclosure. But again and again a quick-footed heifer pressed her slender body against that of some big, long-horned steer, running with him. That she did not pass through the gate was Conniston's lookout.

They were not sluggish-blooded brutes. They were as swift as a horse almost, quick-footed, alert to leap forward or to stop with sharp hoofs cutting the dry dirt, and swing shortly to the side. In a sudden onrush toward him Conniston shut off one cow by forcing his horse in front of her and threatening her with his waving quirt. As she turned and ran back into the mass behind her he saw two more cows running toward the gate. He swung his horse and dashed at them. But they had seen their opportunity, they had grasped it, and they shot through the gate, mingling with the herd outside.

Again Rawhide cursed him, and Conniston made no answer, having none to make. He gave over his place silently at Rawhide's surly order and rode over to aid Toothy. And he marveled at the ease with which Rawhide did the thing which he himself had found simple from a distance and impossible near at hand.

At last, behind the scattering herd of running cattle, they left the corrals and the Lone Dog men behind, and began their drive forty miles to the Sunk Hole. Now a man must be a hundred places at the same time. In twenty minutes the three horses were wet and dripping with sweat. The herd was one which ordinarily, when there was not so much requiring to be done at once on the ranges, half a dozen men would have handled. The steers were wild; they were as stubborn as hogs; there was no narrow, fenced-in road to keep them in the way they should go. They broke back again and again; they turned off to right and left by ones and twos, by scores. While Conniston galloped after one of them that had left the others and broken into a run to the right the main part of the herd over which he should have been watching took advantage of the opportunity to lose themselves in the timbered gulches to the left. Both Rawhide Jones and Toothy had to ride with him to drive them out of the gulches and back to the herd.

Conniston learned that day how a cattle-man can swear— and why. He learned that a steer is not the easiest thing in the world to handle, that sometimes he is not content with fleeing from his natural enemy, but charges with lowered horns and froth-dripping mouth upon man and horse. He learned many, many little things that day, and some big things. And the biggest thing came to him suddenly, and brought a look into his eyes which had never been there before. He learned that Greek Conniston, the son of William Conniston, of Wall Street, was the most inefficient man upon the range.

CHAPTER VIII

Day followed day in an endless round of range duties, and two weeks had passed since Greek Conniston began work for the Half Moon outfit. He admitted to himself over many a solitary pipeful of cheap tobacco that Miss Argyl Crawford had been the reason for his coming out into the wilderness. And he asked himself what good his coming had done. He had not so much as caught a fleeting glimpse of her since her father had engaged him to go to work at thirty dollars a month. He did not even know that she was still on the range, that she had not gone to Crawfordsville, where her father had a house, where he owned the electric-lighting plant, the water system, and a general merchandise store, and where both father and daughter spent many weeks each year.

The range-house, although but a few hundred yards distant from the bunk-house, might as well have been in the next county. News from it seldom filtered to the men's sleeping-quarters. The foreman, Brayley now, Bat Truxton before him, reported frequently to Mr. Crawford at his office in the big building, took orders from him there, advised with him. The other men went there only when they were sent for, and that was not more than half a dozen times yearly, when that many.

Conniston knew that Hapgood had stayed with the

Jackson Gregory

Crawfords two or three days, resting up, as he overheard Brayley say with a fine scorn, and that then he had gone on into Crawfordsville. Conniston supposed that by now he had borrowed money and, if not again in New York, was on his way thither. Of all else of the doings in the big house he was as ignorant as though he had never crossed the desert lands between the Half Moon and Indian Creek.

Conniston most of all men working for Mr. Crawford felt that he could not go to the house. He had come to these people as an equal, as one of their own station in life, even from a plane a bit higher than theirs. When he had gone to work he had not thought that he was to be put upon the same footing as every ignorant laborer who drew his pay from the owner of the Half Moon. He had thought that it would be a lark, that he would come to the house and laugh with the girl over his days of rubbing elbows with thirty-dollar-a-month men. That he would be, in a way, a guest.

Now it was evident that they had forgotten him, that if they thought of Conniston it was merely to remember that he was one of the common outfit. And Conniston's pride told him that if they chose to ignore him, to look down upon him, to shut him out of their world socially, he could do equally as well without them. Which was all very well, but which did not in the least hinder him from dreaming dreams inhabited solely by a slender, lithe, graceful girl with big gray eyes like dawn skies in springtime.

The two weeks had not been wasted. He had learned something, and he had made a friend. The friend was Lonesome Pete. Night after night, with a dogged perseverance which neither towering barriers in the way of unbelievably long words nor the bantering ridicule of his fellows could affect, the red-headed man sat at the table in the bunkhouse under the swinging-lamp and conned "Macbeth." Upon long rides across the range he carried "Macbeth" in his hand, a diminutive and unsatisfactory dictionary in his hip-pocket.

One day Conniston and Lonesome Pete were riding together upon some range errand. Lonesome Pete was particularly interested in his study, and Conniston asked him the question he had been upon the verge of asking many times.

"How does it happen, Pete," he said, carelessly, "that you're getting so interested in an education here of late?"

Pete did not answer with his usual alacrity. Conniston, looking at him, about to repeat the question, thinking that it had been lost in the thud of their horses' hoofs, was considerably amazed to see the cowboy's face go as flaming a red as his hair.

"Look here, Con," Pete said, finally, his tone half belligerent, while his eyes, usually so frank, refused to meet Conniston's amused regard, "what I do an' why I do it ain't any other jasper's concern, is it?"

"Certainly not," answered Conniston, promptly. "Certainly not mine. I didn't go to frolic into your personal business, Pete."

"I mean other jaspers, not you, Con," Pete continued, after they had galloped on for a moment in silence. "You been helpin' me so's I don't know how I'd 'a' made such fas' improvement without you. It's like this: here I am, gittin' along first-rate, maybe, like the res' of the boys, workin' steady, an' a few good hard iron dollars put away in a sock. An' all the time with no more eddication than a wall-eyed, year-ol' steer. An' some day, in case I might creep a ways off'n the range, I ain't no more fit to herd with real folks than that same steer is."

"You're figuring, then, on leaving the range? On going to a city to live? To cut something of a dash in society? Is that it, Pete?"

Again Pete blushed.

"Git out, Con! You're joshin'! But what I says is so, an' you know it as well's I do. Now, it's goin' on three months I'm down in Rattlesnake Valley, where the Ol' Man's stringin' his chips on makin' a big play. He's goin' to make a town down in that sand-pile or bust a tug; I ain't sayin' which right now. Anyway, he's already got a school down there, an' they make the kids go. I figgered it out, seein' as them little freckle-nosed sons o' guns could learn readin' an' writin' an' such-like, by gravy, I could do it too!"

The explanation was so simple, and Lonesome Pete had such difficulty in making his halting words come, and had such a way of refusing to look at Conniston, that the latter began to suspect the truth.

"How about the teacher, Pete?" he asked, quietly, innocently. "They have a real fine teacher, I suppose? Man or— woman?"

"Nuther! She's a lady! An' she's that smart as would make a man wonder! In case there's anything as that same Miss Jocelyn Truxton don't know, I ain't wise to it none."

"And—pretty?"

Lonesome Pete's joyous grin was like a beam of summer sunlight.

"They ain't none han'somer as ever wasted her time ridin' herd on a bunch of dirty-faced brats. Say, Con," a bit doubtfully, "I wouldn't mind showin' you—you ain't goin' to blow it off to the boys, are you?"

Conniston swore himself to secrecy and watched Lonesome Pete with twinkling eyes as the cowboy put his hand deep into the inside pocket of his vest—the left pocket. First he removed the safety-pin with which the top edges of the pocket were held securely together. Then he brought out a bit of cardboard wrapped carefully in a wonderfully clean red handkerchief. Whipping the handkerchief from the cardboard, he held out to Conniston's gaze the picture it concealed.

"That's her, Con. An' I'll leave it to you if she ain't in the blue-ribbon class, huh?"

She was pretty, decidedly pretty. Very dark, evidently young, her face rounded, her mouth laughing, her eyes soft and big. And withal it was a doll-like prettiness, a prettiness which was a trifle too conscious of itself; there was a bit too much pose, too much studied effect. Conniston thought that the girl's two chief characteristics were so close under the smiling surface that he could not help seeing them, and that they were, first, vanity; second, weakness.

"So that's Jocelyn Truxton, is it?" He handed the picture back to Lonesome Pete, who, with a long, worshipful glance at it, restored it in its wrapping to his vest pocket. "Not the daughter of Bat Truxton?"

"You wouldn't think it to look at her after seein' him, would you?"

Never having seen either of them, Conniston remained non-committal.

"Mrs. Bat Truxton was a Boston, Mass., girl, an' I reckon as how Miss Jocelyn takes after her."

So there had sprung up between the two men a strange sort of friendship, a strange sort of intimacy. For even when he came to have a strong liking for Lonesome Pete, Conniston could never for a second look upon this illiterate, uncouth cowboy as an equal, could not refrain from feeling toward him an amused and tolerant contempt. If palmy days ever came again, he was used to thinking, he would find a place for the red-headed man in his retinue of hired men. He could have an easy job at a good salary gardening about the Adirondack country home, or perhaps he might grow into a fair chauffeur.

Gradually Conniston had learned how to ride the wild devils they called broken saddle-horses as a cowman should, and without pulling leather. With Lonesome Pete a patient tutor, he was even beginning to learn how to throw a rope without entangling his own person and his own horse in it, and how to make it obey him and drop over the horns of a running steer. These things came slowly and with many discouraging failures. But they served as a stimulant and an encouragement to the man who taught him and whom he taught.

When he had been with the outfit for three weeks Conniston began to feel confident that he could perform the part of the day's work which was allotted to him. His muscles had begun to harden so that they no longer ached and throbbed day and night.

Then one morning he saw Argyl Crawford. He had begun of late to tell himself that he had invested her in his imagination with a charm which was not hers; that after the studied neglect that he had sustained at her hands and at her father's hands he was going to forget all about her. And now, as she came unexpectedly out of the circle of trees, pausing upon a little grassy knoll just where his idle eyes were resting, where the early sun found her out, making her a thing of light against the dull-green background, Conniston caught his breath and told himself that she was in reality the queen of this land of enchantment.

She came out of the forest as a mountain Naiad might have done, her beauty a glorious, wonderful thing, her grace the free, lithe, unconscious grace of the wild things of this country of hers, swift-footed, firm-footed, and, it seemed to the man who watched her, with a sort of shyness which belongs to the creature of the woodlands. As she paused, her hands at her sides, her head lifted with tip-tilted chin, unconscious that any one saw her, not seeing the man who squatted by the spring below the bunk-house, he felt vaguely as though he were looking upon a nymph who, if he so much as moved, would turn swiftly and flash away from him into the depths of her shadowy forest.

Having no desire to be seen just then, Conniston sat very still. The other boys were breakfasting within the bunk-house. He had hurried with his meal, and now was washing a pair of socks. He had no wish to have her see him doing this sort of work. He moved slightly so that the little clump of willows near the spring stood like a screen between them.

He remembered suddenly that he had not had a shave for four days.

Rawhide Jones, Toothy, and Brayley came out of the bunk-house together. They all saw her and as one man lifted their broad-brimmed hats. She called to Brayley, and as the others went down to the stable he walked, lurching, to her. Conniston could not hear what she was saying, but Brayley's heavier voice came to him distinctly. The girl was asking something, and Brayley after a moment's thought agreed to her request. She turned, smiling at him and thanking him, and went back through the trees toward the house. The big foreman came back to the bunk-house. Conniston, his socks washed and now dripping, turned away from the stream and came to the clothes-line running from the corner of the low building to a tree sixty feet away.

"Hey, you, Conniston," Brayley called to him. "You're jest the man I'm lookin' for. Saddle Dandy for Miss Argyl an' take him up to the house for her. An' take your own hoss along. She wants you to go with her."

Conniston flushed up, suddenly rebellious. He had not gone to work to be a lacky to Miss Argyl. He had no desire to lead her horse up to the house for her that she might swing into her saddle, leaving him to follow her at due and respectful distance like a groom. Why had she singled him out from the others to go with her, to play the part of the menial at her orders? Was it simply so that she, a Crawford, the daughter of a man who for all that Conniston knew to the contrary had never been out of this little corner of the West and was in the beginning a nobody, might say in the future that she had been served by a Conniston, by the son of William Conniston, of Wall Street—boasting of it? If she crooked her finger must he run to do her bidding because her father was taking advantage of his temporary exile to have him work for him at a dollar a day?

"Well?" snapped Brayley, as Conniston stood frowning, making no answer, "Did you think I said she wanted you to-morrow?"

For a moment Conniston hesitated. Then, scarcely knowing why he did it, he turned upon his heel and went to hang out his wet socks. Still making no reply to Brayley, he got his hat and strode off to the stable.

Ten minutes later he rode through the circle of trees and to the front of the house, leading Miss Argyl's pony. Miss Crawford, in khaki riding-habit, gray gauntlets, and wide, gray hat, already booted and spurred for her ride, was waiting upon the front steps. As she saw Conniston ride up she nodded gaily to him with a merry "Good morning," and ran lightly down the steps to meet him. He answered her a bit stiffly—with dignity, he would have said—and swung down from his saddle to help her to mount. But before he could come to her side she had mounted, and sat watching him as he again got into his saddle. He saw a vast amusement in her eyes as they omitted no detail of his appearance, missing neither the stubby growth upon cheek and chin, nor the unbuttoned vest with Durham tag and strings protruding, nor the not over-clean chaps, nor the gun at his belt. And when her eyes rested at last upon his they were smiling, and his stubbornly grave and vacant.

"You are going to ride with me?" she asked, quickly.

He inclined his head.

"Orders from Brayley," he said, quietly.

"Oh!" And then, flicking her horse across the flank with her quirt, she turned away from the house and down the roadway which led by the pond and along which Conniston had come that day when he first saw the Half Moon. And Conniston, ten paces behind her, erect, sober-faced, followed her like a well-trained groom.

For a mile they rode at a swift gallop, the girl in front not so much as turning her head to see if he were following, their way leading along the bank of Indian Creek and through the gloomy half-light which sifted down through the mesh of branches of the big trees reaching high overhead. Then she left the road for a narrow trail which wound through trees and bushes down into the creek-bed and across it, coming out through the trees upon the dry grass-covered plain to the east. And now again she rode at a swinging gallop, and he followed her. He knew that twenty miles ahead of them was Rattlesnake Valley. He began to wonder if that were where she was going.

Suddenly she jerked in her horse and sat waiting for him. And Conniston, grown stubbornly determined that if she wanted him she must call to him, stopped his own horse at a respectful distance behind her. She turned her head and looked at him wonderingly.

"What is it, Mr. Conniston? What makes you act so strangely? Don't you want to ride with me?"

He touched his hat with mock solemnity.

"I did not know that you wanted me to. I imagined that the hired man's place—"

"Oh, nonsense!" she broke in, impatiently. And with a swift smile which was so faint, so elusive that it was gone before he could be sure that he had not imagined it, "I thought that you were going—that we were going to be friends."

"That was ages ago," he retorted, bitterly. "Ages before I turned into a dollar-a-day laborer. Before I went to work for your father, Miss Crawford."

"And that is nonsense. A man does a man's work, honorable work with his two hands, and makes his own money, much or little. The most independent men in the world, Mr. Conniston, are men like Brayley and Toothy and Rawhide Jones and the rest. Are you not as good a man as these, as independent, as free to do as you like, as they are?"

"Am I as good a man!" He laughed shortly. "Conceit, no doubt, Miss Crawford, but none the less I really do fancy that a Conniston is as good as the sort of men I have been herding with here of late!"

She seemed not to notice his sarcasm, although his tones rang with it.

"Your going to work for father—I think it was brave of you. If it makes any difference at all it will be because you make it do so. I should be glad to have you ride with me as a companion if you wish."

She pricked her horse with her spur and rode on. And Conniston, after a brief moment of hesitation in which he began to see that he had been acting rather foolishly, galloped up to her side.

"I am afraid I have been boorish, Miss Crawford. You must forgive me."

"In three weeks you have learned a great deal, but there is still a great deal which you do not seem to have assimilated."

"I have learned—" There was a question in his unfinished sentence.

"You have learned to ride as a man must who is to do his day's work of twelve, maybe fifteen, hours in the saddle. Surely that is something. You have learned to rope a steer on the dead run. You have learned to rope your own horse, to throw him while you saddle him, and to ride him when he gets up. You have learned to work."

He stared at her in surprise.

"How do you know what I have been doing?"

She laughed, a happy gurgle of a laugh which made a man want to laugh with her without knowing the cause of her merriment.

"Lonesome Pete has brought me news, and Toothy, and even your friend Brayley! Do you know," mischief lurking in the depths of her eyes above the assumed gravity of her face, "I think that the boys are actually beginning to approve of you."

"Flattering, I must say!"

"I think that it is."

"Even," he cried, incredulously, wondering if she could jest so earnestly—"even by such men as Toothy and Rawhide Jones and the rest?"

She looked at him steadily, frowning a little bit.

"I don't know why you should speak of them so contemptuously. If, on the one hand, they have had no great social advantages, on the other hand have they not at least made men out of themselves?"

"I had hardly looked upon them in that light," he answered, with something of the sneer still in his voice. "I had looked upon them rather as I had supposed you were ready to consider me, as machines of the type which ladies and gentlemen have to wait upon them, to do the unskilled labor for them, as common laborers."

"Common laborers! I hate that word. They are men, aren't they? They are stanch friends and good enemies. They are true to their own laws and to their conceptions of right and wrong. And they are strong and self-reliant and free and independent."

"And still they are ignorant, unrefined, coarse. Not your

equals, Miss Crawford, and, I thank God, not mine!"

"Not yours? Are you sure?"

"You are serious—or are you making fun of me?"

"I am very serious." There was no mistaking that when he looked into her eyes.

"They are the sons of Smith and Jones and Brown," he replied slowly. "Smith and Jones and Brown before them were uneducated, ignorant, living lives with low horizons, seeing nothing, knowing nothing of the greater world beyond their ken. They were a degree higher than the horses which they mastered, the cattle which they drove to market. And now their sons, inheriting the limited natures of their sires, have grown like weeds in the environment in which fate put them, with no knowledge of the other things. I think that it is answer enough when I say that I am the son of William Conniston."

He did not mean to boast. He merely stated a simple fact simply. And the scorn leaping up in her eyes, ringing in her clear voice as she answered him, startled him.

"We know a man by his hands, not by his name!" she cried, her face flushing with her eagerness. "Our admiration, our respect is always for the man who does things, not for the man whose father did them for him. And now, because men like Lonesome Pete and Brayley and the rest of the boys live a life which knows nothing of your world, you sneer at them!"

"I'll admit," he granted, although stung by her hot words, "that the poor devils have hardly had a fair chance. They are handicapped—"

"Handicapped!" Her scorn was a fine thing, leaping out at him, cutting into his words. "Can't you see who it is that is handicapped in the great race here—here in the West? Here where there is a fight going on every day, every night of the year, a battle royal of man against mother earth? And the man who fights here successfully a winning fight, not stopping to ask at what odds, must be endowed with a great strength, a rugged physical and moral constitution, self-reliance, a true, deep insight into the natures of other men. Those things my father has. So has Bat Truxton, so has Brayley, so, for that matter, has Lonesome Pete."

He had never seen her so tense, so vehement, so warmly impulsive before. Nor so radiantly beautiful.

"Do you know," she was running on, swiftly, "how it happened that you were selected to ride with me to-day?"

"No. At first I thought merely because you wanted to humiliate me. Now I am beginning to believe that you sent for me to instruct me in certain matters relative to the brotherhood of man!"

"And you were not right at first, and are not right now. I asked Brayley to let me have a man to help me with something I have to do over in the valley, and he said he would send you. Do you guess why?"

"No. It was a kindness from Brayley, and I am not in the habit of expecting kindnesses from him."

"Then I will tell you. He sent you because you are the only man he has working under him whom he could spare. *Because he needs all the good men!*"

Conniston felt his face go red. He tried to laugh at what she said, to show her that it mattered little to him what a man of Brayley's type said or thought. And he was angry with himself because he knew that it did matter. Biting back the words which first sprang to his lips, he tried to say, lightly:

"I'm afraid that I shall have to lick Brayley for that."

"Lick him!" Again she laughed her disdain. "Why didn't you do it that first night in the bunk-house? Unless," she challenged, "in spite of all your blue blood and white hands and father's name, Brayley is the better man!"

"What do you know of that?" His voice was harsh, his question a command for an answer. "Who told you?"

"I knew there was trouble. I asked about it. Brayley told me."

He made no answer. There was nothing for him to say. She had Brayley's account of the fight, she believed it, and Conniston would not let her know that he cared enough to give his own version.

"I have not meant to be unkind, Mr. Conniston," she said, after a moment. A new note had crept into her voice with what sounded like sympathy. He did not look toward her. "And, after all, it is none of my concern how you think, how you carry yourself. But I did want you to realize just what that great handicap is. You said on that day when you first came to the Half Moon that you were going to make yourself my friend, didn't you? Do you mind if I talk to you now like a friend? You may call me presumptuous if you like. No doubt I am. As a friend I have a right to be meddlesome, haven't I?" She smiled at him as brightly as if she had never said or thought the things which she had flung at him a moment ago. "To begin with, then, I think that you have deep down in some corner of your being a strength which might do great things, that nature intended you to be a man, a great, big, splendid man!"

"Thanks," murmured Conniston, dryly. "I don't know what I have done to deserve—"

"Nothing! You have done nothing! That is just it. Oh, you see, when I start to meddle I do it very thoroughly! It is not what you have done but what you might do. And I was going to tell you what the real handicap is. It is not the being-without-things, without advantages, which has restricted the fuller growth of such men as Bat Truxton and Brayley. It is something very different from that—essentially different. It is the being-raised-a-rich-man's-son! It is the being-born-something instead of the being-obliged-to-make-oneself-something!"

"Theoretically, Miss Crawford, I suppose that you are right. But theory is only theory, you know. Frankly, would not a man be a fool to work when there is no need for it? Would not a man be a fool to eschew the pleasures of life when fortune is ready to spill them into his lap for him? Does not the rich man's son get a great deal more out of the game than the poor devil who spends his life punching cows at thirty dollars a month? Even if I began to take myself seriously at this late hour and to take life as a serious sort of thing, too; even if I tucked in and fell in love with my work"—he shuddered for her benefit—"what good would it do me? If I turned out to be the best rider, the best shot, the best roper of steers, what then?"

"My father," she answered, simply, "like every other man who does big things on a big scale, is always looking for good men, for foremen, for men like Bat Truxton, like Brayley, and for men who must do work for which such men as Brayley are unfit—men who have got an education and have retained their strength of manhood through it. You could grow; you could step from one position to another, you could yourself be a strong man, a big man, a man like my father, like your father. Don't you see? You could be that sort of a man, a real man, a man's man, instead of being the sort of man who is sent upon a girl's errand because none of the other men can be spared. You have done the natural thing heretofore; the fault has not been yours. You have merely been unfortunate in being too fortunate. But now, don't you see, it is different. Now you are being submitted to the test. Why, even your friend, Roger Hapgood—"

"Leave out the *friend* part. What about him?"

"He is taking hold. He is shaking off the listlessness which has clung to him ever since he was born. Father learned from him that he had studied law in college and got him a place with Mr. Winston in Crawfordsville. And he is working, working hard, and making good!"

"You seem to know everything, Miss Crawford."

"Oh, this is so simple. Mr. Winston is father's lawyer. Mr. Hapgood has ridden back to the Half Moon several times upon business for the firm."

Conniston frowned, little pleased. The Half Moon range-house, then, was open to Hapgood as a friend, as an equal. It was closed to Greek Conniston as a day-laborer! And he knew well enough why Hapgood was staying, why he was working so hard. He had not forgotten the pale-eyed man's appreciation of the girl—and of her father's wealth. He knew that Roger Hapgood was working for much more than his monthly stipend, for much more than the love of the law.

He whirled suddenly toward the girl, surprising her in her scrutiny of his frowning face.

"Why do you care what I do?" he cried, almost fiercely. "Why do you tell me to go ahead, to do something? What difference does it make to you? Will you tell me?"

She returned his look steadily, answered steadily, not hesitating.

"Because it seemed to me a shame for a man like you to be a pawn in a game all of his life while he might be playing the game himself, directing the pawns."

"And there is no other interest?"

"A friend's interest. For," smiling at him, "I believed what you said when you told me that we were going to be friends."

"We are." He spoke slowly, thoughtfully. "You have talked very plainly to me to-day, and I can do no more and no less than to thank you. You have told me several things. Some of them are true. I don't know that I agree with the others. You have a way of looking at life, at the world, which is new to me. I must think it all over. I shall know how to think, what to do, to-morrow."

She looked at him questioningly.

"For to-morrow I shall have decided. And then I shall ask for my time and quit, or—"

"Or—?" she asked, quickly.

"Or I shall tie into my work in earnest. I wonder which it will be?"

"I don't wonder at all!" she cried, softly, her eyes very bright. "And to-morrow evening will you come up to the house and tell me what you have decided?"

"I think," he answered her, quietly, "that I have already decided. But I shall not tell you until to-morrow evening."

CHAPTER IX

That night Conniston sat up late, perched high on the corral fence, staring at the stars while he tore down and builded up the World.

He had ridden to Rattlesnake Valley with Argyl, and had spent a big part of the day there with her. He saw scores of men at work with scrapers, picks, and shovels, and understood little enough of what they were doing. He rode with her into a town, a brand-new town, of twenty small, neat houses, as alike as rows of peas. In one of the houses he worked for Argyl, tacking down carpets in the empty rooms, moving furniture which he had uncrated in the yard. This was to be her father's camp, she told him, where he would soon have to spend a part of each week superintending the work which Bat Truxton was pushing forward seven days out of the week. Then they had at last ridden home together, and he had left her at the house, going slowly back to the corrals with the two horses. And now, his day's work done, he stared at the stars, rearranging the universe.

He knew that he was William Conniston, the son of William Conniston of Wall Street. That fact was unchanged, unchangeable. But in some new way, vaguely different, it was not the all-important fact which it had been. It was still something to be glad of, something which he was not going to forget or underestimate. But it was not everything.

Sitting there alone, his pipe dead between his teeth, Greek Conniston asked himself many questions which had never suggested themselves to his complacency before. And he answered them, one by one, without fear or favor. In what was he better than Brayley, than Toothy even? Was he a better man physically? No. Was he a better man morally? No. Was he a better man intellectually? He had thought he was; now he hesitated long before answering that question. Certainly he had had an education which they had missed. Certainly his intellect had been trained, in a fashion, by great men, by learned university professors. But was it any keener than Brayley's and Toothy's; was it any stronger; was it, after all, any more highly trained? In a crisis now was his intellect any better than theirs? In his present environment was it any better? And finally he answered that question as he had answered the others.

Was he a better man in the composite, in the grand total of manhood? Measured by all the standards by which men are measured, stripping off the superficialities of surface culture and clothes, the thin veneer of education which in his case, as in the cases of the great majority of young men who have been graduated from this or that university, had imparted only a sort of finish, a neat, gleaming polish, and no great metamorphosis of the inner and true being, was he a better man? If there was any one particular, no matter how small, in which Greek Conniston was a better man than the men among whom he had moved with careless contempt, he wanted to know what it was!

"I have been a howling young ass!" he told himself, his contempt suddenly swerving upon himself. "A conceited fool and a snob! Lordy, lordy, why didn't somebody tell me—and kick me? A snob—a d—d, insufferable, conceited snob!"

Three weeks ago the things which Argyl Crawford had said

to him would have amused the very self-satisfied young man. A week later, when something of the truth had begun to filter in dimly upon him, he would have felt hurt, insulted. Now he was ready to go to her, to thank her, to tell her that a fool was dead, that he hoped a man was being born.

"And I would right now," he muttered to himself, "only I suppose that anything I said would sound like the braying of a jackass!"

The one thing which she had said to him which now returned with ever-increasing significance was the reason, as she had explained it, why he had been chosen to go with her to Rattlesnake Valley. Out of the dozens of men who worked under Brayley's orders he was absolutely the only one who could be spared from the day's work! Every other man had a quicker eye, a stronger body, a firmer hand; every other man was a better rider, a better herder, a better roper, a better all-round man. When there was work that must be done, man's work, he was the one who could be spared from it.

By nature headlong, when Greek Conniston went into a thing he was in the habit of going deep into it. When he drove a new car he drove it night and day and at top speed. When he spent money he spent lavishly, generously, recklessly. When he wasted time he wasted it profligately. And now that he abandoned an old position he did it as thoroughly as he had dissipated his father's money. He was plunging from what had so long seemed to him a great height. Plunging; not cautiously lowering himself inch by inch down a dizzy precipice of self-respect, not looking the while for the first ledge upon which he might rest; plunging headlong from the zenith of self-conceit to the nadir of self-contempt. And the depths into which he hurled himself seemed to him very deep, very black.

He ignored considerations by the way. That he had been handicapped in the race did not suggest itself to him to comfort him. He merely saw that the race was on and that he was far in the rear, choked with the dust of the going. He saw, and saw clearly, that of all the men who took their dollar a day from John Crawford he, Greek Conniston, did the least to earn his. That he was not only not the best man on the range, but that he was the poorest man. He was just his father's son. *A man's son, not a man!*

He had not eaten supper, had forgotten that he had not eaten. Long he sat in the thickening night, alone, feeling the part of a man marooned by his dawning understanding upon a desert island, vast, impassable, restless seas between him and his race. He watched the stars come out until they were thick set in the black vault above him, flung in sprays, flashing and scintillating down to the low horizons about him. His brooding eyes ran out across the floor of the plain toward Rattlesnake Valley.

He remembered that he had promised to call to see Argyl to-morrow night, to tell her then what he had decided. What was he going to decide? The obvious thing was not clear to him yet. He would work over it half the night. Out of the confusion into which he had been hurled two things alone stood out to him now as he tried to review them; two things gathered the light which abandoned all other considerations to darkness. The first thing, the clearest thing, the most important thing in all of the new world which was being built up about him was that he loved Argyl Crawford.

Loved her, not as Greek Conniston would have loved yesterday, could have loved then, but with the love which was a part of the Greek Conniston who was being born to-night. Loved her, not with the shallow affection which would have been the tribute of a Greek Conniston of yesterday, but with that deeper, eternal urge of soul to soul which is true love. Loved her gravely, almost sternly, as a strong man loves.

Upon only two days had it been given him to speak with her. He thought of that, but he knew that made no iota of difference. For he knew her better than he knew any woman with whom he had danced or driven or attended theaters and dinners. In that first glimpse from the Pullman window he had seen the purposeful character of her. To-day he had seen it again. To-day he knew that he knew Argyl Crawford, that she had been herself to him, unaffected, honest, womanly. Her nature was simple, straightforward, open, unassuming. Its beauty struck one as the beauty of a Grecian temple, its lines pure and noble, the whole edifice the more wonderful in that it depended upon itself alone and needed no adornment.

She had shaken hands with him last night when he left her at the house, not perfunctorily, but firmly, as the strong-handed cowboys shook hands, and had said to him, simply:

"I wish you luck, Greek Conniston, in the fight you are about to make."

He remembered the hand-clasp. She seemed unable to do anything, no matter how small, without putting her whole self into it, her frankness, her sincerity, her eagerness. And Conniston of to-night, scowling at the match which he had swept across his thigh to light his pipe and now let die down to his fingers, muttered, not without cause, that he had his nerve with him even to think about her.

The other thing which was clear to him was that he must "lick" Brayley. If he did nothing else in all of his futile life, if he quit work or were fired the next minute, he must "lick" Brayley. It did not strike him as amusing, as even strange, that these two things and these alone should be the only things of which he was sure. He merely accepted them as inevitable. He felt no particular resentment toward Brayley. The man had treated him fairly enough since that first night in the bunk-house. He looked upon the matter calmly, almost impersonally, as a duty to which he must attend. And he was not going to wait for an excuse. An opportunity would do.

It was half-past ten, and very late for cow-puncher land, when Greek strode away through the darkness to the bunk-house.

When morning came it happened that Brayley rose fifteen minutes early, Conniston fifteen minutes late. The foreman left immediately for a far corner of the range, and Conniston, having made a quick breakfast, went about his own work. In the corral he selected a horse which heretofore he had carefully left alone, knowing the brute's half-tamed spirit and not caring to trust to it. But now it was different. He waited his opportunity before throwing his rope. Then, as the horse, seeming to know that he had been singled out, shot by him, he cast his lasso. And there was a grim light, but at the same time a light of deep satisfaction in Conniston's eyes as he saw that his whirling noose had gone unerringly, settling as Toothy's rope would have done.

He blindfolded the big, belligerent horse to mount him. When his feet were securely thrust into his stirrups he leaned forward and with a swift jerk snapped the hand-kerchief from the horse's eyes. For a moment the animal's sides between his knees trembled and throbbed like an overtaxed engine. Then there was the sudden jerk which told of a mighty bunching of muscles, a gathering of force. And as Conniston shot his spurs home, with the reins gripped tight in his left hand so that the horse could not get his head down, the forelegs were lifted high in air as the animal reared. A quick blow of the quirt and the forelegs sought earth again, and Conniston began to realize what it was to ride a bucking bronco.

A series of short jumps, every one threatening to unseat him, every one jerking him so that his body was whipped this way and that, so that he had much ado to keep his feet from flying out of the stirrups, and could hardly hold his right hand back from going to the horn, from "pulling leather." The bucks came so close together that it seemed to him that he did not rest a second in the saddle; that each time the big brute struck the ground with his four feet bunched together, to pause for a breathless moment, gathering every ounce of strength to wrench, leaping sideways, he must surely be thrown. But in spite of all he did not pull leather, he did not cease to ply spur and quirt, and he was not thrown. It was a perfectly quiet horse he rode away across the fields only three minutes later.

He did a man's work that day, all that day, until long after the red sun had gone down. And when he came up from the corral to his supper, if he was tired, if the muscles of his body ached, it did not show in his steady stride or in his quiet eyes.

The suit-case which he had left in Indian Creek had been brought out last week. He shaved himself and changed his clothes, putting on the first white silk shirt he had worn for many a day. He even found an old can of shoe-polish and touched up the pair of dusty shoes. And then, laughing at the looks the men turned upon him, at the few jesting remarks which they chose to make, he walked through the trees and to the range-house.

The glow of electric lights through the wide-opened front doors ran out across the lawn to meet him. Striding along the walk, his heels crunching in the white gravel, he again marveled at the comfort, the luxury even, which John Crawford had brought across the desert. He ran lightly up the broad steps. Before he could ring Argyl was at the door, her eyes quick to find his searchingly. He knew what they sought to find in his. And when she put out her hand to him, swiftly, impulsively, he trusted that they had found what they sought.

He followed her through the big front room and into the library. Here there were many deep, soft leather chairs, here there was a blue atmosphere of tobacco smoke, and here Mr. Crawford, immaculate in white flannels, rose to meet him, his hand outstretched.

"How do you do, Conniston?" Mr. Crawford took his hand warmly, the fine lines of his stern old face softening genially. "I was mighty glad when Argyl told me that she had asked you over. Sit down, sit down. Have something to smoke. Tell us about yourself, and how"—the deep-set eyes twinkling—"you like the work?"

Conniston saw that Argyl had seated herself and dropped into one of the big chairs himself, his whole body enjoying the luxury of it. At his elbow was a little table with cigars and cigarettes. Mr. Crawford laughed when he saw that Conniston, having glanced at the table, drew out his own cheap muslin bag of tobacco and rough, brown papers.

"I'm getting used to them," Greek apologized. "And do you know that I'm beginning to like to roll my own 'cigareet'?"

Argyl clapped her hands, laughing with her father.

"I told you so, daddy!" she cried, merrily. "Didn't I say that Mr. Conniston was born to be a good cow-puncher!"

"And I'm half persuaded that you are right, Argyl," came

from behind the dense cloud of cigar-smoke. "But you haven't told us how you like the work, Conniston."

"If you had asked me a week ago I should have had to ask to be excused from trying to tell you in the presence of ladies. I would have quit if I hadn't been too much of a coward. But now—"

"Now?" asked Argyl, quickly.

And it was to her that he made his answer, not to her father.

"Now I like it. And I am going to stick—unless I get fired for incompetency!"

"I like that," said Mr. Crawford, slowly. "Yes, I like that. I was afraid that it was rather too much for you. It's hard work, Conniston, and long hours and little pay. But Brayley tells me that you have the makings of a rattling good cow-hand."

"Thank you, sir. It was very decent of Brayley."

"I ought not to mix business into a social call, I know, but I want to tell you personally that I am very much pleased with the way you are tucking in. You asked if any one needed a good man the day you came. We all do. I do. Why, I always want more of them than I can find. A young man like you, with your advantages, your education—there are all kinds of opportunities. Yes, right with me. The West is the place for young men—provided simply that they are men! That's as true to-day as it was in forty-nine. And truer. Opportunities are greater, the need of men is more urgent. Right now, right to-day, I am looking for a man, a young man, who knows a thing or two about engineering, who can build bridges and cut irrigation ditches and save me money doing it." He threw out his hands. "And I can't get him!"

"Will you tell me about the position?" asked Conniston, with keen interest in voice and eyes alike.

"Certainly. I am running four cattle-ranges, using close to eighty thousand acres doing it, too. That, of course, you know. But that is getting to be a side issue with me. I am doing something else which is going to be a thousand times bigger—ten thousand times more worth while. Have you been to Crawfordsville?"

"No. I have been within a couple of miles of it. I saw it one day from Blue Ridge."

"Well, then you know something of it. It is in a valley ten miles long which has always been one of the richest valleys I ever saw; sheltered by the mountains, watered by the springs which create the source of Indian Creek. The climate is like that of the California foothills. And the soil is fertile— anything will grow there. I saw that twenty years ago. I knew that the place was made for a town-site—and I made the town. There are a lot of smaller valleys about it; there are orchards there now and vineyards. There are mines, paying mines. There is no end to the herds of cattle running through the valleys and at the bases of the hills. The town has a railroad, a narrow-gage from Bolton on the Pacific Central & Western. Building such a town, giving it railroad connection, electric lights, and all the things which go with unlimited water-power was simple enough."

Conniston sat back and watched the man who spoke of city building as of the making of a summer home. Mr. Crawford was leaning forward in his chair, his cigar between his fingers, his eyes very steady upon Conniston's.

"But now," he went on, his eyes clear, but his brows drawn over them, "we come to something different—entirely different. Out yonder in the lap of the desert is what they call Rattlesnake Valley. It is no valley at all, merely a great depression, a sort of natural sink. It is twenty miles wide, forty miles long. I have found no drop of water within thirty miles of it, no single spring, no creek. It is nothing but sand—dry, barren, unfertile sand—five hundred square miles of it, to look at it. And right there, in the heart of that sink, I am going to build a town."

He spoke quietly, his voice low, no hint of boastfulness in his tone, no hint of doubt. He spoke as a man who has studied his ground and who knows both the difficulties which lie ahead of him and the possibilities. Conniston, seeing only the impossibility, the madness of such a project, looked questioningly from him to the girl. Argyl's face was flushed, her eyes were very bright with an intense eager interest.

"It sounds so big," Conniston hesitated, his gaze coming back to the older man's face. "So daring, so impossible!"

"It is big! Bigger than I have even hinted at. It is daring. Of course, I take a chance of sinking everything I have out there and finding only failure in the end."

He shrugged his shoulders, and Conniston noticed for the first time how big and broad they were.

"But it is not impossible. It is merely the repetition of such work as has been done successfully in the Imperial Valley. The stuff which looks to be sand—barren, unfertile sand— is the richest soil in the world. Put water on it and you can raise anything. Reclamation work is a fairly new thing with us, Conniston. Men have been content heretofore to squat in the green valleys and let the desert places remain the haunts of the horned toad and coyote. But now the green valleys are filling up, and there are hundreds of thousands of square miles like the country you rode over from Indian

Creek to the Half Moon which are calling to us. To redeem them from barrenness, to do the sort of work which our friends have done in the Imperial Valley, is pioneer work. The pioneers ever since Adam, be it the Columbuses of early navigation or the Wrights of aerial navigation, have always taken the long chances. They are the ones who have suffered the hardships, and who, often enough, have been forgotten by the world in its mad rush along the trail they have opened. But they are the men who have done the big things. The pioneers are not yet all gone from the West, thank God! And their work is reclamation work!"

"And it's for the work over there that you want an engineer?"

"Yes. I want him bad, too. Do you happen to know one?"

"I know one. I won't say how much good he is, though. I'm an engineer myself."

"You!" It was Argyl's voice, surprised but eager.

"My father is a mining engineer. He always wanted me to do something for myself, you know." Conniston laughed softly. "He sent me to college, and since I didn't care a rap what sort of work I did, I took a course in civil engineering to please him. Civil, instead of mining," he added, lightly, "because I thought it would be easier."

"Had any practical experience?" demanded Mr. Crawford. Conniston shook his head. "It's too bad. You might be of a lot of use to me over there—if you'd ever done anything."

Conniston colored under the plain, blunt statement. There it was again—he had never done anything, he had never been anything. His teeth cut through his cigarette before he answered.

"I didn't suppose that you could use me." He still spoke lightly, hiding the things which he was feeling, his recurrent self-contempt. "I don't suppose, that I know enough to run a ditch straight. I've been rather a rum loafer."

Mr. Crawford smiled. "I suppose you have. But you are young yet, Conniston. A man can do anything when he is young."

There was the grinding of wheels upon the gravel outside, a man's voice, and then a man's steps.

A moment later Roger Hapgood, immaculate in a smartly cut gray suit and gloves, came smiling into the library, his hand outstretched, his manner the manner of a man so thoroughly at home that he does not stop to ring. He did not at first see Conniston half hidden in his big chair. But Conniston saw him, was quick to notice the air of familiarity, the smile which rested affectionately upon Mr. Crawford and ran on, no doubt meant to be adoring and certainly was very soft, to Argyl—and Conniston was seized with a sudden desire to take the ingratiating Roger Hapgood by the back of the collar and kick him upon the seat of his beautifully fitting trousers.

"Good evening, Mr. Crawford. I ran in on a little business for Mr. Winston. Ah, Miss Argyl! So glad to see you."

His little hand, which had been swallowed up in one of Mr. Crawford's, and which emerged rosy and crumpled, was proffered gallantly to the girl. And then Hapgood saw Conniston.

"Oh, I say," he stammered, a very trifle confused. "It's Conniston. I didn't know—"

His pale eyes, under nicely arched brows, went from father

to daughter as though Roger Hapgood were willing to admit that anything which they thought fit to do was all very right and proper, but that he was none the less surprised to find them entertaining one of the hired men.

"Yes, I'm still with the Half Moon," Conniston said, still nettled, but more amused, making no move to rise or put out his hand. "How are you, Roger?"

"How do, Conniston?" replied Mr. Hapgood, the rising young lawyer. Conniston idly wondered what had made his friend go to work. On the surface the reason seemed to be Argyl. Yet Hapgood showed a new side, a determination most unusual in him. Later Conniston was to know, to understand.

"And you like it?"

"Immensely. You ought to try it, Roger!"

Hapgood shuddered. "Couldn't think of it. A lark, no doubt, but I haven't the time for larks nowadays. I'm in the law." He turned to Mr. Crawford. "Thanks to you. Fascinating, and all that, but it does keep a man busy. I hated to disturb you to-night," with an apologetic smile at Argyl, "but Mr. Winston thought that the matter ought to be brought up before you immediately."

He was bursting with importance, some of which seemed to have popped out of his inflated little being and now protruded from an inside pocket in the form of some very legal-looking papers.

Mr. Crawford, upon his feet, said bluntly: "If we've got business, Hapgood, we'd better be at it. Let's go into the office. Argyl, you will excuse us? And you, Mr. Conniston?"

He went out. Hapgood tarried a moment for a lingering look at Argyl. "You will excuse us, Miss Argyl? I'll hurry through with this as fast as I can."

"I say, Roger," Conniston called after him, "I want to congratulate you. I'm immensely glad that you have gone to work." He turned to the girl who was watching them with thoughtful eyes. "Miss Crawford, what do you say to a little stroll out on the front lawn while these men of business transact their weighty affairs? It's the most wonderful night you ever saw."

CHAPTER X

When morning came, Conniston was the last man to crawl out of his bunk. At breakfast he was the last man to finish. He dawdled over his coffee until the cook stared curiously at him, he used up a great deal of time buttering his hot cakes, he ate very slowly. Only after every other man had left the table did he push his plate aside and go out into the yard. His manner was unusually quiet this morning, his jaw unusually firm, his eye unusually determined. He saw with deep satisfaction that all of the Half Moon men except Lonesome Pete and Brayley had ridden away upon their day's work. The red-headed cowboy was even now going down to the corrals, a vacant look in his blue eyes, the corners of a little volume sticking out of his hip-pocket, his lips moving to unspoken words. Brayley was going through the fringe of trees toward the house, evidently to speak with Mr. Crawford upon some range business. Conniston strolled slowly down toward the corrals, stopping and loitering when he had got there.

Now and then he caught a glimpse of Lonesome Pete mending his saddle just within the half-open stable door, but for the most part his eyes rested steadily upon the little path which wriggled through the grove and toward the house. He made and smoked a cigarette, tossing away the burned stub. He glanced at his watch, noticed that he was already half an hour late in going to work, and turned back toward the house, his expression the set, even, placid expression of a man who waits, and waits patiently. Five minutes passed—ten minutes—and he stood still, making no move to get his horse and ride upon his day's duties. And then, walking swiftly, Brayley came out of the trees and hurried, lurching, toward the corral.

"What are you waitin' for?" he cried, sharply, when twenty paces away. "Ain't you got nothin' to do to-day?"

Conniston made no answer, turning his eyes gravely upon Brayley's face, waiting for the man to come up to him.

"Can't you hear?" called Brayley again, more sharply, coming on swiftly. "What are you waitin' an' loafin' here for?"

"I want to talk with you a minute." Conniston's voice was very quiet, almost devoid of expression.

"Well, talk. An' talk fast! I ain't got all day."

Brayley was standing close to him now, his eyes boring into Conniston's, his manner impatient, irritated. For just a moment Conniston stood as though hesitating, leaning slightly forward, balanced upon the balls of his feet. Then he sprang forward suddenly, without sign of warning, taking the big foreman unawares, throwing both arms about the stalwart body, driving the heavier body back with the impact of the one hurled against it. Brayley, standing carelessly, loosely, his feet not braced, but close together, unprepared for the attack, fell heavily, lifted clean off his feet, born backward, and slammed to the ground with the breath jolted out of him, Conniston on top of him.

"You d—n coward!" he bellowed, as his breath came back into his body. "Sneakin' coward!"

He bunched his great strength and hurled it against the man, who clung to him. Still he was at a disadvantage, being under the other and having both arms locked to his side by the clinging embrace which held him powerless. For a moment the two men lay writhing and twisting upon the ground, half hid in their quiet struggle by the dust which puffed up from the dry ground about them. Then, as Brayley again gathered his strength in a mighty effort to rid himself of the man who held him down, Conniston loosened his hold, springing back and up to his feet. And in each hand Conniston held one of Brayley's guns. A quick gesture, and as Brayley rose to his feet he saw his two revolvers flying skyward, over the high fence and into the big corral.

"You got 'em!" Brayley cried, hoarse with anger. "Shoot, you coward—an' be d—d to you!"

For answer Conniston jerked his own gun from his belt, tossing it to lie with Brayley's two in the dust of the corral.

"We're ruling guns out of this, Brayley," he said, quietly. "It's going to be just man to man."

For a moment Brayley stood, open-mouthed, staring at him. Then, as understanding came to him, a great roar burst from his lips, and with his huge fists clenched he rushed at Conniston. In the sudden access of rage which blinded the man Conniston might have stepped aside. But it was no part of his grim purpose to temporize. As Brayley rushed upon him Conniston, too, sprang forward, and the two men met with a dull, heavy thud of panting bodies. Brayley's weight was the greater, his rush fiercer, and Conniston was flung back in spite of his dogged determination not to give up an inch. He had felt Brayley's iron fist before, but not with the rage behind it which now drove it into Conniston's face. The blow laid open his cheek and hurled him backward, to land upon his feet, his body rocking dizzily, his back jammed against the corral. And only the corral kept him from falling.

Again Brayley's great sledge-hammer fists shot out, Brayley's eyes glowing redly behind them. Conniston knew that one more blow like the last one, full in the face, and again he would have been beaten by Brayley. He remembered—and, strangely enough, the remembrance came to him calmly even while the heart within him beat as though bursting against the walls of his chest and the blood hammered hot in his ears—what Argyl had said the other day as they rode to Rattlesnake Valley. She had told him that Brayley had licked him because Brayley had been the better man. He knew that if Brayley beat him down now it would be because he was the better man. And he had told Argyl that he was going to lick Brayley. She had laughed. None the less, it was a promise to her, his first promise, and he was going to keep it.

As Brayley charged for a second blow, Conniston stepped aside swiftly and swung with his right arm, collecting every ounce of his strength and putting it into the blow. Brayley tried to lift his arm to protect himself, but the fraction of a second too late. Conniston's fist landed squarely upon the corner of the foreman's jaw, just below the ear. Brayley's arms flew out, and with a groan driven from between his clenched teeth he went down in a heap.

For a moment he lay unable to rise, the black dizziness showing in his swimming eyes. A month ago Conniston could not have struck such a blow by many pounds. Already the range had done much, very much, for him. But before a man could count five both the pain and astonishment had gone from Brayley's eyes, giving place to the red anger which surged back. And with the return of clamoring rage Brayley's dizziness passed and he sprang to his feet. Again was Conniston ready, again telling himself that he had a promise to keep, and that now or never was the time to make good his word. He was over the man whom he had set out to whip, and as Brayley struggled to his feet it was only to receive Conniston's fist full in the face again, only to be hurled back to the ground with cut, bleeding lips.

Again bellowing curses which ran into one another like one long, vicious word, Brayley got to his feet. And again Conniston's fist, itself cut and bleeding and sore, drove into his face, knocking the man down before he had more than risen. As the blow landed upon the heavy bone of the cheek, Conniston's hand went suddenly limp and useless, his face went sheet-white from the pain of it. Some bone had broken, he realized dully. He couldn't clench the hand again. The fingers hung at his side, shot through with sharp pain, feeling as though they were being slowly crushed between two stones.

Brayley got slowly to his feet, swaying like a drunken man, reeling when he first stood up, and lurching sideways until his shoulders struck the high fence of the corral. Conniston put up his left arm, his right hanging powerless at his side, and followed him. Brayley, his deep chest jerking visibly as his breath wheezed through his swelling lips, waited for him, the anger gone once more from his eyes, which followed Conniston's movements curiously.

For a moment they stood motionless save for the heaving of muscles with their quick breathing, eying each other, measuring each other. One thing stood uppermost in Conniston's mind: the foreman, with every deep breath he drew, was shaking off his dizziness, was regaining his strength. The spirit within him, with all of the battering he had received, was still unbroken. And Conniston himself felt his right arm growing numb to the elbow. In a very few seconds he would be like a rag doll in the other's big, strong hands....

"Well," panted Brayley, "what are you waitin' for? I'll lick you yet!"

Conniston came on, stepping slowly, cautiously. Brayley stood still, his clenched fists at his waist, his back against the fence. His eyes left the other's face for a second and ran to the broken hand swinging at his side. A quick light of understanding leaped into the big cattle-man's face, and he laughed softly. And as he laughed he stepped forward, lifting his fists.

Conniston swung at him with his left hand. The blow whizzed by Brayley's ear, for he had foreseen it and had ducked. But as he retaliated with a crushing blow, Conniston sprang to the side, ducking. Now it was Brayley again who rushed, a leaping light of hope of victory, surety of victory, in his eyes.

But Conniston saw his one chance and took it. He did not give back. And he did not offer the poor defense of one arm against the flail of blows. Instead he stooped low, very low, jerking his body double, dropping suddenly under Brayley's threshing arms, and hurled himself bodily to meet the attack, his left shoulder thrust forward, striking Brayley with the full impact of his hundred and eighty pounds just below the knees. They both went down, down together, and with Conniston underneath. But to Brayley the thing had come with a stunning shock of unexpectedness just as he saw the end of the fight, and Conniston was on his feet a second the first. Again as Brayley sprang up, Conniston stood over him. Again Conniston's fist, his left, but driven with all of the power left in him, beat mercilessly into the already cut face, driving Brayley down upon his knees. Now he was swaying helplessly, hopelessly. But still the dogged spirit within him was undefeated. A strange sort of respect, involuntary, of mingled admiration and pity; surged into Conniston's heart. He was not angry, he had not been angry from the beginning. This was merely a bit of his duty, a part of the day's work, the beginning of regeneration, the keeping of a promise. He was sorry for the man. But he was not forgetting his promise. Brayley was swaying to his feet, his two big hands lifted loosely, weakly, before him. Through their inefficient guard Conniston struck once more, the last blow, swinging from the shoulder. And Brayley went down heavily, like a falling timber, and lay still.

For a little Conniston stood over him, watchful, wiping the blood from the gash in his cheek. He saw that Brayley's eyes were closed, and felt a quick fear that he had killed him. Then he saw the eyelids flutter open, close, open again, as the foreman's eyes rested steadily upon his. He waited. Brayley lifted his head, even struggled to his elbow, only to fall back prone.

They were not ten feet from the empty corral. Lonesome Pete, his saddle mended, rode slowly around the corner of the stable toward the gate. The horse which he was riding was a half-broken three-year-old, but Lonesome Pete was at home upon the backs of half-broken three-year-olds. And his red head was full of Jocelyn Truxton and "Macbeth." He rode with his hat low over his eyes, one hand holding his horse's reins, the other grasping firmly a little book. So it happened that Lonesome Pete rode through the gate and close to the two men and did not see them.

But the horse did see them, did see a man lying stretched upon the ground, and with the sharp nostrils of its kind the horse scented fresh blood. The result was that the frightened brute reared, snorting, and wheeled suddenly, plunging back through the corral gate. And Lonesome Pete, taken unawares as he sat loosely in the saddle, was jerked rudely out of his dreamings of the fair Jocelyn and the bloody

Macbeth to find his horse shooting out from under him, and to find himself sitting upon the hard ground with his legs in Brayley's lap.

Brayley's strength of lungs came back to him with a new anger. "You howlin' idiot, what are you tryin' to do?"

"I was a-readin'," responded Lonesome Pete, still grinning vapidly, still not quite certain whether the things which he saw about him were real things or literary hallucinations.

"A-readin'!" snapped Brayley, sitting up. "That what I'm payin' you for, you blame gallinipper!"

With a glance from Brayley's lacerated face to the bloody smears on Conniston's, Lonesome Pete got to his feet and, shaking his head and dusting the seat of his overalls as he went, turned and disappeared into the stable after his horse. Brayley glared after him a second, grunted, and got to his feet.

"Well," he snarled, facing Conniston. "You licked me. Now what? Want to beat me up some more?"

"No, I don't," Conniston answered him, steadily. "You know I had to do it, Brayley. You had it coming to you after that first night in the bunk-house. Now—I want to shake hands, if you do."

With a keen, measuring glance from under swelling eyelids, and no faintest hesitation, Brayley put out his hand.

"Shake!" he grunted. "You done it fair. I didn't think you had it in you. And"—with a distorted grin—"I'll 'scuse the left hand, Con!"

CHAPTER XI

Brayley and Conniston went together into the corral and picked up the three revolvers. Then Conniston turned toward the stable to get his horse. Brayley's eyes followed him, narrowing speculatively.

"Hey, Conniston," he called, sharply, "where you goin'?"

"To work. It's late now."

"Yes, it's late, all right. But you better go up to the bunk-house first an' fix your hand up. Oh, don't be a fool. Come ahead. I'm goin' to straighten out my face a bit."

So Conniston turned back, and the two men went to the bunk-house. The cook was pottering around his stove, cleaning up his pots and pans. He looked up curiously as they came in, realizing that by now they should have been at work. The faint, careless surprise upon his face changed suddenly into downright bewilderment as he saw the dust-covered bodies, the cut lips, blood-streaked cheeks, and swelling eyes of the two men. The song which he had been humming died away into a little gasp, and with sagging lower jaw he stood and stared.

"Well," snapped Brayley, pushing back his hat and returning the cook's stare fiercely. "Well, Cookie, what's eatin' you? Ain't you got nothin' to do but stand an' gawk? By the Lord, if you ain't I know where we can git a hash-slinger as is worth his grub!"

Cookie's bulging eyes ranged from one face to the other. Then he turned back to his stove and began to wash over again a pan which he had laid aside already as clean.

Conniston and Brayley washed with cold water in silence. Then they found a bottle of liniment and applied it to their various cuts with a bit of rag. Brayley, his big fingers unbelievably gentle, bandaged Conniston's lame hand for him. And then they went back to the corrals.

"You can go out to the east end an' give Rawhide a hand," said Brayley, as he swung up to his horse's back. "I reckon you won't be much good for a day or two except jest ridin'. An' say, Con. I had a talk with the Ol' Man about you this mornin'. He wanted to know if you was makin' good. Lucky for you," with a twisted grin, "that he asked before we had our little set-to! You're to git forty-five a month from now on. An' at the end of the week you're to report over to Rattlesnake to go to work."

As Greek Conniston rode out across the dry fields toward the east there was a subtle exhilaration in the fresh, clean morning air which he drew deep down into his lungs. For the moment the soreness of bruised muscles, the biting pain in his crippled hand, were trifles driven outward to the farthermost rim of his consciousness. His foot was upon the first step of the long stairway which he must climb. He had whipped Brayley in a fair, square, hand-to-hand, man-to-man fight. He had done it through sheer dogged determination that he would do it. He had set himself a task, the hardest task he had ever essayed. And success had come to him as self-vindication.

But it had been to him more, vastly more, than a mere duty, although from the outset he had looked upon it in that light. It had been a test. Had the outcome been reversed, had he failed, had Brayley worsted him, there was every likelihood that Conniston would have left the range. But now, hand in hand with dawning regeneration, there came confidence. There were many things which his destiny had set ahead of him, and he was ready to face them with the same dogged determination with which he had faced the big foreman.

Then, too, this morning he had received more than mere self-approval. Brayley had indorsed his work in his consultation with Mr. Crawford. And Mr. Crawford had seen fit to increase his daily wage. He had not been worth a dollar a day a month ago, and he knew it. Now he was to be paid a dollar and a half a day, and because he was worth that to the Half Moon. So far, in the circumscribed area of his daily duties, he "had made good." He felt that the first heat of the great race was run, that in spite of his handicap he had held his own. The race itself was almost a tangible thing ahead of him. Greek Conniston was ready for it. And he dared think, with a sharp-drawn breath and a leaping of blood throughout his whole being, of the golden prize at the end of it—for the man who could win that prize.

He worked all that day with Rawhide Jones, his left hand upon his reins, his right thrust into his open vest as a rude sort of sling. He met Rawhide's surprise, answered his quick question by saying, simply, without explanation, "I got hurt." Rawhide had grunted and dropped the subject.

All day long one matter surged uppermost in Conniston's mind to the exclusion of anything else: he was to be transferred from the Half Moon to Rattlesnake Valley. He did not know whether to be glad at the change or sorry. He was growing to know the men with whom he worked, growing to like them, to find pleasure in their rude companionship. Now, just as he was making friends of them he was to be shifted among strangers. To-day he had found heretofore unsounded depths in the nature of Brayley; he wanted to know the man better, to show him that he had not been blind to rough, frank generosity, nor unappreciative of it. Through these latter days, during which the scales had been dropping from his eyes in spite of prejudice, he had been forced into a grudging admiration of the man's capability. Brayley could read little and spell less; he was a clown and a boor in the matter of the finer, exacting social traditions; but he could run a cattle-range, and he read his men as other men read books. Conniston realized suddenly, shocked with the realization, that in Brayley there was that same sort of thing which he had come to respect in Argyl Crawford, the same open frankness, the same straightforward honesty, the same deep, wide generosity.

Argyl, too, entered into the confusion of his gladness and disappointment at the coming change of sphere. He had planned to spend many an evening with her; and now, just as he was finding the door to her comradeship opened to him, he was to be whisked away from her.

But on the other hand Conniston's optimism saw ahead of him, in the new field of work, the dim, shadowy, and at the same time alluring outline of a new and rare opportunity. He had not forgotten the things which Mr. Crawford had said of his big project. And in spite of his own deprecatory answer to Mr. Crawford's straightforward question, Greek Conniston had not forgotten all of the engineering he had absorbed during four years in the university. There was work to be done, there were men wanted, above all, men who could understand something beyond the pick-and-shovel end of the thing, men who knew the difference between a transit and a telescope.

And the work itself appealed to him strangely now that that labor was not without independence, not without a stern sort of dignity even. To take a stretch of dry, hot sand, innocent of vegetation, to wrest it from the clutch of the desert as from the maw of a devastating giant, to bring water mile upon mile from the mountain canons, to make the sterile breast of the mother earth fertile, to drive back the horned toad and the coyote, to make green things spring up and flourish, to carve out homes, to cause trees and flowers and vines to give shade and disseminate fragrance, even as time went on to wring moisture from the lead-gray sky above—it was like being granted the might of a magician to touch the desert with the tip of his wand, bringing life gushing forth from death.

When night came Conniston trudged from the corrals to the bunk-house and his evening meal devoutly thankful that the long day was gone. His hand pained him constantly, and in the sharp twinges which shot through it the lesser hurt of his cut cheek was forgotten. The greater part of the other men was there before him. As he stepped in at the door they were dragging their chairs noisily up to the table. Brayley, one eye swollen almost shut, his lips thick like a negro's with the blows which had hammered them, had just taken his seat. The men's eyes were quick to catch the bruised countenance of the man at the door, and ran swiftly from it to Brayley's face and back again. One man chuckled aloud, Toothy giggled like a girl, and the others grinned broadly. For a moment Brayley's face darkened ominously. Then his frown passed, and he turned about in his chair toward the door.

"Hello, Con," he said, quietly.

"Hello, Brayley," Conniston answered, in the same tone.

Brayley's eyes went back to the men at the table, shifting

quickly from one to another. He ran his tongue along his swollen lips, but said no word until Conniston had washed and taken his own chair. Then he spoke, his words coming with slow distinctness.

"Conniston jumped me this mornin.' I had a lickin' comin' to me. You boys know why. An' I got it."

He stopped suddenly, his eyes watchful upon the faces about him. Conniston saw that they were no longer grinning, but as serious, as watchful, as Brayley's.

"That was between me an' Conniston. There ain't goin' to be no makin' fun an' fool remarks about it. He done it square, an' I'm glad he done it! If there's any other man here as thinks he can do it I'll take him on right now!"

Again he paused abruptly, again he studied the grave faces and speculative eyes intent upon his own. No man spoke. And Conniston noticed that no man smiled.

"All right," grunted Brayley. "That ends it. Cookie, for the love of Mike, are you goin' to keep us waitin' all night for them spuds?"

The meal passed with no further reference, open or covert, to the thing which was uppermost in the minds of all. Many a curious glance, however, went to where Conniston sat. He was conscious of them even when he did not see them, understood that a new appraisal of him was being made swiftly, that his fellow-workers were carefully readjusting their first conceptions and judgments of him.

When he had finished eating, Conniston went straight to his bunk. He had no desire for conversation; he did want both rest and a chance to think. He was straightening out his tumbled covers when Lonesome Pete tapped him upon the shoulder.

"No hay for yours, Con," he grinned. "Not yet. Miss Argyl wants you to come up to the house. Right away, she said, as soon as you'd et. She said special she was in a hurry, an' you wasn't to waste time puttin' on your glad rags."

Why did Argyl want him—to-night? He put his fingers to his cheek where Brayley's fist had cut into the flesh. How could he go to her like this? He was on the verge of telling Lonesome Pete that he could not go, of framing some excuse, any excuse. But instead he closed his lips without speaking, picked up his hat and went straight toward the house.

She was waiting for him at the little summer-house upon the front lawn. He saw the white of her lacy gown, the flash of her arms as he came nearer, her outstretched hand as he came to her side. With his hat caught under his right arm he put out his left hand to take hers.

"You were good to come so soon," she was saying.

"It was good to come," he rejoined, warmly. "You know how glad I am for every opportunity I have to see you."

"What is the matter with your hand?" she asked, quickly. "Your right hand?"

"I hurt it," he answered, easily. "Nothing serious. It will be well in a day or two."

"How did you hurt it?" she persisted.

"Really, Miss Crawford," he retorted, trying to laugh away the seriousness of her tone, "there are so many ways for a man to damage his epidermis in this sort of work—"

She was standing close to him, looking intently up into his face through the gathering darkness.

"Tell me—why did you do it?"

"What? Smash my fingers?"

"Yes. In the way you did!"

"What do you mean?" he hesitated, wondering what she knew.

"On Brayley's face! Why did you fight with him?"

"Who told you?"

"Brayley. He had to come to see father this evening. I saw his face. I heard him tell father that he had had trouble with one of the men. I was afraid that it was you! I followed him out into the yard and asked him. It is no doubt none of my business—but will you tell me why you fought with him?"

"I think that I would answer anything you cared to ask me, Miss Crawford," he replied, quietly. "Will you sit down with me for a little?" He moved slowly at her side, back to the seat in the summer-house, grateful for any reason which gave him the privilege of talking with her, watching her quick play of expression. "You see, my object seemed so clear-cut and simple—and now gets itself all tangled up in complexity when I try to explain it to you. For one thing, ever since my first night on the Half Moon when Brayley put me out I have felt that it was up to me to finish what was begun that night. For another thing, I was trying to prove a theory, I imagine! I didn't really believe that Brayley was the better man. And lastly, and perhaps most important of all, I told you the other day that I was going to lick him. It was a sort of promise, you know!"

She sat with her elbow upon her knee, her chin on her hand, her eyes lost in the shadow of her hair. He knew that she was regarding him intently. He guessed from the line of her cheek, from the slightly upturned curve at the corner of her mouth, that she was half inclined to be serious, and almost ready to smile at him.

"You are inclined to look upon Brayley as an enemy?" was all that she said, still watching him closely.

"No!" he cried, warmly. "I sneered at him the other day, I know. Like the little poppinjay I was I thought myself in the position to poke fun at him. To-day I got my first true idea of the man's nature. To-day I found out—can you guess what I found out? That Brayley in many things is just like—whom, do you suppose?"

"Tell me."

"Like you! The discovery was a shock. It nearly bowled me over. But it's the truth!"

"What do you mean?" she asked, plainly puzzled. "How in the world is Brayley like me?"

"Aside from externals, from refinement, from polish, from all that sort of thing"—he spoke swiftly—"his nature is much like yours. There is the same frankness, the same sincerity, the same heartiness. There is the same sort of generosity, the same bigness of—of soul." He broke off abruptly, surprised to find himself talking this way to her. "You must think I'm a fool," he blurted out, after a second. "I talk like one. You have a right to feel offended—to liken Brayley to you—"

"Since I believe you mean what you say—since I think I understand what you mean—I am not offended! I am proud! Yes, proud if I can be like Brayley in some things, some things which count! If you do nothing beyond making a friend of that man your exile in this Western country of ours will have been worth while. But you will do something more. I did not ask you to come to me just to hear what you had to say about your trouble with Brayley. He told me before you came—told me that you had licked him, as you both put it, and that it served him right! That is your business and Brayley's, and I should keep out of it. But there was something else—I wonder if you think me meddlesome, Mr. Conniston? If I *am* meddlesome?"

"If we are going to be friends, you and I—and you promised that you would let me make you my friend—hadn't we better drop that word?"

"Then I am going to tell you something. You are to go to work in the Valley. Brayley told you that? Do you guess why—have you an idea—why father is sending you over there?"

"I supposed because he is pushing the work—because he needs all the men there he can get, can spare from the Half Moon."

"I am going to tell you. And I am afraid that father would not like it, did he know. But I know that I am right. I may not see you again before you go—I am going into Crawfordsville in the morning for a few days. What I tell you, you will remember, is in strict confidence—between friends?"

"In strict confidence," he repeated, seriously. "Between friends."

She leaned slightly forward, speaking swiftly, emphatically, earnestly:

"You have heard of Bat Truxton? He is in charge there of all the men, general superintendent of all the work. You will be put to work under him. You will be in a position to learn a great deal about the project in its every detail. Bat Truxton is an engineer, a practical man who knows what he has learned by doing it. And he is a strong man and very capable. Then there is Garton—Tommy Garton they call him. You will work with him. He, too, is an engineer, and he, too, knows all there is to know about the work."

She paused a moment, as though in hesitation. Conniston waited in silence for her to go on.

"Father is sending you to the Valley because he has begun to take an interest in you. Before the year is over there is going to be an opportunity for every man there to show what there is in him. He is giving you your chance, your chance to make good!"

Argyl got to her feet and stood looking away from him, out across the duck pond. Presently she turned to him again, smiling, her voice gone from grave to gay.

"The race is on, isn't it? The great handicap! And, anyway, I have given you a tip, haven't I? Now you are coming up to the house with me, and I'm going to make you a bandage for your broken hand."

She didn't stop to heed his protest, but ran ahead of him to the house. And Conniston, pondering on many things, saw nothing for it but to allow her to play nurse to him.

Saturday morning Greek Conniston pocketed the first money he had ever earned by good, hard work. Brayley handed him three ten-dollar gold pieces—his month's wage. Conniston asked for some change, and for one of the gold pieces received ten silver dollars. He knew that Mr.

Crawford and Argyl had gone into Crawfordsville, so he gave one dollar to Brayley, saying: "Will you hand that to Mr. Crawford for me? I owe it to him for telegraph service on the first day I spent here." And then he made a little roll of the indispensable articles from his suit-case, tied it to the strings behind his saddle, and rode away across the fields toward Rattlesnake Valley.

He was to report immediately at the office of the reclamation work in Valley City. Following the trail he and Argyl had taken the other day, he rode into the depression, or sink, about the middle of that long, low hollow between the southern end and the clutter of uniform square buildings which was planned to grow into a thriving town in the heart of the desert.

Every foot of ground here now had a new personal interest for him. He studied the long, flat sweep of level land with nodding approval, trying to see just where the main canal should run, just how its course could be shaped most rapidly, most cheaply, most advantageously. For the mounds, the ridges where the winds had swept the sand into long winnows, he had a quick frown. After all, he realized suddenly, this desert was not the flat, even floor he had imagined it to be. A mile, two miles to his right as he rode into the "valley" he could see a slow-moving mass of men and horses, could catch the glint of the sun upon jerking scrapers and plows. There the front ranks of Mr. Crawford's little army was pushing the war against the desert. There was where the brunt of Bat Truxton's responsibility lay.

To his left, still several miles away, was Valley City. He swung his horse toward the camp, which as yet was scarcely more than a man's dream of a town, and rode on at a swift gallop. Now more than ever he saw what some of the difficulties were in front of the handful of men scarring the breast of this Western Sahara. For a moment he could see the houses before him, even down to their doorsteps, and a moment later only the roofs peered at him over the crest of a gently swelling rise. Here the water, when it was brought this far, must be swung in a wide sweep to right or left, or else many days, perhaps many weeks, must be sacrificed to the leveling of a great sand-pile. He began to wonder if there was enough water in the mountains for so mammoth a project; if what of the precious fluid could be taken from the creeks and springs would not be drunk up by the thirsty sands as though it had been scattered carelessly by the spoonfuls, as a blotter drinks drops of ink. He even began to wonder uneasily if Lonesome Pete had been right when he had said that another name for such an attempt at reclamation was simple "damn foolishness." The water had not come yet; it was still running in its time-worn courses down the mountain-sides; but something else was being drunk up daily by the parched gullet of the dry country. And that something else was Mr. Crawford's money. His fortune was no doubt very large; it must run into many figures before Rattlesnake Valley grew green with fertility.

He came at last into the little town, passed the cottage where he had worked with Argyl, and drew up before a four-roomed, rough, unpainted building, with a sign over the door saying, "GENERAL OFFICE CRAWFORD RECLAMATION COMPANY." Swinging down from his horse, which he left with reins upon the ground, he went in at the open door. Within there were bare walls, bare floor, and three or four cheap chairs. Under the windows looking to the south there ran a long, high table, covered with papers and blue-prints. Another long table ran across the middle of the room. At it, facing him, perched upon a high stool, a young man, a pencil behind each ear, his sleeves rolled up, was working over some papers. In one corner of the same room another young fellow, hardly more than a boy—eighteen or nineteen, perhaps—was ticking away busily at a typewriter.

The man in shirt-sleeves working at the second long table looked up as Conniston came in. He was a pale, not over-strong—looking chap, somewhere about Conniston's own age, his short-cropped yellow hair pushed straight back from a high forehead, his lips and eyes good-humored and at the same time touched vaguely with a tender wistfulness. Conniston imagined immediately that this was Garton, Bat Truxton's helper.

"You're Mr. Garton?" he said, voicing his impression as he came forward.

"No one else," Garton answered him, pleasantly. "Tom Garton at your service. And you're Conniston from the Half Moon?"

He put out his hand without rising. Conniston took it, surprised as he did so at the quick, strong grip of the slender fingers.

"I'm glad to know you, Conniston. Glad you're to be with us. Oh yes, I knew a couple of days ago that you were coming over. Mr. Crawford dropped in on us himself and told us about you. Have a chair."

They had shaken hands across the table. Now, as Conniston moved across the room to the chair at which Garton waved, the latter swung about on his high stool toward the boy at the typewriter.

"Hey there, Billy!" he called. "Come and meet Mr. Conniston. He's going to be one of us. Mr. Conniston, meet Mr. Jordan—Billy Jordan—the one man living who can take down dictation as fast as you can sling it at him, type it as you shoot it in, and play a tune on his typewriter at the same time!"

Stepping about the table to meet the boy who had got to his feet, Conniston received a shock which for a second made him forget to take young Jordan's proffered hand. For the first time now he saw Garton's body, which had been hidden by the table; saw that Garton had had both legs taken off six inches above the knees. He remembered himself, and tried to hide his surprise under some light remark to Billy Jordan. But Garton had seen it, and laughed lightly, although with a slight flush creeping up into his pale cheeks.

"Hadn't heard about my having slept with Procrustes? Well, you'll get used to having half a man around after a while. The rest do. I've gotten used to it myself. Now sit down. Have a smoke?" He pushed a box of cigarettes along the table. "And tell us what's the news on Broadway."

"You're a New-Yorker?"

"Oh, I've galloped up and down the Big Thoroughfare a good many times in the days of my youth," grinned Carton, helping himself to a cigarette. "I'm an Easterner, all right; or, rather, I was an Easterner. I guess I belong to this man's country now."

"What school?"

"Yale. '05."

"Why, that's my school! I was a '06 man."

"I know it." Garton nodded over the match he was touching to his cigarette. "You're Greek Conniston, son of the big Conniston who does things on the Street. But we didn't happen to travel in the same class. I was shy on the money end of it. Oh, I remember you, all right. I saw that record run of yours around left end to a touchdown. Gad, that was a great day! I went crazy then with a thousand other fellows. I remember," with an amused chuckle, "jumping up and down on a fat man's toes, yelling into his face until I must have split his ear-drum! Oh yes, I had two pegs in those days. The fat man got mad, the piker, and knocked me as flat as a pancake! I guess he never went to Yale."

For ten minutes they chatted about old college days, games lost and won, men and women they both had known in the East. And then, naturally, conversation switched to the work being done in Rattlesnake Valley. Garton's face lighted up with eagerness, his eyes grew very bright, he spoke swiftly. It was easy to see that the man was full of his work, pricked with the fever of it, alive with enthusiasm.

"You seem to be mightily interested in the work," Conniston smiled.

"I am. I am in love with it! A man can't live here ten days and be a part of it without loving it or hating it. It's the greatest work in the world; it's big—bigger than we can see with our noses jammed up against it! It's a man's work. And thank God we've got the right man at the head of it!"

"Meaning Truxton?"

"Meaning the man who is the brain of it and the brawn of it; the heart and soul and glorious spirit of it; yes, and the pocket-book of it! That's John Crawford, a big man—the biggest man I ever knew. Who else would have the nerve to tackle a thing like this, to tackle it lone-handed? And to hold on to it in the face of opposition which would crush another man, and with the risk of utter financial ruin looming as big as a house, like a glorious, grim old bulldog! Oh, you don't know what it means yet; you can't know. Wait until you've been here a week, seeing every day of it a thousand dollars poured into the sand, a few square yards of sand leveled, a few yards of canal dug, and you'll begin to understand. Why, the whole thing as it stands is as dangerous as a dynamite bomb—and John Crawford is as cool about it as an anarchist!"

"You speak of opposition. I didn't know—"

Garton rumpled his upstanding yellow hair and laughed softly.

"I guess none of us know a great deal about it excepting John Crawford. And John Crawford doesn't talk much. Oh, you will learn fast enough all that we know about it. And now I suppose you'll be wanting to know where you fit into the machine. Bring any things with you—any personal effects?"

"A tooth-brush and an extra suit," Conniston laughed. "They're tied to my saddle outside."

"You can bring 'em in here. I have a room in the back of this shack. You're to share it with me, if you care to. You'll find a shed in the back yard where you can leave your horse. There's a barrel of water out there, too. And, by the way, you might as well learn right now not to throw away a drop of the stuff; it's worth gold out here. When you get back I'll go over things with you. Your first day's work, the better part of it, will be to listen while I talk."

Conniston unsaddled and tied his horse in the little shed, coming back into the office with his roll of clothes. Garton swung about upon his stool and pointed out the room at the back of the house which was to serve for the present as the sleeping-room for both men. There were two cots along opposite walls, a chair, and no other furniture. Conniston threw down his things upon the cot which Garton called to him was to be his, and came back into the office. Pulling a stool up to the table alongside of Garton, he began his first day's work for the reclamation project.

CHAPTER XII

Tommy Garton spoke swiftly, clearly, concisely, explaining those essentials of the work in hand which Conniston must grasp at the beginning. Filled with an ardor no whit less than Mr. Crawford's, there seemed to be no single detail which he did not have at his fingers' ends.

Taking from the drawer of his table a map which bore his own name in the corner, he pointed out just where their source of water was, and just how it was to be brought down from the mountains into the "valley." He indicated where the work was being pushed now. He showed where the big dam had already been thrown across a steep-walled, rocky canon; how, when the time came, a second dam (this purely a diversion weir) was to be constructed across a neighboring canon, higher up in the mountains, deflecting the waters which poured down through it into the lower dam, and from it turning them into the main canal at the upper end of Rattlesnake Valley. He pointed out, five miles to the north of these two big dams, the place where a third was to be flung across yet another canon, imprisoning a smaller creek and turning it toward the southwest to join the overflow of the others in the main canal. He ran over blue-print after blue-print, to show the type of construction work being done. He explained where there was leveling called for, where the canal must be turned aside.

"We'd bring her straight through, and d—n the little knolls," he cried, banging his fist down upon his table in sudden vehemence, "but there is a time-limit on this thing, Conniston. And we've got to get water here, right here in Valley City, when the last day is up. Not twenty-four hours late, either. No, not twenty-four minutes!"

He ran the back of his hand across his moist forehead, and sat staring out of the window as though he had forgotten Conniston's presence.

"What sort of a time-limit? I thought that Mr. Crawford was alone in this thing, that he had the rest of his lifetime to finish it in if he wanted to take that long."

Garton snorted.

"He's got until just exactly twelve o'clock, noon, on the first day of October. If he is five minutes late—yes, five minutes!—there'll be men right here holding stop-watches on the thing like it was a blooming foot-race!—he'll be busted, ruined, smashed, and the whole project a miserable abortion!" He paused a moment, biting the end of his pencil. And before he went on he had turned his eyes steadily upon Conniston's face, studying him. "If you're going to work with us, to get into it with your sleeves rolled up like Bat Truxton and Billy there and me and a few others of us, you might as well know in the beginning what's what in this scrap. For it is a scrap—the biggest scrap you ever saw, a fight to the finish, with one man lined up against— do you have any idea what John Crawford is bucking?"

Conniston shook his head. "I know virtually nothing of this thing, Garton."

"Well, I'll tell you. Single-handed that man is fighting the desert! And he'd beat it back, too, and conquer it and muzzle it and make it eat out of his hand if they'd only let him alone. But they won't, the cold-blooded highway robbers! He's got them to fight with his left hand while he hammers away at the face of the desert with his right! Who are 'they'? 'They' are a syndicate; organized capital. 'They' spell many millions of dollars ready to be spent to defeat John Crawford."

He stopped suddenly, frowning and gnawing at his pencil. Conniston was about to ask a question when Garton went on rapidly, such hot indignation in his tones that Billy Jordan dropped his hands from the keys of his machine to listen to what he had heard many a time before.

"You know already how Mr. Crawford built the town which is named after him? He made that town just as a man takes clay into his hands and makes a modeled figure out of it. And when the job was done he went to the Pacific Central & Western and showed them why it would pay them to build a narrow-gage railroad from Bolton, on the other side of the ridge, thirty miles through mountainous country. He had that planned out long before the first shack was put up in Crawfordsville. And he knew what he was doing. The P. C. & W. built the road and have run an accommodation train back and forth daily ever since. And they have made money at it hauling freight, merchandise from the main line, building-material, farming implements—everything which had to go into Crawfordsville; hauling farm produce from the new settlement back into Bolton.

"Because he had shown the P. C. & W. that the thing could be done on a paying basis, because it *was* done and did pay, the P. C. & W. listened to him when he made a second proposition to them. He went straight to Colton Gray, and Colton Gray listened to him. What Gray advises, the P. C. & W. does. In the end, after many interviews and much investigation and discussion, Crawford made Gray see the matter the way he saw it. The P. C. &. W. contracted to begin work on a line from Crawfordsville to Valley City and on across the desert to the main transcontinental railroad at Indian Creek the day that sufficient water to irrigate fifty square miles of land had been brought into this part of the 'valley.' It was agreed by both contracting parties that the water was to be brought to this spot by noon of October first, or all contracts became null and void.

"The day that Gray agreed for the P. C. & W. Mr. Crawford put men to work on the first preliminary survey. He had already the necessary water concessions. He had studied his ground, made his plans with a carefulness which overlooked nothing which a man could foresee, and had every reason to believe, to be positive, that he could have all the water he wanted in the valley a whole month before the first of October.

"And I tell you he could have done it if they had just let him alone! But they wouldn't. Within thirty days after the first shovelful of earth was turned there was a strong organization perfected to defeat him. Why? In the first place there is a certain bloated toad in our local puddle named Oliver Swinnerton who has his hatchet out on general principles for the Old Man. In the town of Bolton he's the mayor and the chief of police and the board of city fathers and the municipal janitor all rolled into one pompous, pot-bellied little body. He's got money and he's got brains. No sooner does word get about of the Old Man's contract with the P. C. & W. than Oliver Swinnerton gets busy. He went straight to Colton Gray, and at first he could do nothing with him. Gray had taken time for his investigations of Mr. Crawford's scheme, had been convinced that it was feasible, and now stood pat. But Swinnerton with his counter-scheme interested a lot of other capital, and through some of the men he got in with him he got the ear of some of the higher-ups on the P. C. & W. He even got his scheme into the private office of the president, and from the president word ran down to Gray. I think even Gray began then to get shaky in the knees. I tell you, Conniston, the Old Man's project is so big that until it is consummated there will always be a doubt in other men's minds whether the thing ever can be done. If it can't, if it proves impracticable to irrigate this country, to build first Valley City and then a string of settlements across the desert, why then of course there would be nothing in it for the P. C. & W. to run a spur across to Indian Creek.

"And Oliver Swinnerton made it his business to show the management of the railroad that the thing was impossible, that it was a mad fool's dream, that when the first day of October came there would be nothing accomplished because there never could be anything accomplished. He scored his point, and then he played his trump card. He showed that the same money which the railroad would have to spend in stringing rails across the sand here could be spent more advantageously in another direction.

"On the other side of Bolton there are grassy foothills, well watered—a big stretch of country very much like that about Crawfordsville. Already there are orchards there, considerable small farming, grain-raising and hay. Swinnerton planned to build a town out there in the heart of that fertile country where there are now a number of settlements and to have the P. C. & W. run a seventy-five-mile spur out that way. The management naturally will not stand for the expense of both roads at the same time, since both would be very largely in the nature of experiments. Swinnerton's scheme looked more promising than the Old Man's. Swinnerton got his contract with the railroad. And that contract says that if on the first day of October Mr. Crawford has not made good he will be given not a day's grace, but work will be begun on the other road into Swinnerton's country. Do you see now what I mean by opposition? Do you see what will happen if we don't come up to time on our end of the game? Swinnerton is so confident that he holds the winning hand that he has already founded his town, already sunk a pile of money in it. Somebody is going to go to the wall when the first day of October comes."

"But," demurred Conniston, "Swinnerton and his corporation are doing nothing actively to retard our work—can do nothing. If—"

"He isn't?" snorted Garton. "That's all you know about it! How do we get all of our implements, our supplies, all of our men? They come to us by rail, don't they? And that means they come to us over the P. C. & W., doesn't it? And the P. C. & W. is scared out of its life, praying every day to its little gods for Crawford's failure. What happens? We get delayed shipments, we wait for our stuff, and it lies sidetracked somewhere; we get our men stolen from us before they ever get to Bolton, and shunted off to work for the opposition! There are a hundred ways in which Swinnerton and the bigger men in with him can slip their knife into us every day of the week. And they are not missing very many bets, either. Oh, Gray's all right; he's square enough and willing enough to stand by his word. But he can't do everything. It takes time to get matters up to him, and it takes time for him to adjust them. And right now he's in San Francisco attending a railroad conference, and he'll be there fifteen days, I suppose. What sort of service do you suppose we get in the mean time? You get that idea out of your head that Swinnerton isn't doing anything actively to retard us. He's doing everything he can think of, and I told you at the jump that the man has brains."

As well as a man could understand it without actually going over the ground, Conniston learned that afternoon all that

Bat Truxton's assistant could tell him. He learned, roughly, of course, how much had been done already, what remained to be done first, what could be allowed to wait until more men came to swell the forces now at work, what chief natural difficulties and obstacles lay across the path of the great venture.

Little Tommy Garton's enthusiasm was so keen a thing, so spontaneous, so whole-souled, that long before time came for the noon meal Conniston felt his own blood pounding and clamoring for action. Swiftly he was granted the first true glimpse which had ever come to him of the real nature of work. Such work as he was now about to engage in was so infused with the elements of hazard, of risk, of uncertainty, of opposition, that it was shot through with a deep, stern fascination. It was not drudgery, and almost until now he had looked upon all work as that. It was a great game, the greatest game in the world. He already began to look forward to to-morrow, when he was to leave the office and go out upon the field of action with Bat Truxton with an eagerness such as he had felt in the old college days on the eve of the big Thanksgiving football game. Something of the spirit which had made old William Conniston the dynamic, forceful man of business which he had always been, and which had never before manifested itself in old Conniston's son, suddenly awoke and shook itself, active, eager, the fighting spirit of a fighting man.

At noon Billy Jordan pushed back his chair and got to his feet, stretching his arms high over his head.

"Time to eat," he said, picking up his hat. "Coming, Mr. Conniston?"

"And you?" Conniston asked of Garton.

"Oh, me!" laughed Garton. "I don't travel that far. Not

until my new legs come. I had trouble with 'em," he explained. "Had to send 'em back to Chicago. I'm hoping," with a whimsical smile, "that they don't get sidetracked with the rest of our stuff on the P. C. & W. Go with Billy, Conniston. He'll show you where to eat."

He whirled about on his stool, squirmed suddenly over on his stomach, and lowered himself to the floor. Swinging the leathern-capped stumps of his legs between his hands, which he placed palm down on the floor, as a man may swing his body between crutches, he moved with short, quick jerks into the room where the two cots were. Conniston turned away abruptly.

With Billy Jordan he went nearly to the end of the short street before they came to a rude lunch-counter, set under a canvas awning, where a thin, nervous little man and his fat, stolid wife set canned goods and coffee before them. Billy produced a yellow ticket to be punched, Conniston paid his two bits, and they strolled back to the office. When Conniston suggested that they take something to Garton, Billy told him that a boy took him his meals.

There was so much to be got over that day, Conniston was so eager to learn what details he could, Tommy Garton so eager to impart them, that it was scarcely half-past twelve when the two men were back at the long table going over maps and blue-prints. There were no interruptions. An imprisoned house-fly buzzed monotonously and sullenly against a pane of glass, his drone fitting into the heavy silence on the face of the hot desert so that it became a part of it.

At four o'clock a handful of ragged children, barefooted, bronzed of legs and hands and faces, scampered by on their noisy way home from school. A pretty young woman in neat walking-habit and big white straw hat followed the children, smiling in through the open door at Garton, noting Conniston with a flash of big brown eyes and quickly dropping lids. Billy, in seeming carelessness, had wandered to the door when the children passed, and stepped outside, chatting with her for five or ten minutes.

"Miss Jocelyn," Garton told him. "Bat Truxton's daughter, and the village schoolmistress. Billy thinks he's rather hard hit, I fancy."

"I've heard of her," Conniston replied, frowning at the map he was holding flat on the table. "Dam Number Two is the one which is completed, isn't it? And Number Three is the smaller auxiliary dam? How about Number One, which seems to be the most important of the lot? When do we go to work on that?"

Garton chuckled. "You're going to be as bad as I am, Conniston! Can't even stop to look at a pretty girl? The Lord knows they're scarce enough out here, too. Yes, Dam Number One is the important one of the lot. It will be the biggest, the hardest, and most expensive to build, and it will control the water-supply which is going to save our bacon."

Whereupon he, too, forgot Miss Jocelyn and Billy, and launched into further explanation. At six o'clock Billy Jordan covered his typewriter and put on his coat and hat. He came over to the table and leaned his elbow on it, waiting for Garton to finish something that he was saying.

"I'm going around to Truxton's a little while this evening," he said, trying to speak as a man of the world should, but flushing up under Garton's twinkling eyes. "If you find time dragging on your hands you might come along, Mr. Conniston. Miss Jocelyn"—he hesitated a moment—"Miss Jocelyn said I might bring you around."

Conniston thanked him and asked him to thank Miss Jocelyn, but assured him that instead of having time lagging for him he had more to do than he could manage. So Billy went on his way alone. Nor did he seem disappointed at Conniston's refusal to accompany him. It was only when it began to grow dusk and the boy brought Garton's supper that Conniston got up and went down the street to his own solitary evening meal at the lunch-counter.

It was after nine o'clock, and Conniston was lying on his cot in the little rear room of the office-building listening to Tommy Garton talk about reclamation—it seemed the only thing in the world he cared to talk about during working-hours or after—when the outside door was flung open and a man's heavy tread came through the office and to their sleeping-room.

"That'll be Truxton," Garton said. "Wants to see you, I guess."

The heavy tread came on through the office, and the door to Garton's room was flung open with as little ceremony as the front door had been. In the light of a kerosene-lamp upon the chair near his cot Conniston saw a short, squat, heavy-set man of perhaps forty-five, very broad across the forehead, very salient-jawed, his mustache short-cropped and grizzled, his mouth large and firm-lipped, his eyes steady and keen as they turned swiftly upon Conniston from under shaggy, tangled, iron-gray brows. The man had nodded curtly toward Tommy Garton, and then stood still in the doorway regarding young Conniston intently.

"You're Conniston."

It was a positive statement rather than a question, but Conniston answered as he sat up on the edge of his cot:

"Yes. I'm Conniston."

"All right." Truxton removed the lamp from the one chair in the room, placed it upon the window-sill, and sat down, pulling the chair around so that he faced Conniston. "You're goin' to work with me in the mornin'. Now, what do you know?"

His manner was abrupt, his voice curt. Conniston felt a trifle ill at ease under the man's piercing gaze, which seemed to be measuring him.

"Not a great deal, I'm afraid. You see, I—"

"I thought you were an engineer?"

"I am—after a fashion. Graduate of Yale—"

"Ever had any actual, practical experience?"

"Only field work in college."

"Ever had any experience handlin' men? Ever bossed a gang of men?"

"No."

"Ever do any kind of construction work?"

"In college—"

"Forget what you did with a four-eyed professor standin' over you! Ever build a bridge or a grade or a dam or a railroad?"

"No." Conniston answered shortly, half angrily.

"Then," grunted Truxton, plainly disgusted, "I'd like to know what the Old Man meant by sendin' you over here! I can't be bothered teachin' college boys how to do things. What I need an' need bad is an engineer that can do his part of the day's work."

"Look here!" cried Conniston, hotly. "We all have to begin some time, don't we? You had your first job, didn't you? And I'll bet you didn't fall down on it, either! It's up to you. If you think I'm no good, all right. If you give me my work to do I'll do it."

"It *ain't* up to me. The Old Man sent you over. You go to work in the mornin'. If I was doin' it I wouldn't put you on. I don't say you won't make good—I'm just sayin' I wouldn't take the chance. I'll stop here for you at four o'clock in the mornin'." He swung about from Conniston and toward Garton. "How're they comin', Tommy?"

All of the curt brusqueness was gone from his tone, the keen, cold, measuring calculation from his eye. With the compelling force of the man's blunt nature the whole atmosphere of the room was altered.

"First rate, Bat," Tommy answered, cheerfully. "How's the work going?"

"Good! The best day I've had in two weeks. We get to work on those seven knolls to-morrow. You remember—Miss Argyl calls 'em Little Rome."

"What have you decided? Going to make a detour, or—"

"Detour nothin'. I'm goin' right straight through 'em. It'll take time, all right. But in the end we'll save. I'll cut through 'em in four days or four an' a half."

"And then—it's Dam Number One?"

Truxton swore softly. "If I can get the men, it is! Swinnerton stole my last gang—seventy-five of 'em. The blamed little porcupine offered 'em two bits more than we're payin' an' grabbed every one of 'em. The Old Man has wired Denver for a hundred more muckers. Swinnerton can't keep takin' men on all year. He's got more now than he knows what to do with. I guess this gang 'll come on through. As soon as they come, Tommy, I'll have that big dam growin' faster'n you ever saw a dam grow before."

For half an hour the two men talked, and Conniston lay back listening. In spite of Bat Truxton's sour acceptance of him, Conniston began to feel a decided liking for the old engineer. After all, he told himself, were he in Truxton's place he would have small liking for putting a green man on the job. He realized that there was nothing personal in Truxton's attitude toward him. Truxton was not looking for a man, but for an efficient, reliable machine, one that had already been tested and found to be strong, trustworthy, infallible.

Again the question had been put to him, "What have you done?" And it was nobody's fault but his that he had done nothing.

"I wish you had two legs, Tommy," Truxton said, when at last he got up and went to the door. "You an' me workin' together out there—well, we'd make things jump, that's all."

Tommy laughed, but his sensitive mouth twitched as though with a sharp physical pain.

"Oh, I'm doing all right inside," he answered, quietly. "Somebody's got to attend to this end of the game. And

Conniston will be on to the ropes in a few days. He'll help you make things jump."

Truxton made no answer. For a moment he stood frowning at the floor. Then he turned once more to Conniston for a short, intent scrutiny.

"You have your blankets ready, Conniston," he said, shortly. "You'll sleep on a sand-pile to-morrow night."

And he went out, slamming the door behind him.

CHAPTER XIII

At half-past three, Conniston, awakened with a start by the jangle and clamor of Tommy Garton's little alarm-clock, got up and dressed. At the lunch-counter the man who had been fidgety yesterday and was merely sleepy this morning set coffee and flapjacks and bacon before him. Before four he had saddled his horse, rolled into a neat bundle a blanket and a couple of quilts from the cot upon which he had slept last night, tied them behind his saddle, and was ready for the coming of Bat Truxton. Then Truxton on horseback joined him. Conniston mounted, acknowledged Truxton's short "Good mornin'," and rode with him away from the sleeping village and out toward the south.

"Tommy's told you somethin' about what we got ahead of us?" Truxton asked, when they had ridden half a mile in silence.

"Yes. We went over the whole thing together as well as we could in a day's time."

"That's good. If any man's got a head on him for this sort of thing, that man's Tommy Garton. He'd make it as plain as a man could on paper, without goin' over the ground. To-day we're tyin' into those seven sand-hills I mentioned last night. I've got two hundred men workin' there. So they won't get in each other's way I've divided 'em up in four gangs, fifty men to the gang. There's all kinds of men in that two hundred, Conniston, and about the biggest part of your day's work will be to sort of size your men up. I've divided 'em, not accordin' to efficiency, but partly accordin' to nationality an' mostly accordin' to cussedness. I'm givin' you the tame ones to begin on. I'll take care of the ornery jaspers until you get your hand in. But I can't spare more'n a day or two. Then it'll be up to you. You'll have to swing the whole bunch, if you can. An' if you can't it'll be up to you to quit! Oh, it ain't so all-fired hard, not if you've got the savvy. I've got a foreman over each section that knows what he's doin' an' will do pretty much everything if you can furnish the head work."

"Where is the trouble with them? What do you mean by the ornery ones? They're all here because they want to work, aren't they? If they get dissatisfied they quit, don't they?"

Truxton looked at him curiously. "You got a lot of things to learn, Conniston. Just you take a tip from me: You keep your eyes an' ears real wide open for the next few days an' your mouth shut as long as you can. Tommy explained to you about the opposition? About what Oliver Swinnerton is doin' an' tryin' to do?"

"Yes."

"Then you remember that; don't overlook it for a minute, wakin' or sleepin'. It'll explain a whole lot."

When they rode into the camp at Little Rome the two hundred men employed there were just beginning to stir. Conniston's eyes took in with no little interest the details of the camp. There was one long, low tent, the canvas sides rolled up so that he could see a big cooking-stove with two or three men working over it. This, plainly enough, was the kitchen. From each side of the door a long line of twelve-inch boards laid across saw-horses ran out across the level sand. Upon the parallel boards were tin plates stacked high in piles, tin cups, knives and forks, and scores of loaves of bread. There were in addition perhaps twenty tin buckets half filled with sugar.

Scattered here and there upon the sand, some not twenty feet from the tent, some a hundred yards, some few with a little straw under them, the most of them with their blankets thrown upon the sand or upon heaps of cut sage-brush, were Truxton's "muckers." They lay there like a bivouacking army, their bodies disposed loosely, some upon their backs, still sleeping heavily; many just sitting up, awakened by the clatter of the cook's big iron spoon against a tin pan.

Behind the tent, picketed in rows by short ropes, were the horses and mules. And lined up to the right of the tent were twenty big, long-bodied Studebaker wagons, each with four barrels of water. Two more wagons at the other side of the tent were piled high with boxes and bags of provisions.

Truxton and Conniston unsaddled swiftly, and after staking out their horses, Conniston throwing his roll of bedding down behind the tent, they walked around to the front. Already most of the men were up, rolling blankets or hurrying to the rude tables. Several of them had gone to the aid of the cooks, and now were hurrying up and down between the parallel boards, setting out immense black pots of coffee, great lumps of butter, big pans of mush, beans, stewed "jerky," and potatoes boiled in their jackets. The men who had rolled out of their beds fully dressed, save for shoes, formed in a long line near the tent door and moved swiftly along the tables, taking up knives, forks, plates, and cups as they went, helping themselves generously to each different dish as they came to it. Many stopped at the farther ends of the boards, standing and eating from them.

Many more took their plates and cups of coffee away from the tables and squatted down to eat, placing their dishes upon the sand. There was remarkably little confusion, no time lost, as the two hundred men helped themselves to their breakfast. They did not appear to have seen Truxton; they glanced swiftly at Conniston and seemed to forget his presence in their hunger.

Never had Conniston seen a crowd of men like these. There were Americans there, and from the broken bits of conversation which floated to him he knew that they hailed from east, west, north, and south. There were Hungarians, Slavonians, Swedes—heavy, stolid, slow-moving men whose knowledge of the English language rose and set in "damn" and "hell." There were Chinamen and Japs—a dozen of the slant-eyed, yellow-faced Orientals—the Chinamen all big, gaunt men with their queues coiled about their heads. There were Italians, the lower class known to the West as "Dagoes." And almost to the last man of them they were the hardest-faced men he had ever seen.

There was a big, loose-limbed giant of an Englishman who walked like a sailor, who carried a great white scar across his cheek and upper lip, and who wore a long unscabbarded knife swinging from his belt. There was a wiry little Frenchman who showed a deep scar at the base of his throat, from which his shirt was rolled back, and who snarled like a cat when another man accidentally trod upon his foot. Conniston saw a dozen faces scarred as though by knife-cuts; twisted, evil faces; dark, scowling faces; faces lined by unbridled passions; brutal, heavy-jawed faces.

But if their faces showed the handiwork of the devil, from their chins down they were men cast in the mold of the image of God. From the biggest Dane standing close to six feet six inches to the smallest Jap less than five feet tall, they were men of iron and steel. Quick-eyed, quick-footed, hard, they were the sort of men to drive the fight against the desert.

Breakfast finished, the men dropped their cups and plates into one of two big tubs as they passed by the tent, their knives and forks into another, and went quietly and promptly to work. Each man had his duty and went about it without waiting to be told. They filled buckets at the water-barrels and watered their horses; they harnessed and hitched up to plows and scrapers; half a dozen of them hitched four horses to each of six of the wagons whose barrels had been emptied, and swung out across the plain toward the Half Moon for more water.

Truxton beckoned to Conniston and led him toward the south. And suddenly, coming about the foot of a little knoll, Conniston had his first glimpse of the main canal.

Here it was a great ditch, ten feet deep, thirty feet wide, its banks sloping, the earth which had been dragged out of it by the scrapers piled high upon each side in long mounds, like dikes. Truxton stood staring at it, his eyes frowning, his jaw set and stern.

"There she is, Conniston. A simple enough thing to look at, but so is the business end of a mule. This thing is goin' to make the Old Man a thousand times over—or it's goin' to break him in two like a rotten stick."

The workmen were coming up, driving their teams with dragging trace-chains to be hitched to the scrapers and big plows standing where they had quit work the night before. Truxton, tugging thoughtfully at his grizzled mustache, watched them a moment as they "hooked up" and dropped, one behind another, into a long, slow-moving procession, the great shovel-like scrapers scooping up ton after ton of the soft earth, dragging it up the slope where the end of the ditch was, wheeling and dumping it along the edge of the excavation, turning again, again going back down into the cut to scoop up other tons of dirt, again to climb the incline to deposit it upon the bank. Here Conniston counted forty-nine teams and forty-nine drivers. One man—it was the big Englishman with the scarred lip and cheek and the unsheathed knife—was standing ten feet away from the edge of the ditch, his great bare arms folded, watching.

"That's one of your foremen," Truxton said, his eyes following Conniston's. "Ben, his name is. He knows his business, too. He'll take care of this gang for you while you come along with me. I'll show you your other shift."

They followed a line marked by the survey stakes for a quarter of a mile past the camp. Here another fifty men were at work; and here, where the top of the sand had already been scraped away, a harder soil called for the use of the big plows before the scrapers could be of any use. The foreman here, a South-of-Market San-Franciscan by his speech, shouted a command to one of the drivers and came up to Truxton.

"Whatcher want to-day?" he demanded. "Ten foot?"

"Nine," Truxton told him, shortly. "Nine an' a half by the time you get to that first stake. Nine three-quarters at the second. Can you get that far to-day?"

The foreman turned a quid of tobacco, squinted his eye at the two stakes, and nodded.

"Sure thing," he said.

And then he turned on his heel and went back to the point he had quit, yelling his orders as he went.

"Another good man," Truxton muttered. "Thank the Lord, we've got some of them you couldn't beat if you went a thousand miles for 'em."

Still farther on was the third gang, and beyond that the fourth. These hundred men were at work on the "Seven Knolls." And there Truxton himself would superintend the work to-day. He stopped and stood with Conniston upon one of the mounds, from which they could see all that was being done. And with slow, thoughtful carefulness he told Conniston all that he could of the work in detail.

"You do a good deal of watchin' to-day," he ended. "Ben an' the Lark—that's what they call that little cuss bossin' the second gang—listen to him whistle an' you'll know why—know well what to do. Right now an' right here the work's dead easy, Conniston. Only don't go an' let 'em drive you in a hole where you have to admit you don't know. You've *got* to know."

The work here was in reality so simple that men like Ben and the Lark grasped it quickly. Conniston had little trouble in seeing readily what was to be done. The details Truxton furnished him.

When noon came they ate with the men. And at one o'clock Truxton called Ben and the Lark aside and told them shortly that Conniston was the new engineer and that they were to take orders from him. Whereupon Conniston took upon himself the responsibility of "bossing" a hundred men, the biggest responsibility which he had ever taken upon his care-free shoulders.

He had seen the slow, measuring glances which both of his two foremen had bestowed upon him when Truxton told them; knew that they accepted him as their overseer because they took orders from Truxton, but saw in their faces that

Jackson Gregory

they reserved judgment of him personally until such time as they could see how much or how little he knew. He was not greatly in fear of the outcome. The work was running so smoothly, there were so few possible difficulties to come up now, that it seemed to him that all he had to do was to stand and watch.

And at first he did little but watch and, as Truxton had suggested, try to study his men. He saw that both the Lark and Ben said very few words, that when they did speak they barked out short, explosive commands surcharged with profanity, that when they interfered there was a good reason for it, that their commands were obeyed without hesitation and without question. Not once in two hours did either of them so much as look toward him. And the long processions of men and horses came and went, scooped and dumped their big scraper-loads, and swung back into the ditch, each man of them moving like a machine.

It was after three o'clock when he noticed something which he would have seen before had he been used to the work and the men. He saw the long string of scrapers come to a halt for perhaps two minutes; saw that the cause of the halt was a big Northlander who had stopped just as he came upon the bank and was working over at race-chain which seemed to be causing trouble. In a moment he started up again, the other scrapers began to move, and Conniston dismissed the matter as of no consequence. This was the gang over which Ben was foreman. He glanced quickly at the big Englishman and saw that his eyes were upon the Northlander. Again, not twenty minutes later, came a second brief stoppage, again the Swede was working over a trace-chain—and now Ben had swung about and was striding toward Conniston.

"Hi say there," he said, as he came to Conniston's side. "Bat says Hi'm to take horders off you. Do you want me to 'andle those Johnnies? Hor do you figure on a-stepping in? Hi?"

"What do you mean?" demanded Conniston, a bit puzzled. "I haven't interfered with you, have I?"

"No. Hi just want to know, you know. Hi 'andle 'em my wi, hor Hi quit, you know."

"You are to do just as you have always done," Conniston told him, shortly. "If you can handle them, all right. Go to it. If you need any help—What's the matter?"

"Hi don't awsk any 'elp," muttered Ben. "Just one man—"

"You mean that Swede with the big white mare in the lead?" interrupted Conniston, quickly.

Ben looked at him swiftly. Grunting an answer which Conniston did not catch, he turned and went back along the edge of the ditch.

The Swede was again coming up the bank. At the top he did as he had done more than once before: turned out in a wide circle, letting two men pass him. The Englishman strode swiftly toward him.

"Hi, there, you big Swede!" he yelled, his words accompanied by a volley of insulting epithets born in the slums of London. "Wot you trying to do? Want the 'ole works to pawss you w'ile you rest? You blooming spoonbill, get inter that! Step lively, man!"

The Northlander's heavy, slow-moving feet stopped entirely as he turned a stolid face toward the foreman.

"I bane to like I tam plase," he muttered, slowly. "Yo bane

go hell."

The big Englishman sprang back, swept up a broken pick-handle half buried in the sand, and leaped forward. As he leaped he swung the bit of heavy, hard wood above his head. The Swede dropped his reins and threw up his arms to guard himself, but the pick-handle, wielded in a great, sinewy right hand, beat down his arms and struck him a crashing blow across his forehead. Conniston heard the thud of it where he stood. The Swede's arms flew out and he went down like a steer in a slaughter-house.

"You bloody spoonbill!" cried the Englishman, standing over the prostrate body. "Wot are you laying down for? Get hup, hor Hi'll beat the bloody 'ead hoff your bloody shoulders! Get hup!"

Slowly, weakly, reeling as he got upon his knees, the Swede rose to his feet. A great, smoldering, cold-blooded wrath shone in his blue eyes, mingled with a surly fear. He made no motion toward the man who stood three feet from him threatening him. Nor did he stir toward his fallen reins. Instead he turned half about toward the camp.

"I bane quit," he muttered, thickly. "I bane get my time."

"Quit!" yelled Ben—"quit, will you!"

The Swede muttered something which Conniston did not catch. Ben took one short, quick step forward, swinging his pick-handle high above his head. For a moment the Swede paused, hesitating. And then, again muttering, he stooped, picked up his reins, and swung his team back into the cut.

The other men had all stopped to watch. Now Ben swung about upon them, his voice lifted in a string of cockney oaths, commanding them not to stand still all day, but to get to work. At almost his first word the teams began to move again, the men laughing, calling to one another, jeering at the defeated Swede, or merely shrugging their shoulders. And Greek Conniston, his face still white from what he had just witnessed, began to see, although still dimly, what it was he had taken into his two hands to do.

He glanced down at his hands. The middle finger of the right one, with which he had struck Brayley's heavy cheek-bone, was swollen to twice its natural size, stiff and sore. The nails were broken and blackened. There were a dozen scratches and little cuts. The palms were hard and calloused, with bits of loose skin along the base of the fingers where blisters had formed and broken and healed over.

He lifted his head, and his speculative eyes ran back along the ditch. The work was again running smoothly, quietly, save for the clanking of the scrapers and the men's voices calling to their horses and mules, each man intent upon his own duty, the face of the desert as peaceful as the hot, clear arch of the sky above.

CHAPTER XIV

Three days passed, four, a week, and still no word came of the men for whom the "Old Man" had wired to Denver. Conniston had nearly forgotten them. His day was from daylight until dark, often until long after dark. Upon more than one evening, after the men had had their suppers and crawled into their blankets, he and Truxton had sat in the tent at the cook's rude table, a lantern between them, figuring and planning upon the next day.

He began to notice a vague change in the older engineer as the days went by. At first he was hardly conscious of it, at a loss to catalogue it. But before the middle of the week he realized that each evening found Truxton more irritable, more prone to explode into quick rage over some trifle. The man's eyes began to show the restless fever within him, and some sort of an unsleeping, nervous anxiety. Throughout the days the men stood clear of him. His flaming wrath burst out at a blundering mistake or at a man's failure to follow to the last letter some short-spoken instructions. It was only one night when Conniston made careless mention of Oliver Swinnerton, and Truxton flew into a towering, cursing rage, that he began to believe that he saw the real reason for Truxton's growing ill temper.

"The thievin', mangy, pot-bellied porcupine!" Truxton had shouted, banging his fist down upon the cook's table so hard that the lantern jumped two inches in the air. "I'll just naturally rid the earth of him one of these days. Those men ought to have arrived from Denver three days ago. How am I ever goin' to get anything done, an' no men to work for me? With Colton Gray gone an' the rest of the P. C. & W. thieves playin' into that scoundrel Swinnerton's hands, where do we get off? We send for a hundred men, an' it saves Swinnerton the trouble an' expense of a wire. By now every man jack of them is makin' fences an' buildin' houses for him, or I'm the worst-fooled man in the country." And he swung off into a string of curses which would not have been unworthy of Ben the Englishman.

One afternoon when they had run the ditch through the Seven Knolls and were cutting rapidly through a level stretch with a double line of smaller hills a mile ahead of the foremost team, Truxton came striding along the ditch to where Conniston was standing.

"Think you can handle all four gangs without me for the rest of the afternoon?" he asked, as he came to Conniston's side.

"Yes," answered Conniston. "I can handle them."

Truxton laughed softly.

"You're comin' ahead, youngster. Wouldn't have wanted the job a week ago, would you? I believe you could handle 'em, too. But I'll do it this trip. I want you to go to the office for me. See Tommy and run over these figures with him. I told you last night that I was sure of 'em. To-day I'm gettin' balled up. Tell him that I'm puttin' a gang on that double line of hills first thing in the mornin'. Run over the thing with him and verify our figures. If there's anything left of the afternoon when you get through you can take it off an' see the sights in Valley City. Find out how they're fixed for water an' grub an' wood. Tommy's got all that dope at the tip of his tongue. An' be back here the first thing in the mornin'."

He went back to his work, and Conniston hurried away, decidedly glad for the change of work. Just to grip his horse between his knees, to swing out alone across the rolling fields, to drink deep of the untroubled stillness of the wide places, to be an independent, swiftly moving figure with nothing to break the silent harmony of the still, hot sky above and the still, hot sands beneath—a harmony which the soul leaped out to meet—brought a quiet, peaceful content. The day was serene and perfect, like yesterday and to-morrow in this land of dreary barrenness and of infinite possibility; the faint blue of the cloudless sky met the gray monotone of the earth between two mounds in front of him; and as his horse's hoofs fell noiselessly, as though upon padded felt, his sensation was that of drifting across the wide sweep of a gently swelling ocean toward a landlocked sea of pale turquoise.

It was shortly after four o'clock when he rode into Valley City. He passed the one-room school-house, with its distinctive little belfry and flag-pole, and a glance in at the open windows told him that the children had been dismissed. At the corner of the building he came suddenly upon a saddled horse biting and stamping at the flies which defied swishing tail and savage teeth. Half smiling, he stopped. He had recognized the horse as a Half Moon animal, one he had ridden several times, and thought that he could guess who was inside paying his respects to the schoolmistress. Even as he paused Jocelyn Truxton came out, opening her white parasol. And in all the holiday regalia of shaggy black chaps, bright-blue neck-hand-kerchief, and new Stetson hat, Lonesome Pete followed her.

Pete, as he emerged from behind the parasol, saw Conniston

and called a hearty "Hello, Con!" to him. And Conniston turned his horse and rode back to the front steps.

"Miss Jocelyn says as how she ain't been interdooced," Lonesome Pete was saying, his hat turning nervously in his hands, his face flushing as he met Conniston's eyes. "Shake han's with Mr. Conniston, Miss Jocelyn."

Miss Jocelyn lifted her dropped eyelids with a quick flutter, favored Conniston with a flashing smile, banished her smile to replace it with a pouting of pursed lips, and said, archly:

"I have half a mind *not* to shake hands with Mr. Conniston! If he had wanted to meet me he would have come with Billy Jordan the other night."

But, none the less, she finished by putting out a small, gloved hand, and Conniston, leaning from the saddle, took it in his.

"I was sorry, Miss Truxton," he said, lightly. "Didn't Jordan tell you? Garton and I had a lot to do that night, and worked late. It was very kind of you to say that I might come."

"If you had wanted to come *very* much—" she said, shaking her head saucily. "*You* would have found time to come, wouldn't you, Pete?"

Lonesome Pete, his spurred boots shifting uneasily, put on his hat, noticed immediately that Conniston still held his in his hand, snatched it off again, spun it about upon a big forefinger, and grinned redly.

"I sure would, Miss Jocelyn," he declared with great emphasis.

Miss Jocelyn turned back to lock the school-house door, and then came down the steps and into the road.

"I'll go git my hoss an' walk along," Lonesome Pete said, and hurried around to the back of the house.

"Are you going my way, Mr. Conniston?"

Conniston said that he was, and swung down, walking at her side and leading his horse.

"If you really *do* care to come to see me," Jocelyn said, quickly, before the cowboy had rejoined them, "you may call this evening."

Conniston thanked her, and, not to seem rude, said that he would drop in after he and Tommy Garton had finished their work. Jocelyn smiled at him brightly.

"You may come early, if you like. I am sure that you will have a whole lot of things to tell me about the progress you and papa are making with the ditch. I'm *so* interested in the work, Mr. Conniston."

Pete had taken up his horse's dragging reins and led him into the street. Jocelyn, her chin a trifle lifted, her air more than a trifle coquettish as she smiled at Conniston, pretended not to see her red-headed adorer. Walking between the two men, she even tilted her parasol so that it did no slightest good in the world in the matter of protecting her from the sun, but served very effectively in shutting out Lonesome Pete. Conniston laughed and talked lightly with her, vastly amused at the situation and the discomfiture upon her ardent lover's expressive face. And so, with Pete trudging along in silence, unnoticed, they came to the office and stopped, Jocelyn and Conniston still talking to each other, Lonesome Pete tying and untying knots in his bridle-reins.

"Can't you give up enough of your precious time to walk on home with me? I have some icy cold lemonade waiting for me," she tempted.

"I'm sorry. I'd like to, but I've got a lot of work to get over with Garton—"

Only three or four doors from the office was the little cottage which he had helped Argyl to prepare for her father. Even while he was making his excuses he saw the door open, and Argyl herself, lithe and trim in her gray riding-habit, step out upon the tiny porch.

"I beg pardon," he broke off, suddenly. "I—Will you excuse me?"

And, jerking his horse's reins so that the animal started up after him at a trot, he strode down the street, his hat off, his face lifted eagerly to Argyl's. A moment later he was holding her hand in his, oblivious of Jocelyn, Pete, Valley City, everything in the world except the girl with the big gray eyes, the girl whom he had seen through his shifting day-dreams.

When the cowboy and the schoolmistress passed him Lonesome Pete was talking once more and she was being very gracious to him, but Conniston had no eye for such trifles. Jocelyn nodded a bit stiffly to Argyl, and, smiling at Conniston, cried gaily, "You won't forget, Mr. Conniston!"

But he had already forgotten. He had not hoped to see Argyl for many days yet, perhaps many weeks, and the unexpected sight of her thrilled through him, driving all thoughts of Jocelyn out of his mind. And when in a few minutes he was forced to remember that he had business with Garton he left reluctantly and with a promise to have dinner at six o'clock with her and her father.

Tommy Garton he found as cheerful as a cricket and heartily glad to see him. Billy Jordan had looked out as Jocelyn and her two escorts came by, and now was back at his typewriter, pounding the keys for dear life, the ticking and clicking of his machine keeping time to "Yankee Doodle," which he was whistling softly. He, too, shook hands, but his cheerfulness was of a grade noticeably inferior to Garton's. And immediately he went back to his machine and his rhythmical pounding.

Conniston was of a mind to get the business of the day done with before six. The first part of his errand took up the greater part of an hour. Then Garton reported upon the other matter which Truxton had wanted ascertained. There was water enough to last four days. Provisions were holding out well, but soon there would be a need for fresh supplies of sugar, flour, and jerked beef. There was enough of canned goods at the general store to last for a month, a fresh shipment having been recently received—two big wagon-loads from Crawfordsville.

"I expect Mr. Crawford to drop in on us some time before dark," Garton said, as he put away carefully into a drawer the papers he had taken from it during the consultation. "Miss Argyl is already here. Stopped in a minute to let us know that the Old Man is coming."

"Yes, I know. I saw her a minute just before I came in."

They chatted for a while longer, until Conniston saw by his watch that it was six o'clock. Then he got up and reached for his hat.

"You'll spend the night with me, Conniston," Tommy

Garton offered. "I've got plenty of bedding; a man doesn't suffer for covers these nights. Drop in as soon as you and Billy get through supper. I think that I can beat you a game of crib."

"Much obliged, Garton. But I may not run in for an hour or so. Miss Crawford has asked me to eat with them to-night."

"Oh." There was a great lack of expression in Garton's monosyllable, but as he swung about upon his stool, bending over the box of cigarettes which he swept up, Conniston thought that he saw a little twitch as of pain about the sensitive lips. Not understanding, feeling at once that he would like to say something and not knowing what to say, he went slowly to the door. As he was going out Garton called to him, his voice and face alike as cheerful as they had been throughout the afternoon.

"I say, Conniston. Remember me to Miss Argyl, will you? She's a glorious girl. I never saw her match. She's got the same capability for doing big things that her father has. I said the other day that he was the whole brain and brawn of this war for reclamation. I ought to have been kicked. Do you know that the whole project, from its inception, has been as much hers as his? Why, that girl has ridden over every foot of this valley, knows it like a book. Dam Number Three, that auxiliary dam, is her idea. And a rattling good idea, too. The men call it 'Miss Argyl's Dam.' Better brush up on your engineering before you talk reclamation with her, old man. She's read all the books I've got. A glorious girl, Conniston."

Conniston came back into the room.

"See here, Garton," he said, gently. "Why don't you come along. She told me that she wanted you, that she had asked you and—"

Garton waved an interrupting hand, smiling quickly. But
Conniston saw that his face looked tired.

CHAPTER XV

At Conniston's knock Argyl's voice from somewhere in the back of the cottage called "Come in!" He opened the door, went through the cozy sitting-room, which was scarcely larger than the fire-place at the range-house, and at a second invitation found his way into the rear room. There an oil-stove was shooting up its yellow flames about a couple of stew-pans, and there Argyl herself, in blue gingham apron, her sleeves rolled up on her plump, white arms, was completing preparations for the evening meal. She turned to nod to Conniston and then back to her cooking.

"You'll find a chair in the corner," she told him, as he stopped in the doorway, looking amusedly at her. "That is, of course, if you care to call on the cook? Otherwise you will find cigars and a last month's paper in the sitting-room."

"There isn't any otherwise," he laughed back at her. And after a moment, in which she was very busy over the stove and he very content to stand and watch her: "We're even now. Last time we were here I was the hired man and tacked down carpets for you. Now I'm the guest of the family, if you please, and you're the cook."

"You can have two cupfuls of water to wash your hands and one for your face. You'll find the barrel and basin upon the back porch. And don't throw the water away! I'll save it for you to use the next time you come."

"Thank you. But I washed over at Garton's. He lets me have two cupfuls for my face. And now I'm going to help you. What can I do?"

"Nothing. If you wanted to work, why did you wait until the last minute? Unless you know how to set a table?"

"I can set anything from an eight-day clock to a hen," he assured her, gravely. "Where's Mr. Crawford? Has he come yet?"

"No. I expect him any minute. But we won't wait for him. It's against the law in the Crawford home to wait meals for anybody."

Under her direction he found the dishes in a cupboard built into the walls, knives, forks, spoons, and napkins in drawers below, and journeying many times from kitchen to dining-room, stopping after each trip to stand and watch his hostess in her preparations for dinner, he at length had the table set. And then he insisted upon helping play waiter with her until she informed him that he was positively retarding matters. Whereupon he made a cigarette and sat upon the kitchen table and merely watched.

For many days Conniston had longed to see Mr. Crawford, to talk with him concerning the big work. Now, as he and Argyl sat down together, his one wish was that Mr. Crawford be delayed indefinitely. As he looked across the table, with its white cloth, its few cheap dishes, its simple fare, he was conscious of a deep content. He helped Argyl to the *piece de resistance*—it consisted of dried beef, potatoes, onions, and carrots all stewed together; she passed to him the biscuits which she had just made; they drank each other's health and success to the Great Work in light, cooled claret made doubly refreshing with a dash of lemon; and they dined ten times as merrily as they would have dined at Sherry's.

He told her of Tommy Garton, and suddenly surprised in her a phase of nature which he had never seen before. Her eyes filled with a quick, soft sympathy, a sympathy almost motherly.

"Poor little Tommy," she said, gently. "He laughs at himself and calls himself 'half a man,' while he's greater than any two men he comes in contact with once in a year. I call Tommy my cathedral—which sounds foolish, I know, but which isn't! Do you know the feeling you get when you steal all alone into one of those great, empty, silent churches, where it is always a dim twilight? Not that Tommy is as somber and stately as a great cathedral," she smiled. "Just the opposite, I know. But his sunny nature, his unruffled cheerfulness affect me like a sermon. When I allow myself to descend into the depths and see how Tommy manages it, I feel as if I ought to be spanked. I think," she ended, "that I have pretty well mixed things up, haven't I? But you understand what I mean?"

"I understand. And since we have drunk to the Great Work, shall we drink to a Great Soul who is a vital part of it? I don't know how we'd manage without Tommy Garton."

They touched glasses gravely and drank to a man who, as they sat looking out upon life through long, glorious vistas, dawn-flushed, lay alone upon his cot, his face buried in his arms.

They finished their meal, cleared away the dishes together, and still Mr. Crawford had not come. Then Conniston dragged two of the chairs out to the front porch, took a cigar from the jar where it had been kept moist with half an apple, and they went out to enjoy the cool freshness of the evening. The sun had sunk out of sight, the mood of the desert had changed. All of the dull gray monotone was gone. All the length of the long, low western horizon the dross of the garish day was being transmuted by the alchemy of the sunset into red and yellow gold, molten and ever flowing, as though spilled from some great retort to run sluggishly in a gleaming band about the earth.

A little wandering breeze had sprung up, and went whispering out across the dim plains. It swirled away the smoke from Conniston's cigar; he saw it stir a strand of hair across Argyl's cheek. The glory of the desert was still the wonderful thing it had been, but it was less than the essential, vital glory of a girl. Suddenly a great desire was upon him to call out to her, to tell her that he loved her more than all of the rest of life, to make her listen to him, to make her love him. And with the rush of the desire came the thought, as though it were a whispered voice from the heart of the desert: "What are you that you should speak so to her. *What have you done to make you worthy of this woman?* You, a laggard, as frivolous a thing until now as a weather-cock, and by no means so useful a factor in the world, your regeneration merely begun; she the Incomparable Woman!"

It was Argyl who spoke first, and only after nearly an inch of white ash had formed at the end of Conniston's cigar.

"People who do not understand—they are aliens to whom the desert has never spoken!—ask why father gives the best part of a ripe manhood to a struggle with such a country. Does not an evening like this answer their question? No people in the world can so love their land as do the children of the desert. For when they have made it over they are still a part of it and it has become a part of them."

He told her all that he could of the work and Truxton and

the men, going into detail as he found that she followed him, that Tommy Garton had not exaggerated when he had said that she knew every sand-hill and hollow. She listened to him silently, only now and then asking a pertinent question, her eyes upon his face as she leaned forward in her chair, her hands clasped about her knees. And when he had finished he found that his cigar had long since gone out and that she was smiling at him.

"It has got you, too!" she cried, softly. "You are as enthusiastic already as Tommy Garton is. I wonder if you realized it? And I wonder," her eyes again upon the fading colors in the west, the smile gone out of them, "what it would mean to you if, after all, our dream came to nothing, if it proved that we were more daring than wise, if we lost everything where we are staking everything?"

"I have been a small, unnecessary cog in a great machine for only a week," he told her, slowly. "And yet you will know that I am telling you the plain truth when I say that such a failure would bring to me the biggest disappointment I have ever felt. Failure," he cried, sharply, as though he had but grasped the full significance of the word after he himself had employed it—"there won't be failure at the end of it for us! There can't be. It means too much. I tell you that we are going to drive the thing to a successful conclusion. It's got to be!"

"Yes," she repeated, quietly, after him, "it has got to be. I don't doubt the outcome for one single second. Down in my heart I *know*. And I know, too, how much there is yet to be done, how much you men have to contend with, how swiftly the time is slipping by us. Do you realize, Mr. Conniston, how little time we have ahead of us before the first of October?"

"Yes, I know. And there are four miles of main canal to dig, mile after mile of smaller cross ditches, to irrigate the land after we get the water here, and two dams to complete." He got to his feet, his cigar again forgotten, his eyes frowning down upon her. "Truxton is right. We've got to get more men—many more men. And we've got to get them in a hurry."

"Father, when he comes to-night, will know about the men we have been expecting from Denver. He has been all day in Crawfordsville. What do you think of Bat Truxton?"

"He is a good man who knows his business. He is a skilful, practical engineer, and he knows how to get every ounce of power out of the men under him. He is as much the man for the place as if he and the job had been created for each other."

She was now standing with him, watching his face eagerly.

"Have you noticed," she asked, quietly—through the gathering dusk he thought that he could see a faint shadow upon her face which was not a part of the thickening night—"any sort of change in the man since you went to work with him?"

Conniston hesitated, frowning, before he answered. "He has been irritable," he finally admitted, with slow reluctance. "But the reason is not far to seek and does not discredit him. He is heart and soul in this work, Miss Crawford. Like all of us—you, your father, Tommy Garton, me—I think that he feels his responsibility heavily, very heavily. And when day after day rushes by and finds the work far from being finished, and he has to have more men, and the men don't come—good heavens! isn't it enough to make a man restive?"

For a long time Argyl made no answer, but, rising, stood

looking far out into the misty obscurity, as though she would look beyond to-day and deep into the future for an answer to many things. The short twilight passed, the warm colors in the west faded, the breeze of a moment ago died down in faint and fainter whispers, the stars grew brighter, ever more thick-set, in the wide arch of the heavens.

"I hope that you are right," she said, slowly, at last. And then, with a queer little laugh which jarred upon Conniston strangely: "I am getting fanciful, I suppose, and faint-hearted! Never has our undertaking seemed so big to me; never have the obstacles loomed so high. I find myself waking up with a start night after night from some horrible dream that the water has failed in the mountains, or that Oliver Swinnerton has stolen all of our men, or that Bat Truxton has gone over to the opposition! Oh, I know that I am foolish. For, as you say, we *can't* fail. Everything has got to come out right! And now," in the manner native and natural to her—frank, hearty, even eager—"I am going to tell you some good news. In the first place, I see that I have been doing nothing too long, and that always makes one morbid, I think. I am going to get back to work. Isn't that good news? It is to me, at least. And, secondly, I have made a discovery. You'd never guess."

Conniston shook his head. "What is it?"

"What," she asked him, laughingly, and yet with a serious note in her voice, "is the one thing which we should like to discover here? If a good old-style genie straight from between the covers of the *Arabian Nights* were to drop down in front of you and say, 'Name the thing which thou wouldst have, and thou shalt have it!' what would that thing be?"

And Conniston, with his thoughts upon the Great Work,

knowing that her thoughts were with his there, answered quickly:

"Water! But that is impossible!"

"My secret—yet," she answered him. "I had not meant to say anything about it so soon. Promise to say nothing about it until I give you leave, and I'll tell you a little—oh, a very little—about my secret."

Conniston promised, and she went on, speaking swiftly, earnestly:

"It was last week. I was riding out into the desert to the north of here—no matter how far—when I came upon it. It is a spring. Oh, not much of a spring to look at it. Just a few square feet of moist soil, here and there a sprig of drying grass, three or four brown willows. But those things mean that there is water there. How it came there while all of the rest of the desert so far as we know it is bone-dry does not matter so much as *what can we do with it?* I hardly dare hope," she finished, thoughtfully, "that my spring is going to prove a factor in our irrigation scheme. But I hope that it may help to supply us here with drinking-water, water for our horses. That in itself would mean a good deal, wouldn't it, Mr. Conniston?"

"There is no end to what it might mean—may mean. If your spring can be made to supply Valley City and the men working out yonder with water, to supply the horses and mules, it will mean that all the men and teams being used daily to haul from the Half Moon creek can be put to active work on the ditch. And—who knows?—if you can find water at all in the desert we may be able to use it to irrigate! God knows we want water on this land soon—and the mountains are still a long way off! But," and he tried to make out her features in the darkness, "how does it happen that this spring has never been found before?"

"The country all about it is what the desert is everywhere. No one would dream of water in it. Then there is a rude circle of low-lying sand-hills. Within their inclosure, consequently shut off from view unless one rides to the crest of the hills as I happened to do, is the spring."

He thought that she was going to add something further, perhaps more in the way of a description of the location of the spring, when he heard horses' hoofs and the rattle of dry wagon-wheels, and she broke off suddenly.

"It is father at last," she said, softly. "Remember, Mr. Conniston, I want to keep this a secret from father for a while—until I know what it is worth."

"I'll remember," he answered, rising with her and turning toward the two figures which had leaped down from the wagon and were hastening toward the cottage. The man slightly in front of his companion, coming first into the rays of the lamp streaming through the window, was Mr. Crawford. And Conniston saw with a quick frown that the other man was Roger Hapgood.

"Argyl, my dear," said Mr. Crawford, as he kissed the girl who had gone to meet him, "I am sorry we are late. You'll be sorry, too, for I'm amazingly hungry. Anything left? Ah, Mr. Conniston, isn't it? Glad to see you." He took Conniston's hand in a strong grip. "Haven't seen you since you came to the Valley. I'm glad you're here. I want to talk with you about the work."

He went on into the house, Argyl with him. She had shaken hands with Roger Hapgood, and, with an invitation to him and Conniston to follow, went ahead with her father.

For a moment the two men faced each other in silence through the half-darkness. Then Hapgood turned upon his heel and went into the house. In a moment Conniston followed him, smiling.

He took a chair at the side of the room and lighted a fresh cigar while he watched the two men at table and Argyl bringing them their supper. He saw that Mr. Crawford's manner was what it always had been—bluff, frank, open, cheery. But he saw, too, or thought that he saw, little lines of worry upon the high forehead which had not been there a month ago.

Hapgood's face, seen now clearly, was as smug as ever, but there had been wrought in it a subtle change. In place of the fresh, pink complexion, the desert had given him a healthy coat of tan. But that, while Conniston was quick to note it, was not the change that startled him. There was an indefinable something in Hapgood's eyes, at the corners of his thin-lipped mouth, that had not been there before. Conniston wondered if the hand of this Western country had touched the inner man as it had the outer, if the new life had found certain small seeds of strength in the hereto-fore futile Hapgood and were developing them?

Hapgood's manner, however, was unchanged, irreproa-chable. He placed salt and pepper, bread, butter, whatever it was that Mr. Crawford wanted, before him before the older man had realized that he wanted it. His attitude toward Argyl was at all times deferential, eloquent of respectful admiration. Hapgood was nothing if not urbane. Toward Conniston, however, he did not once glance. To his way of thinking, evidently, there were but three people in the room—the wonderfully masterful Mr. Crawford, the radiantly beautiful Argyl, the deeply appreciative Hapgood —and certain negligible, necessary furniture.

During the short meal Mr. Crawford spoke little, contenting himself with a few light remarks to Argyl and the others. Often he ate in silence, abstractedly. Argyl had looked curiously at him and thereafter offered few words. Hapgood took his cue from the masterful Mr. Crawford. Conniston smoked and watched the three of them, his eyes finding oftenest Argyl and resting longest upon her. Finally, when he had finished and pushed away his plate, taking the cigar Argyl offered him, Mr. Crawford spoke shortly, emphatically.

"I got word to-day from the men we have been expecting from Denver. They have gone to work by now."

"Under Bat Truxton?" demanded Conniston, quickly.

The older man cut off the end of his cigar, rolled the black perfecto between his lips, and lighted it before he replied.

"They have gone to work," he repeated, as though discussing a matter of no moment, "for Oliver Swinnerton. Shall we go into the front room? I want to ask you some questions about the work, Conniston. I did not have a chance to see Truxton this afternoon."

He rose and led the way into the other room. Conniston, casting a swift glance at Argyl's face, which had suddenly gone white, followed him. Argyl had stepped forward as though to go with them when Hapgood laid a detaining hand lightly, respectfully, upon her arm.

"May I speak with you a moment, Miss Argyl?" he whispered, but not so low that Conniston did not catch the words distinctly. "It will take just a moment, and—and it is very important."

Reluctantly she paused. Conniston went out and heard

Hapgood shut the door after him. He shrugged his shoulders.

Mr. Crawford did not again refer to the bad news which he had brought, but instead seemed to have forgotten it. He asked Conniston question after question, seeking significant details, demanding to know how many feet the ditch had been driven upon each separate day of the week, what difficulties had been met, how the men did the parts allotted them, what Truxton counted upon accomplishing upon each day to come. And after ten minutes of sharp, quick questions he leaned forward and, with his eyes steady and searching upon Conniston's, demanded, abruptly:

"Is Truxton showing any signs of nervous irritability?"

"Yes." Conniston hesitated, wondering what was in the other man's thoughts. He began an explanation such as he had made Argyl, but Mr. Crawford cut him short.

"That will do. Thank you. That is all that I wanted to know."

He got to his feet and strode back and forth in the little room, his brows bunched together. Conniston, seeing for the first time in this man whom he had held unendingly resourceful, indomitable, signs of a militating anxiety, felt a sudden chill at his heart. Were they, after all, playing a losing game? Was the combination of desert and Swinnerton and capital going to prove too much for them? Was John Crawford even now looking clearly into the future and seeing himself a beaten, broken man?

For a moment of torture, during which he realized to the uttermost what success would mean, what failure, he feared that the vision which he had thought to have glimpsed through this sturdy pioneer's eyes was the true vision, feared that the fight was going out of John Crawford.

And a moment later a little shiver tingled through him as John Crawford stopped in front of him, looking down at him, as he saw that the make-up of this man was not broken, but that it was being bent like a powerful spring which draws its strength from outside pressure. He thought swiftly that the greater the weight put upon a powerful spring the greater was its recoil, the greater weights might it fling aside. Mr. Crawford was half smiling. His lips were calm. In his eyes there was no hint of fear or of failure. Instead a steady light there spoke with clear forcefulness of an unshaken determination, and more than hinted of a certain grim joy of combat.

"Young man," he said, almost gently, "you are mighty fortunate."

Conniston rose, making no reply, as he waited for an explanation.

"Yes, mighty fortunate. You are taking hold. I know what you were when you came to us; I know what you are now. I can see what you are going to grow to be. I congratulate you. And I congratulate you upon being placed in a position from which you are going to see the biggest fight that was ever heard of in this part of the country. Things are going dead against us these days. Do you know what that means?" He squared his shoulders, and for a moment his lips came together in a straight line. Then he smiled again.

"Are you never—afraid of the outcome?" asked Conniston.

"I believe in God, Mr. Conniston. I believe in my work. I believe in myself. We are not going to fail."

In that one brief, fleeting second Conniston had a view of

John Crawford he had never glimpsed before. He made no reply. For a moment there was complete silence, broken after a little by Hapgood's voice from the dining-room. Mr. Crawford, walking composedly back and forth, drawing thoughtfully at his cigar, gave no evidence of so much as hearing the low-toned voice. To Conniston, who thought that he could guess what it was that had put the pleading note into the guarded tones, the words came in an indistinguishable murmur. Conniston, having no desire to play the part of eavesdropper, strolled out upon the porch.

It was only a moment later when the door which he had softly closed behind him was thrown violently open, and Roger Hapgood, his hat crushed in his hand, hastened out, ran down the steps, and with no word of farewell disappeared into the darkness. Conniston gazed after him in wonderment a moment, and then turned toward the open door behind him.

Argyl had come into the room, her face flushed, her eyes bright with anger. Mr. Crawford, looking up from his papers, was saying, quietly:

"What is it, Argyl? What is the matter with Hapgood?"

"I told him to go," she cried, hotly. "I told him never to speak to me again, never to come into this house!"

Mr. Crawford stroked his chin thoughtfully.

"For good and sufficient reasons, Argyl dear?" he asked, gently.

"Yes. And—and I slapped his face, too!"

A little smile rippled across her father's face.

"Then I am sure that the reason was good and sufficient. And I shall take pleasure in horsewhipping the little man for you, dear, if you wish."

Argyl ran to him and threw her arms about his neck.

"God bless you, daddy!" she cried, softly. "I just love you to death. And," holding him away from her and smiling brightly at him, "I don't think that it is necessary. I slapped him *hard*!"

Conniston came back into the room.

Argyl was speaking swiftly, emphatically. "Mr. Hapgood has just done me the honor to ask me to marry him. He told me that he had acquainted Mr. Conniston with his intentions, so it is no secret. No, I did not slap him for that. But you, father, and you, too, Mr. Conniston, since you are one of us in our work, ought both to know what he threatened. He says that we are upon the very brink of failure; that Swinnerton has almost sufficient strength to ruin us and our hopes. And he threatened, if I did not marry him, to turn his back upon us and join the opposition. And I slapped his face."

Mr. Crawford took her hand and kissed it.

"I can think of no more forceful answer you could have made him, Argyl girl. Fortunately, I have not confided in him to any dangerous extent. He knows—"

"He knows," she cried, quickly, "all that you have let Mr. Winston know! Everything you have told your lawyer—"

She paused, hesitating. Mr. Crawford looked at her sharply.

"What?" he demanded, a vague hint of anxiety in his tone.

"He knows—for he told me—the exact condition of your finances."

"Had I not better go?" suggested Conniston. "I do not want—"

"No. You are with us. If Hapgood knows, if he is going to peddle what he knows, you might as well know too! What did he say, Argyl?"

"He said, father, that you had played to the end of your string. He said that you did not have ten thousand dollars in the world. He said that you did not know where to turn to raise the cash for the rest of the work we have before us. I— I—" She looked anxiously at him. "Did I do wrong, father? Should I have temporized with him—ought I to have kept him from going away angry?"

"You should have let me throw him outdoors. I am not afraid of him." He turned from her to Conniston. His face was very grave, his eyes troubled, but he spoke firmly, confidently. "You see, Mr. Conniston, that we have a fight ahead of us. Some people would say that we are on a sinking ship. What do you think?"

"I think," said Conniston, simply, "that we will win out in spite of what people say. I hope I may help you."

"Thank you. To-morrow morning I am coming out to see what you and Truxton are doing. I shall want to have a talk with him—and with you. You will of course say nothing of what has happened to-night."

Out in the darkness Conniston walked slowly toward the office building, his brows drawn, his eyes upon the ground, a fear which he could not argue away in his heart. With untold capital to back them the fight against the desert was such a fight as most men would not want upon their hands. With Oliver Swinnerton and the gold behind him which he was spending with the recklessness of assurance, the fight was tenfold harder. And now, when it was clear that the great bulk of John Crawford's fortune was already sunk into the sand, the fight seemed hopeless.

It had been a bad night for lovers. At the office building, leaning against the wall, a cigarette dangling dejectedly from his lips, Lonesome Pete was waiting for him.

"That you, Con?"

"Yes. What are you doing here?"

"Waitin' for you, an' meditatin' mos'ly." He cast away his cigarette, sighed deeply, and began a search for his paper and tobacco. "I was wantin' to ask you a question, Con."

Conniston said, "Go ahead, Pete," and made himself a cigarette.

"It's this-a-way." The cowboy lighted a match and let it burn out without applying the flame to his brown paper. For a moment he hesitated, and then blurted out: "You've knowed some considerable females in your time, I take it. Huh, Con?"

"Well?" Conniston repeated.

"I gotta be hittin' the trail back to the Half Moon real soon. I wanted to ask you a question firs'." Again he hesitated, again broke out suddenly: "I take it a lady ain't the same in no particulars as a man. Huh, Con?"

Conniston, thinking of Argyl, said "No," fervently.

"If a man likes you real well you can tell every time, can't you? An' if he ain't got no use for you, you can tell that, too, can't you?"

Conniston nodded, thinking that he began to guess Pete's troubles.

"Don't you know—can't you tell—how Miss Jocelyn feels toward you, Pete? Is that it?"

"That's it, only how in blazes you guessed it gets me! Con, I tell you, I can't tell nothin' for sure. It's worse 'n gamblin' on the weather. One day I'm thinkin' she likes me real well, an' she shows me things about grammar an' stuff, an' we git on fine. An' then—maybe it's nex' day an' maybe it's only two minutes later—she's all diff'rent somehow, an' she jest makes fun of the way I talk, an' you'd suppose she wouldn't wipe her feet on me if I laid down an' begged her to."

CHAPTER XVI

After a long night, during which he slept little and thought much, Conniston rose early, breakfasted at the little lunch-counter, and without waking Tommy Garton rode swiftly toward Truxton's camp. He hastened, for although it was still early morning it was time for work to begin upon the ditch.

From the top of a knoll half a mile out of camp he could look down into the little hollow where the men and teams should be already at their daily grind. A little frown gathered his brows as he saw instead that the horses were standing at their stakes in a long row, that the men were gathered together in clumps, obviously idle. And even then he had no way to guess what new trouble had come to the Great Work.

Shooting his spurs into his horse's panting sides, he swept down the gentle slope of the sand-hill and galloped straight toward the cook's tent. He saw that not only were the men idle, but that they gave no evidence of an intention to go to work. He saw, too, that they looked at him as he rode among them, that they watched him curiously, that many of them were laughing.

Fifty paces from the tent he came upon his two foremen—Ben the Englishman and the Lark—talking in low tones

Jackson Gregory

with the two foremen who had worked under Truxton's eye.

"What's the matter?" he called, sharply, angrily, although he did not know it. "Where's Truxton?"

"Inside the tent," the Lark answered him, shortly.

And, asking no further questions, waiting for no explanation, Conniston swung down from his horse, hurried to the tent, flung back the flap, and entered. Only then did the truth dawn on him, and he staggered back as though a man had struck him a stunning blow full in the face.

The air in the tent was reeking and foul with the fumes of cheap whisky. At the little table Bat Truxton sat slouched forward, his face hidden in the arm he had flung out as he slipped forward. An empty quart bottle lay on its side at his elbow. A second bottle, with an inch of the amber fluid in it, stood just beyond his clenched fist.

Truxton made no sign, did not so much as stir, as Conniston dropped the flap of canvas and stood over him. His breath came heavily, saturated with whisky. Conniston laid a rude hand upon the slack shoulder, shaking it roughly. Still Truxton did not lift his head, did not even mutter as a drunken man is apt to do in his stupor. With the full purport of this thing upon him, Conniston was driven to a fury of rage. He jerked Truxton's head back and slapped him across the face until his fingers tingled. Now Truxton's eyes opened, red-rimmed, bloodshot, fixed in a vacant, idiotic stare. And before Conniston could speak the eyes were closed again, the head had sunk forward upon the table.

"My God!" cried Conniston, feeling now only a great despair upon him, seeing only the death to all hopes of success for the reclamation project with Truxton lost to it.

He started to leave the tent, and suddenly swung about again, grasping Truxton's two shoulders in his hands.

"It ain't no go, pardner. He's very—hic—drunk!"

He had not seen the other man, had seen little enough but the sprawling, inert figure. It was the camp cook. And as Conniston turned upon him he saw that this man's face was flushed, that he was little better than Truxton. And if he needed further indication of the reason for the cook's plight it was not far to seek. The man held in his left hand, thrust clumsily behind him, a third bottle, half empty.

"You, too!" shouted Conniston. "Drop that bottle, and drop it quick!"

The cook, with a drunken assumption of dignity, tried to straighten up, grasping his bottle the more firmly.

"Who're you?" he leered. "G'wan; chase yourself. I ain't throwin' away—"

He did not finish. Conniston stepped forward quickly and jerked the bottle out of the cook's hand, hurling it against the stove, where it broke into a score of pieces. The bottle upon the table he treated in similar fashion.

"Now," he said, sternly, "you get to work and get something cooked for the men. Haven't even a fire, have you?" He stepped close to the cook again, thrusting his face close up to the other's. He did not know his own voice, which had gone suddenly hoarse and low, as he went on: "You have a fire going in two minutes. Where are your helpers? And you have breakfast on the tables in half an hour, or I give you my word I'll come back here and beat you half to death!"

He turned and went out with no single look behind him,

glad to be out in the open, thankful for the fresh air, which he drew deep down into his stifling lungs. And, realizing only that nothing could be done with Truxton for the present and that he himself was next in command, he hastened to where the four foremen were standing, grinning at him.

"Get your men busy," he snapped at them. "Ben, send some men up to the tent to help get something to eat. Let them put on anything. If the cook doesn't get coffee ready in fifteen minutes let me know. All of you have your men hook up their teams. They can do that while breakfast is getting ready. And hurry!"

The men looked at him curiously, then at one another. Ben was the first to move.

"Aye, aye, sir," he said, with a grin, lifting his hand from his hip to his forelock, and dropping it to his hip again as he walked away. The others followed.

"Hold on!" cried Conniston, suddenly, before they had gone ten paces. "Do all of the men know about this?"

The men laughed. "They ain't blind," explained one of them.

"And do they know—does any one of you know—where he got the whisky?"

They shrugged their shoulders. Only the Lark answered.

"I know, pal," he said, slowly. "I seen it."

"All right. You wait a minute. I want to talk with you. You other fellows get busy."

The little San-Franciscan dropped back and waited. Conniston came up with him and demanded shortly:

"Tell me about it."

"It was last night, 'bo, about 'leven o'clock, I guess. It was sure some dark, too, take it from me. I woke up thirsty as a water-front bum, an' beat it for the water-barrel. Comin' back, I come past the tent. Bat was in there figgerin' when I went to the wagon. When I come back he was talkin' to another guy. I stops an' listens, just for fun, you know. The other guy I hadn't never saw. An' he said as how Mr. Crawford had sent him out to ask how everything was runnin'. Purty soon he puts a bottle on the table an' says, 'Have one?' Bat says 'No,' but you could see with one eye shut an' in the dark o' the moon as he wanted it worse 'n I'd wanted the water I walked clean over to the barrel to git. The stranger has one, an' fills a glass an' shoves it under Bat's nose. An' if any longshoreman I ever seen had saw the way ol' Bat put that red-eye under his vest he'd 'a' died with jealousy. I knowed as how there wouldn't be nothin' in it for me, so I went an' got another drink of water an' hit the rag-pile. That what you wanted to know, 'bo?"

"Who was the man?" Conniston insisted. "What did he look like?"

"That's dead easy. I'm sure the gumshoe when it comes to pipin' a man off so's I got his photograph in my eye. He was a little cuss an' dressed to kill, with gloves on, an' all that. He was skinny an' pale an' weak-eyed-lookin'."

"That will do!" cut in Conniston, brusquely. "And now get your men going. We've got a day's work ahead of us."

A little more than fifteen minutes later Conniston himself pounded one of the cook's pans as a summons to breakfast.

The cook, surly, glowering as he moved, set forth the big pots of coffee.

Less than half an hour after he had ridden into the idle camp Conniston saw the two hundred men resume their work of yesterday as though nothing unusual had happened, saw the teams string out in the four sections of the ditch where Truxton had left off, watched the long lines of scrapers and plows cutting into the soft soil, scooping it out and piling it upon the banks of the canal.

He climbed to a little knoll from which he could glance over them before and behind the ditch-cutters. Yonder, toward Valley City, Truxton's two foremen were directing their men with the same quick-eyed, steady competence which they had manifested under the eye of the older engineer. From them he turned to the men working under Ben and the Lark. There, too, was machine-like regularity; there, too, each man, each straining animal was in its place, putting forth its utmost of capability.

There came to the man who watched an irritating sense of his own uselessness: the work was going forward with great, swinging, rhythmic effectiveness. This thing had leaped out upon him unawares, and he was half afraid of the responsibility which had fastened itself upon his shoulders. For, after all, Greek Conniston had not yet entirely found himself, was not sure of himself.

Brow drawn and anxious, watchful, deeply thoughtful, Conniston did not see Mr. Crawford until the buckboard driven by Half-breed Joe had stopped close behind him. He wheeled about, startled at Mr. Crawford's voice.

"Good morning, Conniston. How's the work going?"

"All right, I hope." He came to the buckboard and, resting

his hand upon the wheel, looked up into the face of the man who was to learn of another savage blow dealt to the hopes of his project.

"Where is Truxton?" Mr. Crawford was standing up in the wagon, looking as Conniston had looked at the sweep of work being done.

"He—" Conniston hesitated. "He's in the tent."

Mr. Crawford turned suddenly upon him, his eyes narrowing.

"What's the matter?" he demanded, hurriedly.

Conniston shook his head slowly, turning his eyes away from the face which a glance had shown him was drawn with quick anxiety.

"Drive to the tent, Joe!" commanded Mr. Crawford, his voice very stern.

Conniston watched them as their horses leaped forward in the slack traces, saw Mr. Crawford jump down, enter the tent, saw him come out again and spring back into the buckboard.

"Now, Joe," as he got down beside Conniston, "you can unhook your horses. I am going to be here this morning."

Joe drove away to where the camp horses had been picketed. And Mr. Crawford turned to Conniston.

"This is going to make it hard, Conniston," he said, slowly, his face and voice alike very grave. "It is the one thing which I had hoped would not happen. But we've got to make the most of it." He paused suddenly, and his keen eyes ran thoughtfully from one to another of the four gangs of men. "They're working all right," he ended, his eyes coming back to Conniston's.

"Yes. They're good men. The four foremen are as capable as a man could ask for."

"Were they working this way when you got here?"

"No. They were waiting for orders."

Mr. Crawford nodded, making no reply.

"I don't know," Conniston offered after a moment, "that there is any immediate call for worry. I think that I can handle them until Truxton gets around—"

"Truxton won't get around!"

"You mean—"

"That the moment he is sober enough to know anything he will know that he is discharged!"

"But we can't get along without him. He is the one man—"

"We shall have to get along without him. I have told him that if he touched whisky again on this job he could go."

"But would it not be better to wait a few days—to give him a chance to sober up?"

"Conniston, I have never found it necessary to break my word. I am through with Truxton. And if my last hope of success goes with him he must go just the same. I am sorry for the man—the poor fellow can't help these periodic drunks of his. But I am through with him."

Conniston frowned into the eyes which were fixed intently upon him.

"You know best. I am ready to do what I can to help out. I think I can promise you to keep the work going until you can get a man to take his place."

Mr. Crawford bent a long, searching regard upon him. And when he spoke it was slowly, sternly.

"What am I paying you, Conniston?"

"Forty-five dollars a month."

"All right. I'll give you seventy-five dollars a week to take Bat Truxton's place for me—not for a few days, but until the first day of October. Will you do it?"

A hot flush spread over Conniston's face, and surged away, leaving it white.

"Do you think that I can do it?"

"I am not the one to think. You are. You know what the work is, what it means. Can you do it?"

And Conniston stared long out across the wide sweep of the desert, his lips set hard in white, bloodless lines, before he answered, briefly:

"Yes."

"It's a big job, Conniston, and, frankly, I wouldn't put it into your hands if I had a man I thought better qualified to carry it on. A big job! I wonder if you know how big? You will hold the whole fate of this country in the palm of your hand, to make or to mar. You will hold in the palm of your hand my whole life-work. For if you succeed I succeed. And if you fail, all hope of reclamation here dies, still-born, and I am a ruined man. Understand what you are to do? I cannot even stay here to help you. I will leave to-night for Denver. I can't send another man in my place. Would to God that I could! I must go myself; I must raise money—fifty thousand dollars at the very lowest figure. And when I come back I shall bring the money with me, and I shall bring at least five hundred more men. And you will have to oversee the work of seven hundred men then; you will have to drive this ditch night and day; you will have to complete two big dams. And you will have to do that before the first day of October. It is a big job, Conniston. Can you do it?"

Conniston wet his dry lips and hesitated.

"Mr. Crawford, it is a big job. I do not even know that the thing is possible. I believe that it is. I do not know, I cannot know, if I can do it. I believe that I can. If you have a better man, if in Denver or anywhere else you can find a better man, put him in Truxton's place. If you can't, if you want me to go ahead with the work, I'll do it."

"Then that is settled. Confer often with Tommy Garton. If you need advice while I am away, go to him. But remember that in all things it will be up to you to make the final decision. There can be no sharing of responsibility."

"Then," said Conniston, with quiet decision, "I want an absolute and unrestricted authority here. I want the power to take on new men, to fire old men, to raise wages, to do what I think wise and best. I want every man working for you to know that he is under my orders, and that there is no recourse from my judgment. I want to be able to call upon the Half Moon outfit, if I find it necessary, just as you would call upon them."

"You are asking a great deal, Conniston."

"I am asking everything."

"And you can have what you ask!"

"To begin with, I shall want a man here to take my place if I find it necessary to be away at all. I want Brayley here, and right away."

"Brayley is the best man on the Half Moon. You can have him."

"Thank you. There is one further thing."

"Name it."

"I do not draw a cent of wages until the first day of October. Then if I have water in the valley I get it in a block. If I do not have water—I don't touch it!"

A curious little smile flitted across Mr. Crawford's lips.

"You are in a position to dictate, Conniston. Let it be as you say."

"And now, if you have no immediate orders for me, I want to get to work. I am going to shift the gang under the Lark out yonder, in front of the others. He's the best pace-maker I've got."

"Go ahead. I'll be here until noon."

Unconsciously squaring his shoulders as he went, Conniston strode away toward the ditch.

CHAPTER XVII

At noon Mr. Crawford told the men gathered at the long tables that in the future they were to look to Conniston for all orders, that he was empowered to act as he saw fit in any crisis, that he would have absolute command over every part of the reclamation work, here or elsewhere. And then he gripped Conniston's hand warmly, gave him an address in Denver where a telegram would find him, and drove away toward Crawfordsville, promising to telephone to Brayley to report to the Valley immediately.

Before he was out of sight the new superintendent called his four overseers aside.

"What wages are you fellows drawing down?" he asked, bluntly.

"Three bones," the Lark told him.

"Now, look here. Do you fellows know that we have got to get this whole job done by the first of October? That's a lot of work, and maybe you boys know it. It is up to you four fellows as much as it is up to anybody to see that the work is done. You've got to get every inch done every day that you can. You've got to drive your men all they'll stand for. You know what will happen if you make a mistake and try to get too much out of them?"

"Dead easy, Mr. Conniston," grinned the Lark. "They'll quit. They say there is lots of easy graft up in the mountains with a guy named Swinnerton."

"Then," went on Conniston, quietly, "you've got to be careful not to drive them too hard. Keep your men good-natured. If you see any signs of balking let me know. I haven't any kick to make about the way you have been working, but I want you to work harder! Get me? And I am going to pay you four dollars a day instead of three. Wait. I am going to make you another proposition: over and above your wages I'll pay each man of you for every day between the day we get water on the land and the first of October. And for that time I'll pay each man of you at the rate of twenty dollars a day!"

"Gee!" exclaimed the Lark. "You ain't stringing us, are you?"

"No. Understand what I mean: in case we get the work done five days before the first each man of you draws down one hundred dollars above his wages. Drive your men as hard as you can; but don't forget what will happen if you try to do too much. What wages are your men getting?"

"Two dollars and a half."

"Go back and offer them two-seventy-five. And tell them that for every day between the first of October and the day we get water on the land each and every man of them will draw down an extra five dollars. Now get to work. I want to see what you can get done by quitting-time."

That afternoon Conniston left everything in the hands of his foremen. He did not once go to the ditch to see what they were doing. Instead he took Truxton's note-book from the table in the tent—Truxton was still in a deep stupor—and from one o'clock until dark worked over it, seeking desperately to grasp every detail which he must know later and to plan for the morrow and the morrows to come.

When he heard the men coming in from work he got his horse and saddled it, and then waited for the foremen with their daily reports.

"I beat my record by twenty feet to-day," the Lark told him, with a cheerful grin, as he handed Conniston a soiled bit of paper. "I'm hot on the trail of my bonus, take it from me."

That evening Conniston spent with Tommy Garton. He did not even take the time to call on Argyl. He told the little fellow what had happened, received a hearty grip of the hand which meant more to him than a wordy congratulation, laid what few plans he had had time to outline before him, and asked his advice upon them.

"I want the plans and specifications for Dam Number One, Tommy."

Garton took them from a drawer and passed them across the table.

"I will look over them on the job to-morrow. And I want to know how long you think it will take to get that dam built when once we get to work on it?"

"I don't see how it can be done and done right," Garton answered, promptly, "in much less than thirty days. You might be able to do a temporary job of it—put in a bulwark that would do until we could get water down here and live up to our contract—and then build the real dam after the first of October. That might be done in less time."

"How big a shift of men were you planning on putting to work up there?"

"Two hundred. You couldn't use more than that. There isn't room. They'd get in one another's way."

Conniston sat frowning moodily, his fingers tapping the roll of blue-prints in his hands.

"Isn't there any way," he asked suddenly, swinging upon Garton, "of making a go of this without building that dam?"

"No, Greek, there isn't. You see, there isn't any too much water up in the mountains at best. We have to get every drop that the law allows us."

"Figure on it, Tommy. I want your chief work for the next few days to be just figuring out where we can cut down, where we can save not only money but men. It's men we need." He broke off suddenly and leaned forward, putting his hand on Garton's arm. "Damn it, Tommy," he said, huskily, "I want you to know that I don't enjoy giving you orders. I want you to know that *I* know you ought to be doing what I am doing to-day. You are a better man than I am every day in the week, and I know it. If it were not—"

"Oh, shut up, Greek!" laughed Garton, frankly. "You're an old liar, and that's what I know! And," and his voice softened as he put out his hand for a second time that night, "I love you for it. Now let's cut out the slush and get to work."

"Then, since it's up to me, here goes: I want your advice at every jump. I need it, Tommy, need it bad now, and the Lord knows how I'll need it before the time is up! In about three or four days I'll come to you or send for you. I don't know which it'll be. To-morrow morning I am going up into the mountains. Brayley will be in camp some time to-night. He'll take my place for a few days. No, he doesn't know a thing about the work, but my foremen do, and Brayley knows men as you know your multiplication-tables. And I will take a gang of fifty men with me. I don't like to remove them from the ditch, but I've got to get that dam started. I won't be able to sleep until I see that country and get my hands on it. And, Tommy, one thing more: Mr. Crawford tells me that there will be a telephone line into Valley City from Crawfordsville within the week. He is to get five hundred men to me as soon as he can rush them through. When they are within twelve hours of us I want you to let Brayley know. That is, of course, in case I am not back here. Brayley will then double his men's pay and keep them at work all night. Then I'll send half of the new men—half of five hundred, I hope—to Brayley, and he'll put on a day shift and a night shift—with all the work they can stand up under. And I'll have a day shift and a night shift slinging that dam across Deep Creek. It's up there, Tommy, that I expect you'll have to help me out."

"Anything I can do, Conniston. And I'll get busy first thing in the morning along the line you suggest. And," he hesitated a moment, and then finished, gravely, "I'm glad to see the way you're tying into this. And, do you know, I'd bet a man every cent I've got that we put the thing across!"

Conniston stood up, thrusting his papers into his pocket.

"If Truxton—" he began.

"Forget Truxton. He was all right and a mighty good man. One of the best men I ever worked with. But," and his rare smile worked about the corners of his sensitive mouth and lighted up his eyes warmly—"but I have an idea that the man who made that end run for Yale back in the old days is going to score a touchdown such as Bat Truxton would never have thought of. Go to it, Conniston—only let me get into the interference!"

Conniston's plans for the next day had been founded upon his assurance that Brayley would arrive before morning. But Brayley did not come. And even had he arrived on time Conniston would not have dared leave. At first he had thought to remain overnight with Tommy Garton. Then, remembering that he alone was responsible for the camp, he told Garton good night and rode out into the desert. It was late when at last he came to the tent and found his roll of blankets behind it. And ten minutes later cares and responsibilities alike succumbed to bodily fatigue, and he slept soundly.

It was long after midnight, perhaps three o'clock, and still very dark, when he awoke. Two men off in the distance were talking. He paid little attention to them, but rolled over and went to sleep again. And even as consciousness slipped away from him he was vaguely aware that more voices had joined the two which had awakened him. But he thought only that some of the men were calling to one another from their sleeping-places, and attached no further importance to the matter.

It was an hour or two later when he again awoke. There were already faint streaks of dawn lying low, close to the face of the desert. His first connected impression was that he had overslept and that the men were already going to work. For he saw a long line, fifty men at the least count, filing out toward the spot where the water-barrels stood in the long-bodied wagons, while other crowds of men were grouped about one of the wagons. And then suddenly he sat bolt upright, strangely uneasy. It was still long before day—and something was wrong.

He pulled on his boots and, without stopping to lace them, hurried toward the wagons. And before he had gone twenty paces he knew what it was that had happened. The men had been talking in hushed voices, so as not to wake him; but, now that two or three made out who he was, a shout rose sharply into the morning stillness, a shout at once of warning and of derision. And it was clearly the shout of drunkenness. It was taken up by fifty throats, a hundred throats, clamorous, exultant, jeering.

As the men moved back and forth, many of them staggered perceptibly. Conniston saw one of them pitch forward and lie helpless. A man passed by him, swaying and lurching, and in the pale light there was something fiendish in the fellow's leering face, his open mouth, his wide, staring eyes. Off yonder he heard two men quarreling, their voices raised in windy gusts of snapping oaths; saw one of them lift his hand and strike, not as a man strikes with his bare fist, but as a man strikes with a knife; saw the other man fling out his arms, heard his gurgling, choking cry above the sudden clamorous tumult; saw him settle quietly to the ground as though every bone in his body had jellied. His eyes accustomed to the half-light, his ears free of the wax of sleep, it seemed to Conniston that he was peering into a scene which could be no part of earth, but which must be some frenzied corner of hell.

As he ran forward, brushing past tottering forms which cursed him thickly, he saw yet another group of men beyond the wagons; saw that there, too, the spirit of alcohol was rampant; heard a man's voice, high-raised and raspingly shrill, in a monotonous song. And as he ran men did not fall back, but glared at him belligerently, many a coarse-featured countenance distorted hideously, while the men about the wagon bunched up close together threateningly.

He stopped suddenly, trying to think. A mighty laugh greeted his hesitation. He saw a big fellow thrust a tin cup down into one of the barrels, the head of which had been knocked in, lift his cup high above his head, laughing, and then put it to his lips. Then he understood while he did not understand: one of the barrels which should have contained water was nearly full of raw whisky!

Conniston did not believe that there were a dozen sober men in camp. He had recognized the big man standing at the barrel. It was Ben the Englishman. Mundy and Peters, obviously drunk, stood close to him. The little San-Franciscan was standing in the body of the wagon, trying to put his two short arms about the barrel. He had the grotesque look of a dwarf embracing a fat wife.

He could look to no one for help. These two hundred men—men whose hard, brutish natures had known nothing of the excitation of alcohol for weeks, perhaps months, whose brains were now inflamed with it, whose reckless spirits were unchained by it—would listen to words from him, from any man in the world, as much as they would listen to the sighing of the breeze which was beginning to stir the scanty desert vegetation. And above all other considerations, above even the half-formed wonder, "How came it there?" rose the knowledge which would not down, *he and he alone was responsible for what these men did.*

He turned away with white, wretched face, and strode back toward the tent. He must get away from them for a little, he must try to think, he must find something to do. And as he turned a yell of derisive triumph from two hundred throats went booming and thundering out across the desert.

Until now he had been merely grief-stricken that such chaos should have sprung into being under his hand where there should be only order and efficiency. Now there surged into his heart a flaming, scorching rage. The whiteness left his face, and it went a dull, burning red. He prayed dumbly for the might of a Nero that he might wreck the vengeance of a Nero. No words came, but he cursed them in his heart. He saw their blackened fingers choking the life out of the last hope of success of the Great Work, and he longed with an infinite longing to have those yelling throats in the grip of his own two hands that he might tear at them.

He stalked on blindly, his back turned upon them, his ears filled with laughter and shouting, cursing and discordant singing, his brain so teeming with a score of broken thoughts that no single thought remained clear. He told himself that this thing was a nightmare, that it could not be, that it was impossible, ludicrously impossible! He tried to ask himself what it would mean. He tried to answer—and could not. It would mean that there could be no work done to-day! And to-morrow? Would the men be fit to work to-morrow? And the next day? How long would the stuff last?—how long the effects of it when it was gone?

He thought suddenly of the revolver which Lonesome Pete had given him, and which struck against his hip as he walked; and he stopped dead in his tracks at the thought of it. And then he laughed at himself for a fool and strode on. Half of the men were armed. True, they were drunk, but what of that? They were two hundred against one, and they were not cowards. And in the end he would not have helped the Great Work; he would only have done a fool's part and lost his own life. No, there was no chance—

One thought suggests another. He had not gone on a dozen steps before he stopped again, a light of hope and of deter-mination creeping slowly into his eyes. A moment he hesitated. And then, flinging all hesitation from him, seeing clearly his one desperate hope, crying aloud, "I'll do it!" he broke into a run toward the tent. Yesterday they had taken Bat Truxton to Valley City. But they had forgotten Bat Truxton's rifle.

CHAPTER XVIII

With eager fingers Conniston struck a match. Almost the first thing which his searching eyes found was the heavy Winchester, three inches of its barrel protruding from a roll of bedding. He flung the bedding open upon the ground. There was half a box of cartridges with it. He made sure that the magazine was filled, threw a shell into the barrel, thrust the box into his pocket, and ran outside.

No one had seen him. There were no eyes for him. A very few stragglers moved unsteadily here and there; the great majority of the men were packed in a mass about the barrel. Tin cups, dippers, even buckets and pans ran from hand to hand, from those nearest the wagon to the clamorous fellows upon the outskirts of the crowd, spilling the liquor freely as they were jolted and jostled.

This his eyes took in at a quick glance. Then he saw that fifty yards from the group of men there was another wagon which had been drawn aside with its four empty barrels. Walking slowly now, the rifle held vertically close to the side which was turned away from them, he moved toward this second wagon. He reached it, attracting no attention. Springing into its low bed, he dragged the four barrels close together. The broadside of the wagon was turned toward the clamorous crowd. Keeping his body hidden behind the bulwark he had made, he watched and waited for

Jackson Gregory

more light.

Slowly the pale glow in the east lengthened and broadened and brightened. Once Conniston lifted his rifle quickly to see if he could find the sights. It was still too dark for quick, accurate work.

So again he waited. A strange, cool calmness had succeeded to his almost frenzied agitation of a moment ago. He knew the danger of the thing which he was about to do; he knew and realized clearly what he might be called upon to do in self-protection alone when once he had taken his stand. But there was no other way; and, no matter what the consequences, no matter what the results, he accepted the only chance which circumstances had left him. And moments of unswerving determination do not make for nervous excitement. It is the anxious uncertainty, like that through which he had just passed, that makes a man's finger tremble upon the trigger.

Louder and ever louder rose the throaty voices, faster and faster passed the cups and dippers. Ben and Mundy had their arms about each other. In the wagon the Lark had slipped down, and now lay upon his back, staring at the dim, swirling stars and babbling incoherent nothings.

Men sang in strident, raucous, unmusical voices. A swarthy little Italian was playing waltzes upon a harmonica, and heavy-booted feet shuffled and stamped upon the sand as men flung their brawny arms about one another and swayed back and forth. Conniston saw that when a man thrust his arm down into the barrel for a fresh cupful of whisky it did not disappear three inches above the elbow.

Swiftly the desert daylight came. Conniston stooped and tied his boot-laces, that they might not trip him when he moved. He stood up and whipped his revolver from its holster, spinning the cylinder, and then shoving it back. And then, laying the rifle across the top of one of the barrels, he cleared his throat and called out loudly.

One of the men nearest him heard him above the shouting and pointed him out to another. The two laughed loudly and turned away from him, forgetting him as they turned. Again he called, louder than before. No one heard him, no one looked to him. He waved his hat above his head. If any one saw, no one gave sign of seeing. He licked his lips and lifted the rifle.

"God see me through with it!" he muttered.

He fired high above their heads. The sudden report crashed through the babel of shoutings, a veritable babel into which half of the tongues of Europe mingled with Chinese and Japanese sing-song. As the crack of the gun died away all other sounds died with it. The desert grew as suddenly still as it ever is in the depths of its man-free solitudes. Staring, wondering faces which had first turned to one another turned now toward him.

Again there broke out a volley of abrupt cries, followed by as sudden a silence, as they watched him to see what he meant, what he would do. And Conniston took quick advantage of this short hush.

"Leave that wagon, every man of you!" he shouted. "Move toward the ditch. And move fast!"

No man of them stirred. Their numbers, their intoxication, gave them assurance. He was no longer the "boss." They were all just men now, and he was only one while they were two hundred. They began to laugh. The Italian with the harmonica struck up a fresh, jigging air. The heavy-booted feet took up the rhythm. A man climbed into the wagon and scooped up a dipperful of whisky, holding it aloft before he drank.

The light was still uncertain, but the dipper was a bright, clear target. Conniston waited a moment, his teeth hard set, hardly breathing. Then, as the man lowered the dipper from his face and held it out invitingly over the heads of the men on the ground, he fired.

The bullet crashed through the tin thing, hurling it into the crowd. The man who had held it cried out aloud, and, clutching the fingers of his right hand in his left, leaped down from the wagon. The Lark rolled over and to the ground, dived between the wheels, and disappeared. And again came a sudden silence.

Now Conniston did not wait. He fired at the barrel itself, hoping to smash in the staves, to drill holes near the bottom through which the confined liquor could escape. And now the men ceased singing and dancing and leaped back, crowding away from the barrel, plunging and stumbling out of the line of bullets. For a moment Conniston thought that in that wild, headlong scramble for safety he saw the end of the thing. And almost before the thought was formed he knew better.

The men were talking sullenly. He could hear their angry, snarling voices, no longer shouting, but low-pitched. He began to make out their faces and saw nowhere an expression of fear, everywhere black wrath, restless fury. They no longer moved backward, but stood their ground, muttering. In a moment—he knew what would happen. He could read it in their faces, could sense it in their low, rumbling tones. And so he shouted to them again, his voice ringing clear above their mutterings.

"I drop the first man that takes a step this way!"

Tense, anxious, watchful, he waited. He saw hesitation, but saw, too, that the hesitation was momentary, that it would be followed by a blind rush if he could not drive fear into their hearts. And he realized with a sick sinking of his own heart that there was little fear in men like these.

"It looks like an end of things for Greek Conniston," he muttered, dully.

His watchful eyes saw a little commotion upon the fringe of the knot of men who had moved a little toward the tent. He saw one of the men step out quickly and raise a big revolver. The man, as he lifted the revolver, fired, not seeming to aim. The bullet struck one of the front wheels of Conniston's wagon. Almost at the same second Conniston fired. Fired and missed, and fired again. With the second report came a shrill cry from the man with the revolver, and Conniston saw him stagger, drop his gun, wheel half around, and fall. And where he fell he lay, writhing and calling out to his fellows.

For a moment the others hung back, hesitating. The man upon the ground lifted himself upon an elbow, glared at Conniston, and began to crawl slowly back toward the tent. Obviously, he had been struck in the thigh or side. The man who had shot him, and who was new to this sort of work, thanked God that he had not killed the fellow outright.

The next moment he forgot him entirely. Ben and Mundy were a pace or two in front of their men, who from force of habit had begun to flock toward their daily leaders. They were talking earnestly, their voices lowered so that the pressing forms about them had to crane their necks to listen.

Still the whisky-barrel stood scarcely more than touched. Conniston, seeing that as long as it stood there he could hope to do nothing toward a restoration of order, emptied the magazine of his rifle into it. He saw the splinters fly, saw that the bullets had torn great holes into the hard wood, heard the snapping of oaths from those of the men who had drunk only enough to arouse their thirst, and began slipping fresh cartridges into the magazine.

"There'll be precious little of that stuff left, anyway," he grunted, with grim satisfaction.

He had expected a charge, but it did not come. Ben and Mundy had in all evidence taken command now. Their backs were to him as they issued short orders which he could not catch. But their purport was plain enough. He took his revolver from its holster and laid it in front of him upon a board across the top of one of the barrels.

Silently the men were falling back. And as they retreated they spread out into a great semicircle, wider and wider. He saw that fifty, perhaps seventy-five, of them had revolvers in their hands. And he saw that these men stood in advance of their companions. In another five minutes, in less than five minutes, the semicircle would be a circle of which he would be the center. Then they would close in on him, and then—

There must be no *then*. That was the one thing clear. He might shoot down a dozen of them, but they would get him in the end. At one end of the slowly widening arc was Ben the Englishman. At the other was Mundy.

"Ben!" shouted Conniston, sharply. "You've got to stop that! Mundy, stop where you are! I don't want to kill you fellows, but I'll do it if you keep on!"

In the beginning he had hoped to bluff them. Now such hope had died out of him. These were the sort of men who would want to see the other man's cards laid down on the table. And he knew that he must make good his bluff or there would in sober truth be an end of him. His voice rang with cold determination. And Ben and Mundy stopped.

Conniston watched that line of black faces, and as his eyes clung to the threatening arc he thought with a queer twitching of the lips of the football line-ups which he had watched in other days. He was surprised that his feelings now were much as they had been then. It was a game, and that in the other games a goal had been the thing he schemed and battled for while now it was his life made little difference. He was surprised that he was cool, that his heart beat steadily, that his hands upon his gun were like rock.

There was something strange in the way the men were watching him, something in their sudden silence, in their eager faces, which puzzled him. Their whole attitude spoke of one thing—a breathless waiting. What were they waiting for? Had his words put the fear of death in them? Were they watching to see if he was going to shoot down the men who led them? Was there a chance—

His taut senses told him of a danger which he could not understand. Something was wrong; death hovered over him—close, closer. What was it? His eyes flashed up and down the long curve of motionless figures, seeking an explanation and finding none. A little shiver ran up and down his backbone. He could not understand—

A sound, scarcely louder than the footfall of a cat, but jarring harshly upon his straining, over-acute ears, told him. He swung about with a sharp cry. There was the explanation. There, just behind him, barefooted, bent almost double, crouching to leap upon him, a great Chinaman, a long, curved knife clenched in his hand, was not three feet away. Even as he swung about the giant Asiatic sprang forward, the knife flashing up and down. Conniston struck with his rifle—the range was too short for him to use the thirty-thirty save as a club. It struck the big man a glancing blow upon the shoulder.

The lean, snarling, yellow face was so close to his that he could feel the hot, whisky-laden breath. He parried, and the rifle was jerked from his grasp, falling with a clatter to the bed of the wagon. The knife struck and bit into the shoulder he had thrown forward. Again it was raised. Conniston sprang back, and as he leaped he swept up the revolver from the barrel-top. As the knife fell, cutting a long gash again in his shoulder, he jammed the muzzle of Lonesome Pete's gun against the Chinaman's stomach and fired. The Chinaman grunted, coughed, and sank limply, vomiting blood.

For a moment Conniston forgot the men out yonder, growing suddenly sick at the sight of the ugly, twitching thing at his feet. And then as quickly as it had come, the nausea was gone, and he was clear-headed and watchful. He snatched up his rifle and whirled toward Ben and Mundy and the men between them.

They had not moved, had taken no single step forward. He remembered having seen a man near Mundy standing with open mouth and bulging eyes; the fellow's jaw still sagged, his eyes were fixed in the same strange stare, his eyelids had not so much as winked.

"That's one!" yelled Conniston. He laughed out loud, the laugh of a man whose nerves are strained almost to the point of snapping.

"Come on, come on! Who'll be next?"

They muttered among themselves; here and there a man called out sharply. But still they did not move. A thing like that which they had just witnessed drives the fumes of alcohol from a man's brain like a dip in ice-water. They could beat him down, they could take him, they could kill him as he had killed the Chinaman. But he could kill more than one of them before they could drop him. These things were clear. And the men hesitated.

"Afraid?" he laughed, taunting, jeering them, all discretion swept away from him. "Why don't you send some more men? There might be a little whisky left—if you hurry!"

He saw Ben and Mundy stir uneasily, saw them glance at each other, at the barrel with its shattered staves and gushing liquor, at the men whom they were self-elected to lead, and back to him. He saw the Lark and the man Peters standing close together, talking earnestly, seeming to argue with growing heat. And as the wave of hot blood left him and he grew cool and his saner judgment came back to him he called out to them sternly, but not threateningly, not mockingly:

"Ben! Mundy! you, Peters! and you, Lark! what's the use? Hasn't this thing gone far enough? You can kill me, but what good will it do? Your whisky is spilled, and you can't get it back. You know the wages I offered you fellows yesterday. You can go back to them, and nothing said. I have five hundred more men coming from Denver. They can take your jobs if you like. You can go to Swinnerton, but when he knows that I have fired you he won't take you on. You know that he is just taking men to keep us from getting them. You'd be fools to give up your jobs now. What's the word, boys? Will you go back to work, Ben? And you, Peters? And you, Mundy and the Lark? Shall I tell the cook to get coffee ready? Talk up lively. What is it?"

A rumbling chorus of murmurs rose up to greet him. The men were sullen, and they snarled openly at him. But he could see that already the thing had gone further than the more law-abiding spirits had thought to see it go. A sudden soberness had fallen upon many of them, and with it a cooler sanity. They broke into quick talk everywhere up and down the line. He could see that no longer at least were they united against him. He could see that the argument between Peters and the Lark was strong, heated. And he hoped and prayed that good might come of it and of the brief hesitation.

Suddenly the Lark broke away from his comrades and ran forward. Conniston, ever watchful, ever suspicious, covered him with his rifle. But the Lark was grinning, and as he came closer he lifted his two hands.

"I'm with you!" he shouted. "I got a bellyful of this here racket. An'," with a glance over his shoulder, "I got a bellyful of that rotgut, too. Besides, it's all gone. How about coffee, boys?"

"And you, Mundy? How about you?" Conniston called, quickly. "Do you want to keep your job at the wages I offered you yesterday? Or shall I put another man in your place? Quick, man! Speak up!"

Mundy hesitated, glancing at Ben before he answered. And then slowly he stepped out to where the Lark already stood.

"I'll keep my job," he grunted, sullenly.

"Please, sir," grinned the Lark, shaking his hand high above his head like a ragged urchin in school, "kin I go git a drink? Water, I mean," he finished with widening grin.

"Yes," answered Conniston, trying to keep from his eyes the gladness which was surging up within him. "Come this way first. There—stop. Now throw your gun toward me. You've got some sense. Now go get your water."

Ben came forward; and slowly, reluctantly, with evil, red-rimmed eyes, Peters. And, as the Lark had done, they tossed their revolvers to the sand near Conniston's wagon and trudged off toward the nearest water-wagon. A dozen men followed them. Gradually the line broke up as the call of water grew imperative to parched throats.

From the corner of his eye Conniston saw these men go to the first wagon, tilt up the barrels, and go to the next. And suddenly he heard a great shout go up from them—a shout no longer of anger, but of sheer surprise.

In the bottom of every barrel there was an auger-hole. There was not a single drop of water in camp!

In a flash of inspiration Conniston saw the thing which he must say.

"Who wants to go to work for Swinnerton now?" he cried. "You know whose work this is; you know who is trying to block every move we make. You know as well as I do that it was Swinnerton, or one of the men working for Swinnerton, the same man who got Bat Truxton drunk, who has given you your whisky—and taken away your chasers! And you know as well as I do how many miles it is to water."

The rest of the men had flung down their guns and rushed to the empty barrels. Already the burning thirst engendered by the raw, vile whisky was making them lick their dry lips, making their throats work painfully. They pulled over barrel after barrel, seeking to find that somewhere there was a cupful of water. And they found none.

"It's Swinnerton's gang you have to thank for this, boys," Conniston shouted again, seeing and taking his opportunity. "Swinnerton, who wants to break us like a rotten stick. He will be a millionaire many times over if he breaks us. And if we put our work across, if we make a go of it, Swinnerton will be the rotten stick!"

He stopped suddenly and watched them. And as often as he heard them curse him he heard them curse Swinnerton.

"Ben," he cried, when he had waited for them to understand what he had said, "get the harness on some horses and take one of the wagons to Valley City. Take a couple of men with you. Go to the general office and ask for Tommy Garton. Tell him we've got to have water. You, Lark, take the rest of the wagons as fast as you can send your horses to the Half Moon for more water. Take what men you need. Cook, see if you have enough water in your tent to do any good. And then get us something to eat. Ben will be back from Valley City before you know it. The rest of you fellows better lie around and chew tobacco until water comes. We'll get an early start to-morrow to make up for lost time. Peters, you and Mundy see that somebody looks out for the men that are hurt. Take them to the tent. They get first water if the cook has any. If not, Ben, you take them with you to Valley City."

His orders came with staccato precision. There was no tremor of doubt in his tones. And there was no slightest hesitation in obeying the orders from the man who was again "boss." Ben shouted out his own commands to two men who stood close to him, and they ran for the horses. The Lark was at the same time snapping out his orders, and the men he called by name hurried for horses, and many hands made quick work of the hitching-up. Other fingers whittled plugs, wrapped them about with bits of sack, and drove them tight into the holes in the barrels. The cook sped to his tent, found a bucket half full of water, and was drinking thirstily when Mundy jerked it from his hands.

"None of that, you sneakin' skunk!" he shouted. "Them

guys as got hurt gets the first show."

The fellow Conniston had shot in the thigh, and the man whom he had seen a companion strike with a knife, cutting him deeply in the neck, were carried into the tent, water thrust up to their parched lips, their wounds bound swiftly and gently. The Chinaman Mundy rolled over with his foot.

"Deader 'n hell," he grunted. "Might as well leave him where he is until plantin'-time."

Once more order had grown quietly out of chaos. The men stood here and there talking, chewing tobacco, cursing the thirst which as the minutes dragged by grew ever more tormenting. Already the sun had rolled upward above the flat horizon. Already the desert heat had leaped out at them. A dozen men climbed upon Ben's wagon, thinking to go to Valley City with him to get water there. But he drove them back, threatening them with his big fists and cockney oaths, and they dropped down and watched him as the wagon, rocking and swaying and lurching, was drawn away from them by galloping horses.

At a sharp word from Conniston two of the men brought the broken barrel which had contained whisky to where the discarded revolvers lay glinting in the early light and tossed them into it. And then Brayley came.

"What's up, Con?" he asked, swinging down from his panting horse, his keen eyes taking in the fading excitement, the general idleness. And then, as he stooped forward and looked into the barrel: "Good heavens! What *is* the matter?"

In a few words Conniston told him. For a moment Brayley said nothing, shaking his head and eying him curiously.

"You sure got your nerve, Con," he said, simply, after

a minute.

Conniston laughed shakily. Again a sinking nausea made him faint and dizzy. He could remember now the way the nose of his revolver had sunk into the Chinaman's stomach, could see again all of the horror of the thing which he had done.

"I'm sick, Brayley," he said, unsteadily. "The thing will drive me mad. I—I had to kill a man—and I can't forget how he looked!"

"How you managed to stop 'em jest killing *one* gets me. Where is he?"

Conniston nodded to the wagon and turned away shuddering. The Half Moon foreman strode over to the wagon and looked closely at the limp body. And then he came to Conniston with long strides.

"Hell," he grunted, disgustedly. "I thought you said you'd killed a man! That's only a Chink!"

CHAPTER XIX

The few barefooted, tattered urchins of Valley City had scampered homeward through the quiet street, swept along upon the high tide of glee. Bat Truxton had got drunk again; Mr. Crawford had fired him; Miss Jocelyn had gone away with him to Crawfordsville; there was every reason for their glad optimism to see a long vacation before them. What was the importance of reclamation somewhere off in the misty future when vacation, unexpected and thence all the more delectable, smiled upon them now?

"Mr. Crawford has been just as mean to poor papa as he could be," Miss Jocelyn had confided to them, in tear-dampened scornfulness. "Papa doesn't want me to teach, anyway. And"—with a sniff and a toss of her head—"we'll be in town now where we can enjoy ourselves."

It is not a pretty thing to contradict a lady, but certainly if Miss Jocelyn's papa made the remark which she attributed to him it must have been at some time prior to his return from the camp to Valley City; prior, too, to his exit from Valley City to Crawfordsville. For her papa went out of the Valley reclining wordlessly upon a thick padding of quilts in the bed of a big wagon, with his few household effects so arranged about him as to screen him from the sun and the curious gaze of a chance passer-by, and in no condition to express himself upon any matter whatever.

Jackson Gregory

There was in Crawfordsville, upon a pleasant, shady avenue, a little vine-covered cottage belonging to Bat Truxton, and thither the big wagon conveyed him, his scornful daughter, and his few household effects. And there shortly after twilight upon the third day after the closing of school in Valley City Mr. Roger Hapgood, sartorially immaculate in shining raiment, glorious as to tie and silken socks, presented himself.

Miss Jocelyn Truxton, a big, yellow-hearted rose peeping forth at him from a carefully careless profusion of brown hair, came out upon the porch at his knock, smiled at him saucily, and offered him her hand.

"How do you do, Mr. Hapgood? We didn't expect you again so soon. I thought that maybe you had forgotten us." And then, blushing prettily over the hand which Mr. Hapgood was still holding ardently in his, "Won't you come in?"

Mr. Hapgood, having assured her that he should forget all else in the world before he forgot her, called her attention to the fact that it was a deucedly fine evening, and that it would be too bad to lose any of it by going into the house. His smile and eloquent eyes pointed out that there was a not uncomfortable rustic bench, large enough to accommodate two nicely, at the cozy, vine-sheltered end of the porch.

"And how is Mr. Truxton?" he asked, his tone gently solicitous, when they were seated.

"I have had Dr. Biggs call since you were here," she told him, assuming the pose which a certain Broadway favorite had discovered (the photograph of the leading lady in this particular pose had been cut from the latest theatrical gazette which now lay upon the sitting-room table; it is denied us to enter the room set aside for Miss Jocelyn to see if the picture be pinned to the wall over her dresser!)—a pose which was not lost to the appreciative and admiring eyes of Mr. Hapgood. "Dr. Biggs says that papa's is a high-strung, nervous disposition which at times makes the taking of—of a little alcohol absolutely necessary. And that the—the stimulant is liable to upset him. It is entirely a nervous trouble, and in a few days, with perfect rest, he will be well again."

Mr. Hapgood nodded gravely, sympathetically.

"Mr. Truxton has been so great a factor in the reclamation project—he has been the very heart and soul of the actual work done—that I wonder how Mr. Crawford's schemes will get along without him?"

"I hope they fail," cried Jocelyn, hotly. "Papa has given the best in him to help them, and look how they send him adrift when—when he makes one little slip!"

"Do you know why Crawford really let him go?" Hapgood, speaking in hushed tones, continued to eye her keenly. "Don't you know that Crawford was just waiting and looking for an excuse—any excuse?"

Jocelyn turned widening eyes upon him. "What do you mean?"

Hapgood gave the impression of a man hesitating over a serious matter. And then, with a sudden burst of something remarkably like ingenuous ardor, he exclaimed:

"Why should I say anything? Perhaps I should keep my peace and let matters take their own course. I have a distinctive dislike to interfering in any way with the affairs of other people. And yet, Miss Jocelyn, I feel so strong an interest in you—you will forgive me if I have to speak plainly; you will pardon me when you know I mean no offense?—that I cannot keep my peace." A momentary struggle between his desire to befriend her and his dislike to say evil of others, and then with vehement intensity, "I will *not* remain silent."

Whereupon he became immediately silent and remained so until the curiosity which he had fired urged him to go on.

"When Conniston left the Half Moon and went to work in the Valley under your father"—leaning forward, his low-toned voice again deeply confidential—"the whole plot was laid and perfected. He was to work there until he had learned all that Mr. Truxton could teach him, until the greater part of the work had been done, and then your father was to be discharged so that Conniston could take his place. Yes, and so that when the work was completed—the work which your own father had made possible— Conniston would reap the rewards of it, take all the honors."

He paused suddenly, and again his pale eyes, intent upon the girl's face, were keen with the shrewdness in them. Jocelyn sprang to her feet, her face flaming, her body tense.

"The—the wretches!" she gasped.

Roger Hapgood made no reply, content for the moment to rest upon his oars, watching the boat he had launched drift as it would.

"Why," asked Jocelyn, after a little, her face puzzled—"why do you tell me this, when you are one of Mr. Crawford's lawyers?"

He lifted his hand as though warding off a blow.

"Don't say that! Miss Jocelyn, did you think that I was the sort of man, so forgetful of his manhood, that I would remain in the service of such people when I had found them out? Did you dream that I could remain a part of a project a second after such a man as Conniston had been put at the head of it? Did you think," half sadly, half reproachfully, "that I could continue my affiliations with such men after the treatment which Mr. Truxton—*your father*—had received? Miss Jocelyn, I went straight to Mr. Winston and handed him my resignation. Thank God that if I must give up my position I can at least keep my self-respect!"

It was very effectively done, and Jocelyn thrilled with it.

"I am so sorry!" she said, softly, her light touch sympathetic upon his arm. "So sorry that because of us—"

"Don't say it—please don't, Miss Jocelyn! I can never forget that it was I, no matter how innocently, who helped them in getting the excuse they were looking for. And don't you see, I shall feel in a way that my fortune is linked with yours, I shall feel that there are certain bonds between us, I shall feel that in a small, very small way I am being of some light service to your father and," very softly—"and to you."

"But what will you do? You have so few friends here. This is a new country to you—"

"For a moment I thought of returning immediately to the East. But I could not. Why? I won't tell you now; I dare not." He paused long enough to look the things which short acquaintance forbade him saying, and then, as though shaking himself mentally, went on, "What shall I do? I have already done it. Just so long as I thought blindly that the right was with us I worked for reclamation as a man does not often work. And now that the scales have dropped from my eyes, do I hesitate? I have gone to Mr. Swinnerton. I have offered him my services. And he has seen fit to accept them. And now I shall not have to sit idly by, my hands in my lap, waiting to see the Crawfords reap the rewards and assume the honors which belong—elsewhere!"

Jocelyn had read stories of heroes. Never before had she known what it was to find herself in the actual bodily presence of one of these creatures. And small wonder she thrilled again, not alone because of the fact that this great-hearted gentleman had sacrificed himself upon the altar of righteousness, but, further, that in the reasons for such self-immolation had entered thoughts of her. A real, perfectly delightful romance was being enacted, and *she* was its heroine!

"You are very good," she murmured, quite as the heroine should. "And papa will appreciate it when I tell him. And," shyly, "if you care to know it, I think that your generous kindness is the finest thing I have ever known."

It was the psychological time for a love avowal. But Mr. Hapgood had not played out his other role. He rose hastily, looking at his watch.

"I stopped in for just a moment," he said, quickly. "I am on my way to the post-office. I expect some important mail to-night. By the way," stopping with a glove half drawn on, "if your father cares to accept a position again soon I think that I know of one which would suit him. Mr. Swinnerton wants a competent engineer to aid him in a bit of work. I took the liberty to mention Mr. Truxton to him. He was delighted at the bare mention of your father's name. But"—and again the old shrewd look crept into his eyes—"maybe Mr. Truxton does not care to work against the reclamation? Maybe he is willing to see the Crawfords and that Conniston fellow succeed in their scheme?"

"I am going right in to talk with papa," she told him, quickly. "I am going to tell him the real truth. And I think, Mr. Hapgood, that you can tell Mr. Swinnerton that papa will come out to see him to-morrow or the next day."

Mr. Hapgood took the hand which she held out to him, bestowed upon her a look which spoke of warm admiration tinged with half-melancholy longing, sighed, relinquished her hand with a gentle pressure, and ran down the steps.

"Good night, Jocelyn," he called, softly, from the little gate.

"Good night, Roger," she whispered.

CHAPTER XX

A certain old football phrase rang day and night in Conniston's brain, "*It is anybody's game!*" Anybody's game! For there was a chance for success in the Great Work, and he saw that chance clearly, and fought hard for it. If everything went smoothly now, if Mr. Crawford gave him five hundred more men, if there were no unforeseen obstacles set in his way, no smashing accidents, he would see the ditches in Rattlesnake Valley filled with water by the last day of September. He had figured on everything, he had sat late into many a night after the grind of a twelve or fifteen hour day, frowning over details, calculating to the cubic yard what he must do each and every day, going over his calculations with a care which missed no detail. And he knew that he could play this game safely and win—if they would only let him alone! And still he knew that it was anybody's game. Could Swinnerton block him in some way which he could not foresee, could Swinnerton make him lose a single day's work, could Swinnerton steal his five hundred men as he had stolen men in the past, it was Swinnerton's game.

Brayley was driving the work in the Valley now. Tommy Garton had his new legs from Chicago, and from the seat of a buckboard, sometimes from the ground where his crutches sank into the soft sand, he advised Brayley and watched the work. Conniston was in the mountains, and the Lark with fifty men was with him.

Once in Deep Creek, with the site of Dam Number One before him, Conniston studied long before he gave the order to the Lark to begin work. Here were the stakes of Truxton's survey, here were the foundations already laid, here was a nature-made dam-site. He had not needed the stakes to show him the spot. And still he hesitated.

Here, where plans had been made for the chief dam, Deep Creek belied its name. It ran clear and untroubled over a gentle slope, widening out until from edge to edge of the water it measured close upon forty feet. Still farther back upon either hand the sides of the canon stood in perpendicular walls thirty feet high. Above the site the walls widened gradually until they formed a pocket, flat-bottomed, half a mile wide. Still farther up the creek's course these natural walls grew steadily closer together until perhaps three-eighths of a mile deeper in the canon they drew so close together that there was scarcely more than the width of an ordinary room between them.

It was this point—the Lark had been here with Bat Truxton when the survey was made and called it the "Jaws"—that inspired Conniston's hesitation. Here was a second dam-site, and not until he had studied both long and carefully, with a keen eye to advantage and disadvantage, did he give the word to begin work.

If it were only a question of a site, with time not an element to success, he would have chosen as Truxton had done and without a second's doubt. Had he had only to consider the building of a dam across Deep Creek in the shortest possible time, he would have chosen the site at the Jaws. But the thing which he wanted now was the largest possible dam in the shortest possible time. There was a pocket above the Jaws, but it was shorter, narrower. And above it the creek-bed plunged downward, at times broken into perpendicular waterfalls, until, yonder at a sharp bend, the water as it now frothed through its narrow, rocky canon was on a level with the top of the Jaws. He needed to take out water in vast quantities, countless millions of gallons of it, to turn into the ditches thirty miles away across the dry desert.

"The one question," he told himself, as he stood upon a boulder whence he could overlook the two sites, "is, can I get the dam finished where Bat Truxton planned it—get it done in time?"

And in the end he told himself that if the five hundred men came he could have his dam completed in time; and that if the five hundred men did not come the whole task before him was hopeless. Then he waved his hand to the Lark, and the Lark shouted a command which set fifty idle men to work before the echoes of his voice had died away between the rocky walls of the canon.

The materials he should require—the lumber for the great flume which was to turn the water from the weir into the cut which was to be made across the spine of the ridge separating Deep Creek from the wider canon through which Indian Creek shot down upon the uplands of the Half Moon, the kegs of giant powder, the horses and imple-ments—he had brought with him or had conveyed hither yesterday from Crawfordsville. He knew that in a very few days now the main canal would be completed, stretching like a mammoth serpent over the five miles of rolling hills through which it twisted intricately to avoid rocky ridges and knolls to follow natural hollows; that when at last Dam Number One should be an actuality of stone and mortar, with the water rising high above the flood-gates through which he could send it hissing and boiling into the flume, the way was open to shake his victorious fist in the face of nature itself, to drive water across thirty miles of desert and into the heart of Rattlesnake Valley.

Upon one thing Conniston had set his heart before he had been twenty-four hours in Bat Truxton's shoes. He would forget the date which had been marked in red numerals since his first talk with Tommy Garton; he would not think once of the first day of October. He would have everything in readiness upon the twenty-fifth day of September.

He knew that the water would at first run slowly through the dry canals, that the thirsty soil would drink up the first of the precious gallons, that he must allow himself those five days in order that he play safe. And now that he had seen the scope of the work to be done, now that he felt that he could manage without the auxiliary dam until after the first of October, that the two dams here on Deep Creek and Indian Creek would give him enough water to keep to the terms of the contract, he believed that he would have everything in readiness by the twenty-fifth of September.

For this he had hoped, at first half heartedly; for this he was now working. Besides the inducements he had offered his men he now promised them a wage of once and a half for overtime. That meant that from the first light of morning until dark, with often less than an hour off at noon, they worked day after day. They fought with the uneven bed of the stream, they fought with great boulders, until their arms ached in their sockets and their scanty clothing was drenched with sweat. Conniston, while he urged them on to do all that was in them, marveled that they did not break down under the strain.

Nor did he spare himself. Many a night during the swift weeks which followed he had no more than three or four hours' sleep.

Until the Lark yelled to his men to "knock" off at night,

Conniston labored with them. Then, when they had rolled heavily into their blankets, he more than once had saddled his horse and ridden down along the foothills across the stretch of sand and to Valley City to advise with Garton, to learn how the work was going there, to plan and order for the days to follow. He grew gaunt and nervous and hollow-eyed. Heavier and heavier the load of his responsibility rested upon his shoulders. Nearer and nearer came the end of the time allotted to him, and always the things still to do loomed ahead of him like mountains of rock. He went for two weeks without shaving, and scarcely realized it. His hands grew to be like the hands of his men, torn and cut and blackened with dirt ground into the skin. His boots were in strips before he thought of another pair; his clothes were ragged. He thought only of the Great Work.

In the Present, which came to him with tight-clenched, iron fingers gripping the promise which he must rend from them with the strength of brain and brawn, there was only the Great Work. The Past extended back only to the day when Bat Truxton had fallen and he had been called to take the place of command; and since then there had been only the Great Work. And the Future, mocking him now, smiling upon him the next day, then hiding her face in her misty veil, held high above his head the success or the failure of the Great Work.

And as he grew haggard and tense-nerved and unkempt, little lines formed about the corners of his mouth which would have told William Conniston, Senior, that there had been wrought in his son a change which was not of the body, not of the mind alone, but even of the secret soul.

He thought that he should have heard from Mr. Crawford by now, and yet no word had reached him. When the day's work had been done upon the dam he rode the ten miles into Crawfordsville and inquired at the Western Union office for a telegram. No, nothing had come. The next day he was as short-spoken as Bat Truxton had been the day before Hapgood had tempted him, as irritable. He saw half a dozen men struggling with a great rugged mass of rock, and cursed them for their slowness. And then he turned away from the Lark's curious eyes, biting his lips. For he knew that they were doing all that six big iron-bodied men could do, and that he was not fit.

Again that night he rode to Crawfordsville. He thought that the telegraph agent grinned maliciously as he tossed a yellow envelope upon the counter.

"Sign here, Mr. Conniston," he said.

Conniston signed and, stepping outside, read the words which drove a groan to his lips:

"WILLIAM CONNISTON, Jr.,

"General Supt., Crawford Reclamation, Crawfordsville.

"No success yet. May have to go to St. Louis for the money. Hope to have men in four or five days.

"JOHN W. CRAWFORD."

He did not see Jocelyn Truxton in front of the post-office as he rode past, did not see Hapgood come out of the two-story building and join her. He saw only the days which were rushing down upon him, offering him a broken, blunt weapon to fight a giant.

Never once had Conniston doubted as he doubted now. Never before had all glint of hope been lost in rayless blackness. If he had the five hundred men, *if he had them now*, there was a fighting chance. But if he must wait another week before they came—

To-day the telephone line had been completed to Valley City. All day he had looked forward to a talk with Argyl. Now he swept by the little office without lifting his head. He could not talk with her; he could not talk with Tommy Garton even. They would know soon enough, and they would know from other lips than his.

That night he slept little, but sat staring at the stars, searching stubbornly to find his lost hope, struggling over and over to see the way. And all that he could see was a long, dry, ugly cut in the desert, a vain, foolish, stupid thing; Mr. Crawford a ruined, broken man; Argyl smitten with sorrow and disappointment; himself the vanquished leader of a mad campaign; Oliver Swinnerton and his servitors flushed with victory. Still he fought to find the way, and shut his lips tight together, and strove to shut from his mind the pictures which his insistent fancy painted there. And when morning came and he walked to the dam which was taking form, pale, worn with the fatigue of the night after the fatigue of the day, he snapped out his orders half viciously, and watched with a hard smile while his handful of men resumed their mammoth task.

"Take it from me"—the Lark was regarding him curiously —"you better go git some sleep, or it's goin' to be a redwood box for yours."

The sun had just pushed a shining edge of its burning disk over the mountain-tops when Conniston suddenly cried out like a man awaking from the clutch of a frightful nightmare, and pointed with shaking finger to the road winding up the canon.

"What's up, 'bo?" asked the Lark, swinging upon him.

"I don't know," Conniston said, harshly. "I—guess I'm just seeing things. Look!"

A wagon had crept around a turn in the road, and its long bed was close packed with the forms of men standing upright, their hands upon the back of the high seat or upon one another's shoulders to steady themselves as the wagon pitched and lurched over the ill-defined road. Around the bend another wagon, similarly loaded with a human freight which taxed the strength of four puffing horses, came into view. And behind that another and another—

"Am I seeing things?" snapped Conniston, his hand biting into the Lark's shoulder. "What is that?"

"Them," grunted the Lark, wriggling like an eel in Conniston's grip, "is your five hundred new guys, or I'm a liar! An' fergit you're the strong man in a sideshow doin' stunts with a rag doll—"

But Conniston did not hear him. Already he was running toward the wagons. And there was a light in his eyes which had not been there for many days. A little, youngish man, sandy of hair, with bird-like brightness of eye and the grin of a sanctified cherub, swung down from the seat of the foremost wagon, lifted his hand, thereby stopping the laboring procession, and came forward to meet Conniston.

"I want to talk with the superintendent," he said, as the two men met. "Where is he?"

"I'm the superintendent. I'm Conniston. You want me?"

"All right, Mr. Conniston. I'm Jimmie Kent."

He put out his hand, which was painfully small, but which gripped Conniston's larger hand like a vise. "There are your five hundred men. Or, to be exact, five hundred and five. I started with five hundred and seven. Lost two on the road."

"But," interrupted Conniston, staring half incredulously at him, "Mr. Crawford's telegram—"

Jimmie Kent laughed.

"Mr. Crawford kicked like a bay steer over that telegram. And in the end, when he wouldn't put his name to a lie, I did the trick for him."

"But why?"

"Simply, sir, because I am under contract to deliver five hundred men into your hands. Simply because the telegraph agent in Crawfordsville belongs body and soul, bread and butter, to our esteemed friend Mr. Oliver Swinnerton. Know Oliver personally? Capable man, charming host, but the very devil to buck when he has his back aloft! And they tell me that he is playing high this trip. It was just as well, don't you think, that I sent that wire? Had Oliver known that this consignment of hands was coming, and when they were coming—well, I don't know how he would have managed it, but one way or another he would have come mighty close to taking them off my hands. And now," whipping a big, fat note-book from his pocket, "will you sign right there?"

Kent removed the cap from a gold-filigreed fountain-pen, handed it with a bit of paper and the note-book to Conniston, and pointed out where the signature was wanted. And Conniston set his name down under a statement acknowledging the receipt from James Kent of five hundred and five men, "in good and satisfactory shape."

"Thank you, Mr. Conniston," as he blotted and returned

the document to his breast pocket. "Perhaps, however, you would have preferred to have counted before signing?"

"That's all right. I'll take your word for it. If there aren't five hundred, there are as good as five hundred. And thank God, and you, Jimmie Kent, that they are here!"

"Need 'em pretty bad? Well, I'm glad I got 'em to you in time. And you might as well know how I did it. I unloaded my men at Littleton, two hundred miles east of here. And then I chartered a freight and sneaked 'em into Bolton at night. Got into Bolton last night, and came right out. I don't believe," with a genial grin, "that our friend Oliver knows a thing about it yet. I do believe that that wire to you at Crawfordsville has got him sidetracked."

Conniston called the Lark to him.

"I am going to put two hundred more men to work right here and right now," he said, swiftly. "You get double salary to act as general foreman over the two hundred and fifty. Divide your old gang of fifty into five parts, ten each. Break up the new gang of two hundred into five sections, forty men to a section. Then put ten of our old men to work with each section of forty, making, when that is done, five gangs, fifty men to the gang. Understand?"

The Lark nodded, his eyes bright.

"Then pick out from your old gang the five best men you have. No favoritism—understand me? The five best men! You know them better than I do. I want them to do the sort of thing you have been doing, each of them to act as section boss, under you, over fifty men. Send them to me. And get a move on!"

The Lark shot away, losing no time in question or answer. A

moment later five big, strapping fellows stood before Conniston, eying him curiously.

"You fellows," Conniston told them, bluntly, "are to act as section bosses. You are to get the wages the Lark here has been getting. You are to get the same money I offered him for every day between the first of October and the day we get water into the Valley. You are to take orders from him and no questions asked. You can hold your jobs just as long as you do the work. If you can't do the work you'll get fired and another man put in your place. Come along with me. And you," to the Lark, "come too."

He swung off toward the wagons, the five men and Jimmie Kent following him. At the first wagon he called to the men to "climb out." As they clambered down the men in the other wagons got to the ground and came forward.

"I want forty men," Conniston called. "Walk by me single file so I can count."

When the fortieth had passed him he raised his hand.

"You," he said to the one of the new foremen nearest him, "take these forty men, add ten of the old section to them, and go to work on the dam. Wait a minute. Have you boys had any breakfast?"

They had not.

"Go to the cook, then," he ordered. "Tell him to give you the best he can sling out at quick notice. Tell him that there will be one hundred and sixty more to feed. I'll send for more grub right away."

The men passed on to the cook's tent, and one after another Conniston counted off the other sections of forty and sent them to be fed.

"The rest of you," he called to the three hundred men who had watched their fellows move away, "go to the Valley. You can loaf until we scare up something to eat for you and until the horses rest a bit. I'll send right away to Crawfordsville—"

"Mr. Conniston," interrupted Jimmie Kent, "in those two wagons back there is a lot of grub. And tools," he added. "Mr. Crawford had me pick them up in Littleton."

CHAPTER XXI

Never had Conniston known a busier forenoon, never a happier. The fatigue, the despondency, the utter hopelessness of the early morning was swept away. He felt a new life course through his veins, there came a fresh elasticity to his stride, his voice rang with confidence. For he was as a leader of a lost hope within the walls of a beleaguered city to whom, when all hope was gone, reinforcements had come.

He felt that now nothing could tire him in body or in mind, nothing drive from his heart his glorious conviction of success to come.

And yet he had no faintest idea how busy the day was to be. When two hours had passed and the wagons carrying three hundred men had started for the Valley, Conniston had the two hundred and fifty men at Deep Creek working with a swiftness, an effectiveness which would have told a chance observer that they had been familiar many days with the work. He was to leave them before noon, to hurry on horseback to overtake the wagons that he might personally oversee the arrangements to be made upon their coming into the Valley. And there was much to be done, many specific orders to give the Lark, before he dared leave.

Upon the dam itself he put a hundred men to work. The remaining hundred and fifty he set to building the great flume which was to carry the stored water for five hundred yards along the ridge, then into the cut in the crest of the ridge and into Dam Number Two. He saw that he must have more horses, more plows and scrapers. But for the present he could do without them. There was blasting to be done upon the rugged wall of the cañon, there were tall pines bunched in groves, many of which must come down before the flume could be completed or the ditch made. And men with axes and crowbars and giant powder were set to their tasks.

Everywhere he went the Lark dogged his heels, listening intently to the orders which his superior gave him.

"The main thing," Conniston told him, when he had outlined the work as well as he could, "is to keep your men working! Don't lose any time. I'll be back as soon as I can make it, some time to-morrow, and if you don't know how to handle anything that comes up put your men on something else. The dam has got to be made, the flume has got to be built, the cut has to be dug, a lot of trees and boulders have to come out. You will have enough to keep you busy."

"Do you know, Mr. Conniston," Jimmie Kent told him, as they sat down together for a bite of lunch, "I've got a hunch. A rare, golden hunch!"

Conniston laughed—he was in the mood to laugh at anything now—and asked what the rare "hunch" was.

"Just this: there's going to be some fun pulled off in this very same neck of the woods before the first of October! And, by Harry, I'd like to see it! Have you any objection to my sort of roosting around and keeping my bright eye on the game? Oh, I don't want a salary; I'll pay for my grub, and you can have my valuable advice gratis. Can I stick around?"

When Conniston told him that he should be glad to have him stay, and as his and the company's guest, Jimmie Kent beamed.

"That's bully of you! If you don't mind, and we can scare up a horse for me, I'd like to ride into Valley City with you? I can send a wire from there to my firm asking for an indefinite vacation. Oh, they'll grant it, all right. They want a man like me in their business."

It was after one o'clock, work was in progress, and Conniston and Jimmie Kent swung into their saddles and started for Valley City. Before they had ridden a mile down the mountainous road Conniston heard Kent whistle softly, and ahead of them, coming to meet them, saw a light pole buggy swiftly approaching. A moment later and the man driving had stopped his horses and was looking with small, shrewd eyes into Conniston's.

He was a short man, round of face, round of eyes, round of stomach. Very fair, very bland, very red under the flaming sun, the sweat trickling down his face and upon the crumpled white of his shirt-bosom. His eyes were mildly surprised as they rested upon Kent. They were only smiling as they returned to Conniston.

"I was looking for Mr. Conniston, the superintendent," he said, in a soft, fat voice. "Can you direct me—"

"I am Conniston. And I am in a very big hurry. What can I do for you?"

The man in the buggy swelled pompously.

"I am Oliver Swinnerton," he said, with dignity. And then

suffering what he might have been pleased to consider austerity to melt under a soft, fat smile, "Glad to know you, Conniston. Shake!"

He put out a soft, fat hand. Conniston stared at him in amazement.

"Swinnerton!" he cried, sharply. "Oliver Swinnerton! And what in the world do you want with me?"

When it was obvious that Conniston was not going to lean forward in the saddle to take his hand Mr. Swinnerton withdrew it to mop his moist forehead.

"Oliver Swinnerton," he repeated, nodding pleasantly. "And I wanted to talk with you about"—his left eyelid, red and puffy, drooped, and his right eye squinted craftily—"about reclamation."

"I can't imagine what common interests you and I have in reclamation. And I am in a hurry."

Oliver Swinnerton chuckled as at a rare jest.

"How do, Kent?" was what he said, having seen Jimmie Kent, it would seem, for the first time. "And what might you be doing in this part of the country?"

Jimmie Kent's voice was as pleasant as Swinnerton's had been.

"Maybe you remember how you did me up in the matter of the Bolton town lots, Mr. Swinnerton? Well, I am just sticking around for the fun of seeing some one do you up."

Mr. Swinnerton's chuckle was softer, oilier than before. He smiled upon Kent as though the sandy-haired man were in truth the apple of his eye.

"Always up to your little repartee, ain't you, Jimmie? Well, well! And now, Mr. Conniston—Jimmie, you'll pardon us?—may I have a word in private with you?"

"No," Conniston flared out, "you may not! I don't know you, Mr. Swinnerton, and I don't want to."

Only a something akin to the hurt surprise of a child in voice and look alike as Swinnerton queried softly:

"No? Pray, why not? What have I done, Mr. Conniston?"

"You have proven yourself a scoundrel!" burst out Conniston, angrily. "A fair fight in the open is one thing. Such cowardly means as you take to gain your ends is another. And if you will turn your horses and drive back off of Crawford territory I'll be glad to see the back of you."

For a moment Swinnerton stared at him in stupefaction. And then he broke into a delighted giggle which drove the tears into his eyes. Jimmie Kent looked from one to the other, and then, whistling softly to himself and saying no word, rode on down the road.

"I don't know what you are gurgling about," Conniston said, shortly. "But if you will follow Mr. Kent and get off and stay off this land I shall be much obliged to you."

Mr. Swinnerton wiped the tears from his eyes and gasped from the depths of his mirth:

"You'll do, Conniston! He, he! Oh, you'll certainly do!"

"I don't know what you're talking about," snapped Conniston. "But I tell you what I will do if you don't get out of here. I'll just naturally pitch you out!"

"I'd never have guessed it," chuckled Swinnerton. "Never in the world. I'd never even have thought of such a thing. Conniston, it's the bulliest scheme I ever heard of! How you managed it so easily—"

"Managed what?" Conniston's curiosity, in spite of him, had for the moment the upper hand of his anger. "What do you mean?"

"Close-lipped, eh? Close-lipped to the end! That's business —mighty good business, too. Oh, you'll do."

"Are you going to tell me what you mean? I tell you I haven't any time to waste, and I want to see your back, and see it moving, too. If you have anything to say, say it quick."

"That's the stuff, Conniston. Close-lipped to the end. But," and with a glance over his shoulder at Jimmie Kent, now out of hearing, and leaning a pudgy arm upon a pudgy knee as he smiled confidentially into Conniston's frowning face, "ain't it pretty close to the end now?"

"I give you my word, Swinnerton, that if you can't tell me straight out what you are driving at, off of this land you go."

The stern assurance of Conniston's tone seemed to surprise Swinnerton.

"Come, come," he said, rather sharply. "What's the use of this shenanigan? Can't I see through clear window-glass? Am I a fool? Oh, I didn't guess, I didn't know that such a man as you were alive; I didn't so much as know your name until yesterday. But—know a man named Hapgood?" And his eyes twinkled again.

"Yes," bluntly. "What about him?"

"Oh, nothing much. Only he told me about you. And now what he didn't guess I know, Mr. William Conniston, Junior."

"And, pray, what might that be?"

"Want me to tell you, eh? Want to be sure that I know, do you? Want to see if Oliver Swinnerton is a fool, blind in both eyes? All right." His voice dropped yet lower, and he blinked with cunning eyes as he finished. "You are up to the same game I am! You are going to slip the knife into John Crawford clean up to the hilt. You are going to make a bluff at getting work done until the last minute, and then you are going to have nothing done. You are going to throw him into my hands like I would throw a sick pup into a ditch."

"Am I?" asked Conniston, coolly, mastering the sudden desire to take this little fat man into his two hands and choke him. "You know a great deal about what I intend to do, Mr. Swinnerton. And now, if you are not through talking your infernal nonsense, I am through listening to it. There is room to turn right here. Understand?"

"But—" began Swinnerton, only to be cut short with:

"There are no buts about it!"

He stooped, seized the bit of one of Swinnerton's horses, and jerked it about into the road.

"Get out!"

"I tell you," yelled Swinnerton, "Conniston or no Conniston, you can't bluff me. Do you hear?"

Conniston made no reply as he jerked the horses farther around. When their heads were turned toward the way which Swinnerton had come he lifted his quirt high above his head. Oliver Swinnerton went suddenly white and raised his arm to protect his face. But only Conniston's laugh stung him as the quirt fell heavily across the horses' backs. The buggy lurched, the horses leaped forward; Oliver Swinnerton's surprised torrent of curses was lost in the rattle of wheels, his red face obscured in the swirling dust.

"I wonder what he was driving at?" muttered Conniston as he watched the horses race down the road.

Jimmie Kent, reining his horse aside as Swinnerton swept by him, smiled and called, pleasantly:

"Good-by, Oliver. Seem to be in a hurry!"

CHAPTER XXII

Conniston and Kent, riding swiftly, side by side, overtook the wagons conveying the three hundred men to the Valley, and, passing them, arrived at Brayley's camp before the men there had quit work for the day. Brayley was more than half expecting them, as Kent had telephoned to the office from Bolton to learn where Conniston was and had told Tommy Garton of his errand.

"An' now," proclaimed Brayley, with deep satisfaction, "we'll have the big ditch clean through Valley City an' the cross-ditches growin' real fast before a week's up."

"I've told the drivers to stop when they get here, Brayley. Some of the men have blankets with them. We can rush more from Mr. Crawford's store in Crawfordsville. We can make out as to food. Have you figured out what more horses, what further tools you'll need? That's good. Send a man to the Half Moon right now with word to Rawhide Jones to rush us the horses. Put your new men to work in the morning if you have to make them dig ditch with shovels. Also send a hundred of them into Valley City as soon as it's daylight to begin the cross-ditches. Let Ben go with them. He can get his instructions there from me or from Tommy Garton. How is everything going?"

Brayley reported that the work was running smoothly, that

his foremen were as good men as he ever wanted to see, that he had no fault to find anywhere.

"An' this ol' ditch is sure growin', Con," he finished, with a sudden gleam of pride.

Conniston did not wait for the arrival of the wagons to ride on into Valley City. Kent he left behind him at the camp.

"I've a tremendous curiosity to see how you do this sort of thing," Kent confided to him, as he handed Conniston the message he wished sent from Valley City to Clayton & Paxton, of Denver. "I think that if Mr. Brayley has no objections and can spare me a blanket and some bread and coffee I'll roost here and watch the ditch grow in the morning."

Tommy Garton was still perched upon his high stool when Conniston came to the office.

"Just through, though," he said, as he climbed down and with the aid of his crutches piloted his new legs toward the door, grasping Conniston's hand warmly. "Good news, eh, Greek?"

"The best, Tommy. If we don't put this thing across now we ought to be kicked from one end of the desert to the other. By the way, I had a visit from Swinnerton this afternoon."

He told of what had passed, and ended, thoughtfully:

"What do you suppose was his object, Tommy? Just wanted to get a peek at what we have done?"

Garton laughed softly.

"You poor old innocent. Don't you know what the little man was after? Didn't he make it plain that he wanted you to double cross the old man? Didn't he make it plain that he was in a position to make it worth your while? If our scheme fails, don't you see that you can go to Swinnerton and demand and get a good job working for his scheme? He has bought many a man, Greek. It is his theory that he can buy any man he wants to buy."

"And I let him get away without slapping his little red face," muttered Conniston, disgustedly.

He left Garton a few minutes later, promising to return and spend the night with him, to talk at length with him in the morning, and went down the street to the Crawford cottage. He knew that since Argyl's father had left for Denver Mrs. Ridley, the wife of the proprietor of the lunch-stand, had been staying with her. It was Mrs. Ridley who answered his knock.

"Miss Argyl ain't come back yet, Mr. Conniston," she told him. "She went out this mornin' an' ain't showed up since. I reckon, though, she'll be back real soon now. It's after supper-time already."

"Do you know where she went?"

"No, sir. She didn't say. Won't you come in an' wait for her?"

"No," he answered, after a moment. "I'd better not. If Miss Crawford has been all day in the saddle she will be tired. I'll drop in in the morning."

"Maybe that would be better," Mrs. Ridley nodded at him. "We're up early—breakfast at five. You might run in an' eat with us?"

Conniston promised to do so, and returned to the office, more than a little disappointed at not having seen Argyl, wondering whither her long ride could have taken her. Until late that night he and Garton talked, planned, and prepared for the work of to-morrow. It was barely five the next morning when he again knocked at the cottage door. Again Mrs. Ridley answered his knock.

"Am I too early?" Conniston smiled at her. "I noticed your smoke going. Is Miss Crawford up yet?"

"Miss Crawford—" He saw that she hesitated, saw a nervous uneasiness in her manner as she plucked with quick fingers at the hem of her apron. "She ain't come in yet!"

"What!" cried Conniston, sharply. "What do you mean? Where is she?"

"I—I don't know, sir. She ain't come back yet."

"You mean that Miss Crawford left yesterday morning and that she has not returned since that time? That she has been gone twenty-four hours—all night?"

"Yes, sir." The old woman was eying him with eyes into which a positive fear was creeping, her lips trembling as she spoke. "You don't think anything has happened—"

"I don't know!" he cried, sternly. "Why didn't you let me know last night?"

"I didn't know what to do." The tears had actually sprung into her eyes. "I thought she must be all right. I thought mebbe she'd gone to Crawfordsville or to the Half Moon."

Conniston left her abruptly and hastened to the office.

"Tommy," he called, from the doorway, "do you know where Miss Crawford is? Where she went yesterday?"

"No. Why?" Garton, sensing from the other's tones that something was wrong, swept up his crutches and hurried forward.

"She left yesterday morning," Conniston told him, as he went to the desk and picked up the telephone. "She hasn't come back yet. Mrs. Ridley doesn't know anything about her." And to the operator:

"Give me the Crawford house. Quick, please! Yes, in Crawfordsville."

Upon the face of each man there were lines of uneasiness. Garton propped himself up against the desk and lighted a cigarette, his eyes never leaving Conniston's face.

"Can't you get anybody?" he asked, after a moment.

"No. What's that, Central? They don't answer? Then get me the bunk-house at the Half Moon. Yes, please! I'm in a hurry."

It was Lonesome Pete who answered.

"No, Con," he answered. "Miss Argyl ain't here. Anything the matter?"

Conniston clicked up the receiver and swung upon Garton.

"It is just possible," he said, slowly, "that she is in Craw-fordsville, after all. May have left the house already. I can call up the store as soon as it opens up and ask if she has been there."

Billy Jordan had entered at the last words.

"Who are you talking about?" he asked, quickly. "Not Miss Crawford?"

"Yes." Conniston whirled upon him abruptly. "Do you know where she went yesterday?"

"No, I don't know where she went. But as I was coming to the office I met her, just getting on her horse in front of her house, and she gave me a message for you."

"Well, what was it?"

"'If you see Mr. Conniston,' she said, 'tell him that I have gone to investigate the value of the Secret.' I don't know what she meant—"

"She said that!" cried Conniston, his face going white.

"But she's all right," Billy Jordan hastened to add. "She's back now."

"You saw her?"

"No." He shook his head. "But I saw the horse she was riding. Just noticed him tied to the back fence as I came in."

Again Conniston hurried to the cottage. Mrs. Ridley was upon the porch.

"Miss Crawford is back?" he called to her from the street.

She shook her head.

"Not yet. Ain't you—"

He did not wait to listen. Running now, he came to the little back yard, and to a tall bay horse, saddled and bridled, standing quietly at the fence. At first glance he thought, as Billy Jordan had thought, that the animal was tied there. And then he saw that the bridle-reins were upon the ground, that they had been trampled upon and broken, that the two stirrups were hanging upside down in the stirrup leathers as stirrups are likely to do when a saddled horse has been running riderless.

She had been to investigate the Secret! She had been gone all day, all night! And now her horse had come home without her! He dared not try to think what had happened to her; he knew that she must have dismounted while at the spring to examine the ground; he knew that there were sections of the desert alive with rattlesnakes.

The Great Work which had walked and slept with him for weeks, which had never in a single waking hour been absent from his thoughts, was forgotten as though it had never been. The Great Work was suddenly a trifle, a nothing. It did not matter; nothing in the wide world but one thing mattered. Failure of the Great Work was nothing if only a slender, gray-eyed, frank-souled girl were safe. Success, unless she were there to look into his eyes and see that he had done well, was nothing.

Unheeding Mrs. Ridley's shrill cries, he swung about and ran back to the office.

"Tommy," he cried, hoarsely, "her horse is back—without her! She rode away into the desert yesterday morning. She is out there yet. Billy, my horse is in the shed. Don't stop to saddle, but ride like the very devil out to Brayley's camp. Tell him what has happened. Tell him to rush fifty men on horseback to me. Tell him to see that each man takes two canteens full of water. And, for Heaven's sake, Billy, hurry!"

CHAPTER XXIII

Billy Jordan, terror springing up into his own eyes, sped through the door. And Conniston and Garton turned grave faces upon each other.

"Have you any idea," Garton was asking, and to Conniston his voice seemed to come faintly from a great distance, "which way she rode?"

"North. I don't know how far. Tommy, have you a horse here I can ride?"

"You are going to look for her?"

"Yes."

He was already at the door, and turned impatiently as Garton called to him:

"It's up to you, Greek. But—do you think that you could do any more to help her than the men you are sending out?"

"No. But, man, I can't sit here without knowing—"

"Greek!" There was a note in Tommy's voice, a look in his eyes which held Conniston. "I know how you feel, old man. And don't you know that another man might be fool

Jackson Gregory

enough to—to love her as much as you do?"

"Tommy!"

"Yes," with a hard little smile. "Why not? I'm only half a man, old fellow, but the head and the heart of me are left. And I've got to sit here and wait. And," his tone suddenly stern, "that's what you've got to do! You can't help by going—and you are the only man who has got to keep his head clear, who has got to stay here and direct the new forces which our good fortune has given to us."

For a moment Conniston stood staring incredulously. Then he turned, and his frowning eyes ran out toward the north, across the far-stretching solitudes of the desert. Somewhere out there, a mile away, ten miles away, twenty miles away, alone, perhaps tortured with thirst, perhaps famishing, perhaps—He shuddered and groaned aloud as he tried in vain to shut out the pictures which his leaping imagination drew for him. And here Garton's quiet voice was telling him that he had responsibilities, that he had work to do, that he, to whom she meant more than success or failure, life or death, must hold back from going to her.

"I won't—I can't!" he cried, wildly. "She is out there, Tommy, alone. She needs me—and I am going to her! What do I care about your cursed work!"

"There's a horse and saddle in the shed by the lunch-stand." Garton turned and hobbled back to his stool.

And Conniston, without a glance over his shoulder, hastened toward the shed. Before he had gone half the distance he stopped, swung about, and went slowly back to the office.

"You were right, Tommy," he said, as he stopped in the

doorway. "I was a fool. Understand," he added, quickly, "that if I thought I could be of one particle more value than the men I shall send in my place the work here could go to eternal perdition! But I can tell them all that I know of the way she has gone—and she would want me to stay here and push the work as if nothing had happened."

Mrs. Ridley, hysterically crying that Argyl was dead, that she *knew* that she was dead, and that she herself was to blame, came sobbing and moaning and wringing her hands into the office.

"Don't do that!" Conniston cried, angrily. "If you want to do any good, go down to the lunch-counter and help your husband put up fifty lunches. The men may be gone all day. Put up plenty."

She hurried away, drying her eyes now that there was something for her to do; and the two men, never looking at each other, sat and waited the coming of Brayley's men.

All that long, endlessly, wretchedly long forenoon, Conniston went about his work like a man under sentence of death, his face white and drawn, his step heavy, his voice silent save when necessity drove him to short, sharp, savage commands.

Again and again he forgot what it was that he was doing, forgot the ditches which were branching off from the main canal, right and left, as his eyes ran out across the sun-blistered sands, as his fancies ran ahead of them, searching, searching, searching—and half afraid to find what they sought. He had seen the questing riders push farther and farther into the desert, had seen them drop out of sight. Now they were gone; no moving dot told him where their search had taken them, what they had found. In the middle of an order he found himself breaking off and turning again to the north, looking for the return of the party, hoping to see the men waving their hats that all was well, straining his ears for their reassuring shouts. And the desert, vast, illimitable, threatening, mysterious, full of dim promise, full of vague threats, gave no sign.

At eleven o'clock he saw one of the men returning. Why one man alone? What would be the word which he was bringing? His heart beat thickly. His throat was very dry. He felt a quick pain through it as he tried to swallow. He lifted his head, and his eyes asked the question of the man who had jerked in his sweating horse at his side. The rider shook his head.

"Nothin'—we ain't found nothin' yet. Mundy sent me back. He says to tell you they're about ten mile out now, an' the hosses is gettin' done up for water. He says will you send a water-wagon or will you send out a fresh party?"

Conniston's heart leaped at the man's first word. He knew then how he had feared to know what they had found. And then it sank as fear surged higher into it. They had not found her yet—already she had been gone a whole day, a whole night, half the second day—

"Get a fresh horse and go back," he said, when the man waited for an answer. "Tell Mundy that I am starting a six-horse wagon, carrying water, right away. Tell him to keep on looking. You men keep close enough together for the most part to be able to hear a gun fired from the man nearest you. I'll send the wagon due north. You can pick it up by the tracks."

The man rode away, and Conniston strode to the office.

"Tommy"—and his voice was steady and determined— "you'll have to get into a buggy and watch the work this afternoon. I've got the men started—and now I am going to her."

"All right, Greek," Garton answered, gently. "I can keep things going."

Conniston turned and left him. He saddled his horse with eager fingers, gave the order for the wagon carrying water to move steadily northward until it came up with the men who had gone ahead, put a lunch and a flask of whisky into his pocket, filled his own canteens, and rode out across the hot sands.

"I am going to find her," he told himself, with quiet confidence.

He rode slowly at first, curbing his crying impatience with the knowledge that restraint now meant the reserve of endurance to his horse upon which he might be forced to call before he had found her. He held to a course due north, remembering what Argyl had told him about the location of the spring.

When he had gone nearly five miles he began to search to right and left, still holding to a general northerly direction, but often turning out of his course to ride to the tops of the knolls which rose here and there about him. And now he had let his horse out into a swinging gallop, urged to spare neither animal nor himself, prompted to make what haste he might by the thought that already noon had passed, that the day was half gone, that what he was to do must be done before the night came.

Once—he thought that Valley City must be at least eight or nine miles behind him—his heart leaped with sudden hope and fear as he saw, half a mile to the east, a cluster of little sand-hills like those Argyl had told him surrounded her spring.

He did not know that he was cutting his horse's bleeding sides with his spurs as he galloped up the gradual slopes; long ago he had forgotten all thought of conserving the beast's strength. He knew only that the very soul of him cried out aloud that he might at last come to her, and that his eyes, ever seeking, seeking, seeking, were more than half afraid to rest upon every shadowy, stirring bunch of scrub brush, more than half afraid to run ahead of him down the far sides of the low hills.

Nothing before him as he jerked in his panting horse, nothing but the desert, still, hot, thirsty, a great tortured thing under the merciless sky. Nothing but long level stretches so bleak, so barren, that a jackrabbit could not have hidden his gaunt, gray body. Nothing as he looked with narrowing eye far to east and west, north and south, but a vast, silent monotone of plain that would seem to conceal nothing, as open under the bright rays of the sun as the palm of a man's hand, an unsmiling, grave-faced, hypocritical thing which hid and held from him all that he wanted in the world.

A frenzy of terrified rage upon him, he stiffened in his stirrups, he shook his clenched fist at the quiet, jeering face whose very unmoved stillness was like a deep contempt, and cursed it, his voice springing harshly through his dry lips, rising almost into a sobbing shriek, dying away without an echo, leaving the face of the desert quietly contemptuous. For he grew suddenly as silent, a word cut in two by the click of his teeth, the sound of his own voice in his ears tricking him.

Breathless, a man turned to stone, he listened.

He had heard something—he *knew* that he had heard a

voice, not his own, a voice hardly more than a faint whisper, calling to him, calling again, then lost in the all-engulfing silence. About him the miles were laid bare in the sunlight. There was nothing.

Driven from the moment of inactivity into a madness of haste, tormented afresh at the thought that he had lost one precious minute, he cut anew with his red-roweled spurs into the torn flanks of his horse, and rode on, careless of all save that he must hurry, that his was a great race against the racing day, that he must find her before the night had sought her out. The very shadow which he and his horse cast—a distorted, black centaur sort of thing, running silently across the desert—was one with the desert in its cursed menace. For a moment ago it had hidden under his horse's belly, and now it ran beside him, ever lengthening, ever pushing farther to the eastward, a grim avowal that the day was passing.

The miles fled behind him like lean greyhounds. The miles before him reached out in unshortened endlessness. It was one o'clock. He had been gone two hours—he had done nothing. Now, far ahead, he caught sight of moving figures, saw a man yonder on horseback, saw another, hardly more than a drifting dot against the sky-line to the east, another yet to the west.

They were still searching for her, still pushing deeper and deeper into the burning solitudes; they had found nothing. They must be, he estimated roughly, twenty miles from Valley City. Had she ridden so far? Why hadn't she told him more about the location of the spring? If there *was* a spring, had she clung close to it when her horse had left her? Then she would not die for want of water! Or had she dug with breaking nails into the soil which had in it moisture enough to feed the roots of the yellow willows but which would but mock her as the desert mocked him, refusing to yield up one single drop of water?

Gradually, steadily he swung toward the left, riding a little to westward so as not to be seeking over the same territory across which the men before him had ridden. And as he rode he saw, a mile away from him, still farther to the west, a ring of hills, and he prayed that he might come upon the spring there and upon Argyl. And his moving lips were not still before he had found her.

He had swept down into a little hollow, the slightest of depressions in the sandy level, not to be seen until a man was upon its very rim, floored with scanty, dry brush. His tired horse threw up its head and shied. But Conniston had seen her first, a huddled heap, almost at his feet.

"Argyl!" he cried, loudly, dropping to his knees beside her, leaving his horse to stand staring at them. "Argyl!"

She lay as she had fallen, her right arm stretched straight out in front of her, her left arm lying close to her side, her face hidden from him in the sand. She did not move. Had he called to her an hour ago she would have turned her wide eyes upon him wonderingly. Now, if he had shouted with the voice of thunder she would not have heard. She was dead, or death was very close to her. For a moment, a moment lengthened into an eternity of hell, he did not know whether the shadowy wings of the stern angel were now rustling over her head or if already the wings had swept over her and had borne away from him the soul of the woman he loved.

"Argyl, Argyl dear!" he whispered. "I have come to save you, Argyl. To take you home. Oh! don't you hear me, Argyl?"

He put his arms about her, and as he knelt lifted her and put his face to hers. She was not cold; thank Heaven, she was not cold! But she did not move, she was heavy in his arms, the warmth of her body might have been from the ebbing tide of life or from the sun's fire. He could not feel her breathe, could not feel the beating of her heart.

He held her so that he could look into her face, and the cry upon his lips was frozen into a grief-stricken horror. Her hair unbound, hanging loose, tangled about her face, dull and soiled with the gray sand-dust, her lips dry, cracked, unnaturally big, her cheeks pinched and stamped at the corners of her mouth with the misery through which she had lived—was this Argyl?

He laid her back upon the sand, his body bent over her to shut out the sun, and unslung his canteen. He washed her mouth, let the water trickle over her brow and cheeks, forced a little of the lukewarm stuff between her teeth. He bathed her head, bathed her throat, and again forced a few drops into her mouth. And then, when she did not move, he would not believe that she was dead. She could not be dead. It was impossible. She would open her eyes in a minute, those great, frank, fearless, glorious gray eyes, and she would come back to him—back from the shadow of the stern angel's wing, back to herself and to him.

He unstoppered his flask of whisky and, holding her to him, thrust it to her lips. And the thing which had been a curse to Bat Truxton, which had hurled him downward from his leadership of men, which had threatened to wreck the hopes of the Great Work, brought Argyl back from the last boundaries of the thing called Life, back from the misty frontiers of the thing called Death to which she was journeying.

Her eyes opened, she stared at him, her eyes closed again.

Again he forced her reluctant throat to swallow the whisky,

a few drops only. And again he bathed her with water—brow and throat and quiet wrists. Her eyes did not open now, but he saw that she was breathing. Presently he made her take a little water. He washed her dusty nostrils that she might breathe better. And that breath might come into her tired lungs more easily he gently, reverently loosened the clothing about her breasts.

Not once did his eyes leave her face. He did not fire the shot which was to be a signal to the others, because he knew that they could not hear. Soon he would look for the wagon. It would pass closely enough for him to see it, near enough for him to make himself seen. Now he could do alone as much for her as could fifty men, as could any one.

An hour passed, two hours. He had watched the color of life creep back into her face faintly, slowly, but steadily. She had again opened her eyes, had turned them for a puzzled second upon his tense face, had closed them.

Now she seemed to be sleeping.

He had exhausted the contents of one canteen, had gone to his saddle for the other, when far to the south he saw the wagon. He had waved his hat high above his head, standing like a circus-rider in the saddle, and had emptied the cylinder of his revolver into the air. He had seen that the driver had heard him, that he had fired an answering volley, that he had turned westward. And then he had gone back to Argyl.

She had heard the shots. Her eyes were open and turned curiously upon him as he came swiftly to where she lay.

"Will you give me some water?" she whispered.

He lifted her head, and she drank thirstily, looking with

reproachful surprise at him when he took the canteen from her lips.

"That is all now, Argyl," he told her, his voice choking. And then, all power of restraint swept away from him by the joyous, throbbing love which so long he had silenced, he drew her close, closer to him, crying, almost harshly: "Oh, Argyl, thank God! For if you hadn't come back to me—I love you, love you! Don't you know how I love you, Argyl?"

Her hand closed weakly upon his.

"Of course, dear," she answered him, faintly, her poor lips trying to smile. "Of course we love each other. But can't I have a little water, dear?"

CHAPTER XXIV

It was the twentieth day of September by the calendar—ten days before the first of October as every man, woman, and child in the Valley measured time.

Conniston came and went superintending every part of the work, and, although he was still the gaunt, tired man he had been two weeks ago, he was no longer tight-lipped and somber-eyed. He smiled often; he laughed readily, like a boy. Argyl, her clean, healthy, resilient young body and spirit having shaken off the effects of the clutch of the desert, was the same Argyl who had raced for the Overland Limited that day when Conniston had first seen her; her laugh was as spontaneous as his, sparkling and free and buoyantly youthful. Mr. Crawford was quiet, saying few words, but the little lines of care had gone from the corners of eyes and mouth. Tommy Garton was the proverbial cricket on the hearth of the Valley's big family. Brayley looked upon his ditches with the gleam in his eye bespeaking a deep pride like the pride of ownership and a big, strong love. Jimmie Kent assured whomever would listen that he was glad that he had stayed, and that he had a mind to call on his old friend Oliver to see how he was feeling. Rattlesnake Valley had become the Happy Valley. With the first of October ten days off there was no shadow of doubt in a single heart that the Great Work would be a finished, actual, successful thing before the dawn of the

Great Day.

Upon the twentieth day of September Greek Conniston, being in Valley City, received a telegram which puzzled him. It was from Edwin Corliss, private secretary and confidential man of affairs of William Conniston, Senior, of Wall Street. Conniston replied immediately and by wire. During the three days following he received and despatched several telegrams. Since the messages have a certain bearing upon the Great Work, they are given below in the order in which they were received in the Valley and despatched from it:

"WM. CONNISTON, Jr.,

"Rattlesnake Valley.

"Drop everything. Come home immediately. Your father insists. Particulars when you arrive.

"CORLISS."

"EDW. CORLISS,

"New York.

"Can't get away. Under contract. Love to dad.

"WM. CONNISTON, Jr."

"WM. CONNISTON, Jr.

"Rattlesnake Valley.

"Smash contract. Will pay damages. Your father wants you in New York in five days.

"CORLISS."

"EDW. CORLISS,

"New York.

"Impossible. Can make hurried trip East after October first.

"WM. CONNISTON, JR."

"WM. CONNISTON, JR.,

"Rattlesnake Valley.

"Orders imperative from your father. Cables from Paris drop everything immediately and come home.

"CORLISS."

"EDW. CORLISS,

"New York.

"I refer you to wire of yesterday.

"WM. CONNISTON, Jr."

Then came a message which puzzled Greek Conniston more deeply than the others had done—a message *via* cable and telegraph and telephone from his father himself:

"WM. CONNISTON, Jr.,

"Rattlesnake Valley.

"Come home. Leave that work alone. Start minute you

get this. Wiring you thousand dollars Crawfordsville. Corliss will advance all you want in New York. Do as I command immediately or I disinherit you.

"WM. CONNISTON, Sr."

"WM. CONNISTON, Jr.,

"Rattlesnake Valley.

"At your father's orders have wired thousand to you Crawfordsville.

"CORLISS."

"EDW. CORLISS,

"New York.

"Money you wired remains subject your orders. I don't need it. Inform dad.

"WM. CONNISTON, Jr."

When William Conniston, Junior, received the second message from William Conniston, Senior, a swift understanding came to him, an understanding not only of the reason for the attitude Corliss had taken, but of what Oliver Swinnerton had had in mind when he had talked slyly of Conniston's intentions, and had expressed his confidence that the young superintendent was preparing to double cross his employer.

"WM. CONNISTON, JR.,

"Rattlesnake Valley.

"Am starting for New York. Meet me. Drop work. I have a million dollars at stake in Oliver Swinnerton project. Will lose all if you don't quit.

"WM. CONNISTON, Sr."

And it gave Greek Conniston a great, unbounded joy to answer:

"WM. CONNISTON, Sr.,

"Paris.

"Sorry, dad. You lose million. I have reputation at stake.

"WM. CONNISTON, Jr."

CHAPTER XXV

The days ran on, each twenty-four hours seeming shorter, swifter than the preceding twenty-four. Although everywhere in the Valley there was a glad confidence that the reclamation project was an assured thing, although feverish anxiety had been beaten back and driven out, there was no slightest slackening of unremitting toil. Upward of seven hundred men worked as they had never worked before. As the end of the time drew nearer, as success became ever more assured, they worked longer hours, they accomplished swifter results. For each man of them, from Brayley to the ditch-diggers, was laboring not only for the company, but for himself. Each and every man had been promised a bonus for every day between the time when water was poured down into the sunken Valley and the coming of high noon upon October the first. And Conniston still held to his determination to have everything in readiness by the twenty-fifth of September.

Upon the evening of the twenty-fourth of September Conniston called upon Mr. Crawford at his cottage in Valley City. He found his employer smoking upon the little porch alone.

When he was seated and had accepted a cigar, Conniston began abruptly what he had to say.

"If you have time, Mr. Crawford, I want to make a partial report to you to-night. Thank you. To begin with, I have completed the big dam, Dam Number One. It is all ready for business. The flume is finished, the cut made across the ridge to Dam Number Two across Indian Creek. Dam Number Two is ready. From these two dams the main canal runs, completed entirely, thirty miles and into Valley City. Dam Number Three, Miss Crawford's Dam, is finished, and the branch canal from it to the main canal will be completed in two days. I do not believe that this dam is going to be an absolute necessity to us now. I think that we are going to have all the water from Deep Creek and Indian Creek that we need. But Dam Number Three makes us more than confident. And when later you want to extend your area of irrigated acreage you will want it.

"I have examined the country about the spring which Miss Crawford discovered, and have men working there now boring wells. There is water there—how much I do not yet know. I have a hope, which Tommy Garton thinks foolish, that we may strike artesian water out there in the sand. At any rate, we'll get enough out of it eventually to aid in the irrigation of that location, to be useful when you get ready to found your second desert town. About Valley City itself I have all the cross-ditches required by your contract with Colton Gray of the P. C. & W."

He paused, and Mr. Crawford after a moment's thoughtful silence said, quietly:

"In other words, Mr. Conniston, you have completed all of the work which the contract calls for?"

"Except one thing." Conniston smiled. "I have not put the water on the land yet. A rather important matter, isn't it?"

"But you are ready to do that?"

"I shall be ready to do that to-morrow at noon. And I want you to help me. Will it be possible for you and Miss Crawford to come out to Dam Number One in the morning?"

"You are kind to ask it," Mr. Crawford said, inclining his head. "We shall be glad to come, Mr. Conniston. Is that the extent of your report?"

"Yes. I have something else I want to say to you—but it is not about reclamation."

"Shall I make my report to you first? For I feel that after all you have done for me I should like to report, too. Every one of my cattle-ranges is mortgaged to the hilt. I do not believe that I could raise another thousand dollars on the combined ranges. I have been driven so close to the wall that I could not go another step. I have been forced to sell during the last two weeks over a thousand of my young cattle—to sell them at a sacrifice in order to obtain ready money. I have enough money in the bank to conclude the financing of our reclamation project. After the first day of October, when the P. C. & W. begins its road out to us, I can raise whatever more funds I want, and raise them easily.

"You have succeeded, Mr. Conniston, and thereby you have saved me from being absolutely, unqualifiedly ruined. Within six months I shall have doubled my fortune. And I shall have lived to see the most cherished dream of my older manhood materialize. I owe very much to you, I am very grateful to you, and I am very proud to have been associated in business with a man of your caliber. And there is my hand on it!"

"I am glad to have been of service," Conniston replied, as the two men gripped hands. "And I appreciate your confidence. Besides," with a quick, half-serious smile, "I think that I have profited as greatly as any one else could possibly do."

"I know what you mean. And I agree with you. Now, you said that there was another matter—"

"Yes. I have had a cable from my father in Paris. Because I could not agree to do a certain thing which he requested he has seen fit to disinherit me."

"I know. Tommy Garton told me about it. And I know what the thing was which he required of you. I did not thank you for your answer to him, Conniston, for we both know that you did only your duty. But I know what it meant, I know what your stand cost you, and I am prouder to have known you, to feel that outside of our business relations I can say that William Conniston, Junior, is my friend, than I have ever been in my life to have known any other man!"

His voice was deep with sincerity, alive with an intensity of feeling which drove a warm flush into Conniston's tanned face.

"As you say, I did only what a man must do were he not a scoundrel. But, too, as you say, it means a great deal. It means that when you will have paid me my wages I shall have not another cent in the world. And being virtually penniless, still my chief purpose in coming to you this evening has been to tell you that I love Argyl, and that I want your consent to ask her to marry me."

For a moment the older man made no reply. For a little he drew thoughtfully at his cigar, and as in its glow his grave face was thrown into relief Conniston saw that there was a sad droop at the corners of the firm mouth.

"You have told Argyl?" he finally said.

"Yes. I told her that day in the desert. I had meant to wait until the work was done, until she could have seen that I was honestly trying to live down my utter uselessness. But—I told her then."

"And she?"

"She said that I might speak to you."

"I am selfish, Conniston—selfish. Argyl has been daughter to me and son, and the best friend I have ever had. I shall miss her. But if she loves you—Well," with a gentle smile, "she is too true a woman to hold back from your side, no matter what I might say. And since she must leave me some day, I am very glad that you came into her life. I congratulate you, my boy."

While the two men were talking and waiting for Argyl to come in, Tommy Garton, his new legs discarded for the day, was lying on his cot in the back room of the general office, blowing idle puffs of cigarette-smoke at the lamp-chimney, watching the smoke as the hot draft from the flame sent it ceilingward. He was thinking of the talk he had had with Conniston, how Conniston had gone to Argyl's father.

"After all," he grunted to himself, as he pinched out his cigarette and lighted another, "they were made for each other. And I lose my one chief bet this incarnation. Hello! Come in!" For there had come a sudden sharp knocking at the outer door.

The door was pushed open and a big man, dusty from riding, came slowly into the front room, cast a quick glance about him, and came on into Garton's room. Garton started as he saw who the man was.

"Hello, Wallace!" he said, sitting up and putting out his hand. "What in the world brings you here?"

Wallace laughed, returned the greeting, and sat down upon the cot across the room. And as he came into the circle of light thrown out by the lamp a nickeled star shone for a moment from under his coat, which was carelessly flung back.

"Jest rampsin' around, Tommy," he answered, quietly, making himself a cigarette. "Jest seein' what I could see. You fellers keepin' pretty busy, ain't you?"

"Yes. Too busy to get into trouble, Bill." He lay back and sent a new cloud of smoke to soar aloft over the lamp-chimney. "We haven't had a visit from a sheriff for six months."

"Oh, I know you been bein' good, all right. If everybody was like you fellers I'd have one lovely, smooth job. Goin' to make a go of this thing, ain't you, Tommy?"

"You bet we are!" cried Garton, enthusiastically. "There's nothing can stop us now. I expect," with a sharp look at the sheriff, "Swinnerton is feeling a bit shaky of late?"

"Couldn't say," replied Wallace, slowly. "Ain't seen Oliver for a coon's age."

They talked casually of many things, and Tommy Garton, to whom the sheriff's explanation of the reason for his visit to the Valley was no explanation whatever, sat back against the wall, his head lost in the shadow cast by a coat hanging at the side of the window and between him and the lamp, a frown in his eyes.

"Any time big Bill Wallace drifts this far from his stamping-ground just to look at a ditch I'm dreaming the whole thing," he told himself, as his eyes never left the sheriff's face. "And as for not having seen Swinnerton, that's a lie."

Tommy Garton was already scenting something very near the actual truth when the telephone in the front room jangled noisily.

"Want me to answer it?" Wallace was already on his feet.

"Thanks," Garton told him. "But I've got it fixed so that I can handle it from here."

He picked up the telephone which was attached to the office instrument and which he kept on the floor at his bedside. And as he caught the first word he pressed the receiver close to his ear so that no sound from it might escape and reach his alert visitor.

It was the Lark's voice, tense, earnest, trembling with the import of the Lark's message.

"That you, Con? Garton? Conniston there? No? Tell him for me to keep under cover. Lonesome Pete has jest rode into camp, an' he's seen that canary of his, an' she's been blowin' off to him. Hapgood's thicker'n thieves with Swinnerton. He's put him up to this. Swinnerton has sent the sheriff after Con. He's to jug him for killin' that Chink! Get me? Jest to hold him in the can so's he can't work until after October first. Get me, 'bo? You'll put Con wise? Wallace ought to be there any minute—"

Garton answered as quietly as he could:

"All right. I'll attend to everything. Good-by." And then, setting the telephone back upon the floor, he took a fresh cigarette from his case, lighted it over the lamp, his face showing calm and unconcerned, and, leaning back, began to think swiftly.

Conniston was now with the Crawfords. Presently he would leave them and return to the office to spend the night with Garton. Bill Wallace evidently knew this, and was content to wait quietly until his man came. Lonesome Pete had done his part, had ridden with all possible speed to Deep Creek, where he had supposed Conniston was. The Lark had done his part. The rest was up to Tommy Garton. For he knew that with Conniston left to continue his work the work would be done. He knew that Conniston had every detail now at his fingers' ends. He knew that if Swinnerton could succeed in this coup he might be able to put some further unexpected, some fatal obstacle in the way of the Great Work. And that then, with Conniston out of it, it again would be "anybody's game."

Wallace was talking again about unimportant nothings, Garton was answering him in monosyllables and striving to see the way, to find out the thing which he must do. It was plain that Conniston must be prevented from coming to the office to-night. And when he saw the way before him he asked, carelessly:

"You'll stay with me to-night, Bill?"

"If you got the room, Tommy." He glanced about the little room. "This bed ain't workin'?"

"Conniston, our superintendent, will sleep there to-night. He'll be in in an hour or so. But I've got blankets, and if you care to make a bed on the floor, there's lots of room."

"I'll do it," laughed the sheriff, stretching his great legs far out in front of him. "It'll do me good. I been sleepin' in a bed so many nights runnin' lately I'll be gettin' soft."

"All right. And if you'll pardon me a minute I want to telephone my assistant. I've just got word of some work which must be ready by morning. Not much rest on this job, Bill."

He picked up the telephone again and called Billy Jordan.

"I wish you'd run around for a minute, Billy," he said, his tone evincing none of the tremor which he felt in his heart. "Bring the fifth and seventh sheets of those computations you took home with you. Yes, the figures for the work we are to do at the spring. Yes, you'd better hurry with them, as I want to look 'em over before morning. There's a ball-up somewhere. So long, Billy."

He had seen that Bill Wallace, whose business it was to be suspicious at all times and of all men, had regarded him with narrowed, shrewd eyes.

When Billy Jordan came in, ten minutes later, in no way surprised at the summons, since he had been called on similar errands many times, he found Bill Wallace telling a story and Tommy Garton chuckling appreciatively.

"You know each other?" Garton asked. "Wallace says he's just over here to look around at the beauties of nature, Billy. I've an idea," with a wink at Wallace, "that he's looking for somebody. You haven't been passing any bad money, have you, Billy? Much obliged for the papers." He glanced at them and pushed them under the pillows of his cot. "That's all now, Billy. Except that on your way home I want you to drop in and see Mr. Crawford. Tell him that if he sees Conniston I want him to tell him to be sure and come right around. There's a ball-up in the work out at the spring. Wait a second." He scribbled a note upon the leaf of the note-book which lay upon the window-sill. "Give that to Mr. Crawford. It's an order to Mundy to cut the main ditch out there down to four feet, and to stop work on the well that is causing trouble, until further orders. Mundy will be going out again to-night, and will stop at Crawford's first. Good night, Billy. And come in early in the morning."

Mundy's name did not appear in the note. Mundy was at the time twenty miles from Valley City. But Mr. Crawford's name was there, and after it was "*Urgent*," underlined. The note itself ran:

"*Wallace is here to arrest Conniston for murder of Chinaman shot in whisky rebellion! A put-up game with Swinnerton to stop his work. Tell Conniston to go back to Deep Creek to-night. Send Brayley to me immediately. Let no one else come. I'll entertain the sheriff to-night.*

"GARTON."

Billy loitered a minute, yawned two or three times, and finally said good night and strolled leisurely away.

"I think," said Wallace, rising as the door closed behind Billy Jordan, "I'll go out an' unsaddle my cayuse. Got a handful of hay in the shed, Tommy?"

"Sure thing, Bill. Help yourself."

Wallace picked up his hat and turned to the door. Garton rolled over suddenly, thrust his hand again under his pillow, and sat up.

"Say, Bill!" he called, softly.

Wallace turned, and as he did so he looked square into the muzzle of a heavy-caliber Colt revolver upon which the lamplight shone dully.

"Stop that!" cried Garton, sternly, as the sheriff's hand started automatically to his hip. "I've got the drop on you, Bill. And, sheriff or no sheriff, I'll drop you if you make a move. Put 'em up, Bill."

Snarling, his face going a sudden angry red, the sheriff lifted his two big hands high above his head.

"What do you mean by this?" he snapped.

"I mean business! Now you do what I tell you. Walk this way, and walk slowly."

"D—n you, you little sawed-off—" roared the big man, only to be cut short with an incisive:

"Never mind about calling names. And remember that no matter if only half a man is behind this gun it 'll shoot just the same. Keep those hands up, Bill! Now turn around. Back up to me. And let me tell you something: you can whirl about and bring your hands down on my head, but that won't stop a bullet in your belly. The same place," he said, coolly, "that Conniston shot the Chinaman!"

Bill Wallace had got his position as sheriff for two very good reasons. For one thing, he belonged to Oliver Swinnerton. For another, he was a brave man. But he was not a fool, and he did what Garton commanded him to do. And Tommy Garton, with the muzzle of his revolver jammed tight against the small of Wallace's back, reached out with his left hand and drew the sheriff's two revolvers from their holsters, dropping them to the floor behind his cot.

"And now, Bill, you can go and sit down. And you can take your hands down, too."

"I'd like to know," sputtered Wallace, as he sat glaring across the little room at the strange half-figure propped up against the wall and covering him unwaveringly with a revolver, "what all this means!"

"Would you? Then I'll tell you. It means that no little man like Oliver Swinnerton, and no smooth tool belonging to Oliver Swinnerton, is going to keep us from living up to our contract with the P. C. & W. Not if they resort to all of the dirty work their maggot-infested brains can concoct!"

When Brayley came in he found two men smoking cigarettes and sitting in watchful silence. And when Brayley understood conditions fully he took a chair in the doorway, moved his revolver so that it hung from his belt across his lap, and joined them in quiet smoking.

*   *   *   *   *

"To-morrow," Conniston was saying to Argyl, just as Tommy Garton called to Wallace to put his hands up, "we are going to open the gates at Dam Number One, and the water will run down into the main canal and find its way to Valley City. I think we have won, Argyl!"

CHAPTER XXVI

Conniston instantly saw the need of haste, the urgent necessity of acting speedily upon the advice tendered by Tommy Garton in his note.

"Arrest you!" Argyl had cried, indignantly. "Arrest you for being a man and doing your duty!"

"No, Argyl," he told her, a bit anxiously. "Their reasons for causing my arrest now are simply that that man Swinnerton, not knowing when he is beaten, wants me out of the way for a few days. He is ready to spring another bit of his villainy, I suppose. But I do not think that Wallace is going to serve his warrant in a hurry."

They laid their plans swiftly, Mr. Crawford agreeing silently as Conniston outlined the thing to be done. When the horses were ready Conniston walked cautiously to Tommy Garten's window and peered in. And he was grinning contentedly when he returned to Mr. Crawford and his daughter.

"Tommy is the serenest law-breaker you ever saw," he told them, as he swung to his horse after having helped Argyl to a place at her father's side in the buckboard. "It's a cure for the blues to see him sitting there on his cot covering his tame sheriff with a young cannon. There'll be a fine, I

Jackson Gregory

suppose, for interfering with an officer in the pursuit of his duty."

"I think," Mr. Crawford said, quietly, as he sent his horses racing into the night, "that Oliver Swinnerton won't be looking for any more trouble from now on."

Where the road forked, one branch running straight on to Crawfordsville, the other turning off toward Deep Creek, Mr. Crawford took Conniston's horse, and Conniston got into the buckboard. Mr. Crawford was to ride alone to Crawfordsville, see Colton Gray, of the P. C. & W., tell him that the Crawford Reclamation Company had made good its part of the contract, invite him out to Dam Number One to see what was done, and to insist that the P. C. & W. keep to its part of the contract, beginning work immediately upon the railroad into the Valley. Conniston and Argyl were to drive on to the dam, and to open the gates controlling the current to be poured into the big flume.

The darkness had not yet gone, but was lifting, turning a dull gray, when Argyl and Conniston came to the dam. And now the engineer told her of two things which until now he had mentioned to no one save the men whom he had been obliged to call in to do the work for him. From Dam Number One for thirty miles, reaching to Valley City, there were small groups of his men stationed a mile apart. Each group had piled high the dry limbs of trees, scrub brush, and green foliage brought from the mountains. Each group was instructed to watch for the water which was to be turned at last into the ditch and to set fire to its pile of brushwood when the precious stuff came abreast of them. And so, by day or night, there was to be thirty miles of signal fires to proclaim with flame and smoke that the Great Work was no longer a man's dream, but an accomplished, vital thing.

The second thing he explained as Argyl walked with him to the dam across Deep Creek. He showed her the accomplished work, showed her the deep, wide flume, and as they stood upon the dam itself pointed out an intricate set of levers controlling the great gates.

"Argyl," he told her, speaking quietly, but knowing that there was a tremor in his voice which he could not drive from it—"Argyl, do you know how much to-day means to me? Do you know that it is the most gloriously wonderful day I have ever known? Do you know that I have fought hard for this day, and that the hardest fighting I had before me was the fight against Greek Conniston the snob? Do you know that at least I have tried to make a man of myself, even as I have tried to build ditches and dams? You do know it, Argyl? You do know that as hard as I have worked for reclamation I have worked for regeneration! And I have not failed altogether."

His tone was suddenly firm, suddenly stern. He was a man weighing himself and his work, and he was speaking with a voice which rang with simple frankness and deep sincerity.

"There is the work to say that I have not failed utterly. There it is, ditch and dam, to say that I have done a part of the thing I have set my hand to. I am not boasting of it, for what many men could have done I should have been able to do. But I am proud of it. And, Argyl, while I am not a man yet as I would be, not a man full grown as your father is, while I can never hope to be the man your father is, yet I have done what I could to be less of a fop, less of a drone in the world. Do you understand me, Argyl?"

"Yes, Greek." She answered him softly, her face turned up to his, her eyes frankly filled with love and pride for what he had done, what he was. "I understand."

Jackson Gregory

"Then, Argyl Crawford, just so sure as I have done a little thing or a big thing in working the reclamation of this desert, just so certainly have you done a big thing or a little thing in making less barren the waste places in my own soul. Don't you see what you have done, Argyl? It is not I who have done anything; it is you who have done everything. If I am in any way responsible for success to our work, then are you responsible for every bit of it. That dam, that ditch, everything, all of it belongs to you! The success belongs to you!"

"Greek"—she smiled at him through a sudden gathering of tears—"you mustn't say such things—"

"And so," he went on, quietly, "since the whole work has been your work, I want the completion of the work to be yours. Look here, Argyl."

He touched a long, slender lever reaching from the flume to the bank where they stood.

"When the sun comes up it is going to bring a new day for all of us," he continued, slowly. "A new day which, for me, you have made possible. And just as the sun comes up will you put your hand to this lever and press it down?"

She looked up at him quickly. "Oh," she cried, her hand clutching at his arm, her voice quivering, "you mean—"

He laughed happily. "I mean that when you press that lever it will throw open the water-gates. I mean that it will be your hand which turns the first mad current down into the flume. I mean that it will be you, Argyl, who actually sends the first water to reclaim Rattlesnake Valley. Are you glad, Argyl?"

If Argyl was glad, she did not say so. For a moment she

stood with her face in her two hands, sobbing. And then, laughing softly, the tears upon her cheeks catching fire from the first rays of the rising sun, she lifted her face to Greek Conniston's, and, drawing his face down, kissed him.

The new day had leaped out at them, whipping the last shreds of misty darkness from the face of the earth. Down yonder, below them upon the slope of the hills, they saw the Lark and his hundred men preparing for breakfast. Only in the bed of Deep Creek alone, below the dam where a trickle of water ran thread-like, was there any shadow. And suddenly something moving within the breaking darkness there caught Conniston's eye.

It was a man running, running swiftly downstream, running as though pursued by no less terrible a thing than death, stumbling, rising, running again. Something in the man's carriage struck Conniston as familiar, while he could not make out who it was. Then the light grew stronger, rosier, and he cried out in surprise.

"Hapgood!" he exclaimed. "Roger Hapgood!"

And almost before the words had left his lips he cried out in a new tone, a tone of horror, and, seizing Argyl's hand in his, ran with her, crying for her to hurry, urging her to run with him, away from the dam. For his eyes had seen another thing in the creek-bed, a something just at the base of the dam at its lowest side. It was a little sputtering flame, such a flame as is made by a burning bit of fuse.

Hapgood, still running, had climbed up the steep right bank, had run almost into the men's camp, had turned suddenly and dashed back down the bank, to run across the creek and climb the farther side. Conniston and Argyl as they fled from the threatened dam could see him as he clambered upward, could see the loose stones and dirt set sliding, rattling from under his hurrying feet and clawing hands.

Then came the thundering roar of the explosion. The great dam, the citadel of all hopes of success, tottered like a stone wall smitten with a thousand battering-rams, tottered and shook to its foundations. And then, as a dozen explosions merged into one, the whole thing leaped skyward, as though hurled aloft from some Titan's sling, and, leaping, burst asunder, flying in a thousand directions, raining rock and mortar far and wide along the slopes of the mountains. And Conniston, dragging Argyl after him, cried out brokenly. Upon the dam he had toiled for weeks, and now there was no one stone left of it! And the first day of October was but five days off.

"Look!" Argyl was clinging to him wildly, her arm trembling as it pointed. "Look! Oh, God!"

She did not point toward the dam. Her quivering finger found out a moving figure far below it in the creek-bed. It was Hapgood. The explosion which had demolished the work of weary weeks had shaken the ground under his flying feet so that the loose soil no longer held him. He had cried out aloud, had fought and clawed, had even bit with blackened teeth into the steep bank. And it mocked him and slipped away from him and hurled him, bruised and cut, to the bottom of the canon.

Even as Conniston looked the freed waters which had chafed in the great dam leaped forward, a monster river of churning white water and whirling debris, and like a live thing, wrathful, vengeful, was charging downward through the steep ravine. Hapgood had heard. They had seen his white face turned for an instant over his shoulder. And then his shriek rose high above the thunder of waters as he ran from the merciless thing which his own hands had unchained.

They saw his one hope; saw that he, too, had seen it. With the water hurling itself almost upon him, he gained the bank ten feet farther downstream, where the sides were more gently sloping. They saw him climb to a little shelf of rock a yard above the bottom of the creek. They saw his hands thrust out above his head, grasping at the root of a stunted tree. One more second—

But the fates did not grant the one single second. The churning, frothing, angry maelstrom had caught at his legs, whipping them from under him. They heard his shriek again, throbbing with terror, vibrant with a fear which was worse than despair. They saw his face, white and horrible, as he glanced again for a moment at the thing behind him. And then the swirling water leaped up at him, snarling like some mighty beast, and clutched at his throat, at his hands, and flung him like a thing of no weight far down into its own tumultuous bosom. For a moment they saw his arms, then they saw his hands clutching at the foam-flecked face of the water—and then even the hands disappeared.

CHAPTER XXVII

"Who was it?"

It was Mr. Crawford's voice, calm, expressionless. Conniston and Argyl swung about, the horror of the thing which they had seen still widening their eyes, and saw Mr. Crawford, Jimmie Kent, and a man whom Conniston took to be Colton Gray.

"Hapgood," he answered, his eyes going back to the tumult of water sweeping away the hopes of many men.

Mr. Crawford stepped forward and put his hand on Conniston's arm.

"We lose, my boy." His voice was as steady as it had been before, but Conniston saw that his lips quivered despite the iron will set to keep them steady. "And it could not be helped. And Conniston, my boy, my son," his tones ringing out so that all there could hear, "I am proud of you, and proud that I may call you my son!"

"Greek! Poor Greek!" Argyl was clinging to him, everything lost to her but a great pity for him. "Is it to be only defeat, after all?"

"Defeat!"

He whirled about, his clenched fist raised high above his head, his body rigid, his haggard face dead white. "Defeat!" He laughed, and Argyl shivered at the strange tone in his laughter. "Defeat!" he cried a third time. "We have five days!"

He was upon a boulder, standing where all men might see him, might hear him. And his voice as it rang out through the roar of the leaping water was sharp, clear, decisive, confident.

"Here you, Lark! Rush fifty men with crowbars to the Jaws! Make the rest of your men hitch up to their plows and scrapers and rush them to the Jaws as fast as their horses can run! Send me five good men. Pete," as Lonesome Pete's red head surged forward through the crowd of working-men, "come here!"

Pete came, and came running.

"Get on your horse. Kill him getting to Miss Argyl's Dam. Open the gates there and turn the water into the canal. And for God's sake hurry!"

And Lonesome Pete, with one wild yell of understanding, fled. The Lark had swung about, calling upon his men by name, and as he called fifty big, quick-eyed men leaped forward to fall quickly into the sections bossed by the men whose names the Lark was shouting. The dirt and stones had not ceased rolling and rattling down the rocky walls of the canon when fifty men with picks and crowbars were rushing along its banks to the Jaws. And as Greek Conniston hurled his orders at the Lark and the Lark snatched them up, shouting to the men about him, horses were hitched to plows and scrapers and driven, galloping, to the Jaws.

The five men for whom Conniston had called and whom the Lark had selected came to him quickly.

"Get into Mr. Crawford's buckboard," he called, sharply, to two of them. "Drive to Dam Number Two and open the gates there, turning every bit of water you can into the canal! You three men get saddle-horses. You," to one of them, "rush to Crawfordsville and telephone to Tommy Garton. Tell him what has happened. Tell him to send me two hundred men on the run. *On the run*, do you hear? Tell him to tie Bill Wallace up and put two men to watch out for him. Now go! And you two fellows get your horses saddled and bring them here and wait for orders."

He got down from the boulder, and as he did so Mr. Crawford came to his side.

"Do you mean, Greek," he said, anxiously, "that there is a chance yet?"

"A chance? Yes! There is more than a chance! We are going to make a go of it. Listen: Truxton put in his foundations here, and I went ahead with the superstructure for the simple reason that here is a perfect dam-site, here are solid rock walls and creek-bed that would hold any concrete structure in the world. And up there at the Jaws you have to contend with shale, full of seams, in places lined with clay. And right there I am going to make a rock-filled dam, and make it fast! It's going to be a temporary job and a makeshift, but it's going to sling the water into a flume that will carry it back into the old cut and down into the Valley. And it will do until Mr. Colton Gray and his people are satisfied."

The man who had accompanied Mr. Crawford and Jimmie Kent from Crawfordsville came forward and put out his hand.

"Mr. Conniston," he said, quickly, "I am Colton Gray. And I am already satisfied. If my influence is worth anything the P. C. & W. is going to stand by its old contract. And I believe that when I tell the P. C. & W. what I know they will complete what you have done and inform Mr. Oliver Swinnerton that they can have no further dealings whatever with a criminal of his type."

Conniston shook hands with him warmly.

"Thank you. But you are going to have no points to strain. We are going to have water, plenty of water, in Rattlesnake Valley before the first day of October."

Conniston left them and ran to join his men at the Jaws. Never had he heard of a dam to match the one he saw growing under his eyes. There was no time for scientific perfection of work; here and now was only a crying need for an obstruction, any kind of an obstruction which would withstand the great and growing pressure of water, which would drive it up to the banks, which would turn it into the flume which was being made for it even as the dam grew. Trees were lopped down, great, tall pines, their branches shorn off with flashing ax-blades, the trunks cut into logs upon which many men laid hold.

In the bed of the creek between the Jaws the logs were laid as one lays logs to build him a log house. Sand and gravel and rock went rattling and hissing into the log-surrounded spaces, piled high and higher, with the water backing angrily up against it. Boulders were rolled down from the mountain-side, hurled into the bottom of the canon by blasts of giant powder and dynamite, gripped with rapidly adjusted log-chains, and dragged to their places by straining horses.

Steadily the dam rose, and steadily the muddy water crept

up with it. Men toiled in the bed of the stream with the foaming, coffee-colored water washing about their hips, seething as it climbed up to their great, hairy, panting chests. With no thought of finishing the breakfast which they had barely begun, they worked upon the banks with sweaty, hot bodies and calm, cool minds. Stripped to their waists, almost naked many of them, black with dirt and running sweat, they strained and strove against the rising stream. The morning died, noon came, and Conniston had a dozen men distribute sandwiches and hot coffee. The afternoon wore on and brought with it the men whom Tommy Garton had sent.

Then Conniston called to every man of the hundred who had toiled for him since sunrise to drop his tools. In their places he put a hundred new men. And again the work went on in great strides, and the strange dam rose swiftly. The other men whom Garton had sent, Brayley with them, he put to work to begin the restoration of the broken dam, that the thing which the hapless Hapgood had torn down might be ready against the time of need after the first of October. For he could find no place for more than a hundred men working between the Jaws and upon the banks above them.

* * * * *

Night had come down upon the mountain-slopes. Argyl and Conniston were standing by a sinking camp-fire talking quietly. Lonesome Pete, returned from his errand, had gone into the grove at the edge of which their fire burned for fresh fuel. There came to them through the silence the clatter of hoofs; the vague, shadowy form of horse and rider rose against the sky-line, and Jocelyn Truxton threw herself to the ground. Moaning hysterically, she ran to Argyl!

"Argyl, Argyl," she cried, stopping abruptly, her two hands pressed to her breast, "I am so wretched! I don't deserve to live! I have been so mean, so little—" She broke off into passionate weeping.

Argyl went swiftly to her, putting her arms about the girl's shaking shoulders.

"Jocelyn, dear," she said, softly. "Don't!"

"I have been wicked, wicked!" Jocelyn was sobbing. "They told me what has happened—about the dam—about Roger Hapgood!" She broke off, shuddering.

"But," Argyl was saying, trying to soothe her, "that is not your fault, Jocelyn."

"Oh!" cried Jocelyn, wildly. "You don't know. It was I, I who suggested the horrible thing to Roger Hapgood. It is I who am to blame for everything."

"Hush, child! You have been a naughty little girl, that is all. You didn't know what it was that you were doing—and you are not a bit to blame!"

"And—and—and I have been such a little fool! I have just been a vain, conceited little fool. And I hated you—because I knew all the time that you were prettier than I am. And—and I was ashamed of Pete, and I made fun of him—and now he has gone away and—and I love him. I don't care if he has got red hair and can't read! I love him—so there!"

Lonesome Pete, coming back with his armful of firewood, dropped it, and for a moment stood staring from one to another, his mouth wide open. And then, forgetful of Conniston, pushing Argyl away as he came forward, he took Jocelyn's quivering form into his arms and drew her close to him.

"Miss Jocelyn," he cried, suddenly, "I ain't goin' away! Don't you think it. An' you ain't to blame for nothin' whatever! You're jest a little girl as has made a slip or two—who in hell ain't, huh?"—with belligerent, flashing eyes—"an' I'll dye my hair any color you say as you like better 'n red!"

*   *   *   *   *

"I am going East to-morrow, Mr. Conniston." Jimmie Kent was speaking, his eyes very keen. "Before I go I'd like to make you a proposition. First, do you know what firm it is I represent? Maybe you have heard of the W. I. R.? That means the Western Improvement and Reclamation Company. The board of directors met the other day in Denver, and against his protest made Mr. Crawford its first vice-president. The company plans on the reclamation of many thousands of square miles of sand and sage-brush in Colorado and Nevada. The company wants a competent engineer to act as general superintendent of all of its operations. Do you want the job? Who am I to offer it to you?" He laughed softly. "Oh, I'm just its president."

*   *   *   *   *

Filled to bursting with hopeful toil, the days ran by. Again it was night, the night before the first day of October. With the desert about them, with the stars low flung in the wide arch of heaven, Argyl and Greek Conniston stood at the edge of a deep canal which ran with water to its level banks. And as they spoke to each other, looking down into the future which belongs to them, contented, confident, eager for the coming of the Great Day, a boy rode up to them upon a shaggy pony and called:

"Mr. Conniston?"

"Yes," Greek answered. "What is it?"

It was a telegram. He read it by the light of the match he had swept across his thigh. Argyl, bending forward, read it with him. It was from New York.

"Mr. WILLIAM CONNISTON, Jr.,

"Superintendent Crawford Reclamation,

"Rattlesnake Valley.

"Good boy! Congratulations. They tell me you win.

"WM. CONNISTON, Sr."

Conniston, the bit of yellow paper crumpled between his fingers, turned to Argyl.

"In the only thing which counts—to the uttermost—do I win, Argyl dear?"

And Argyl, lifting her eyes to him frankly, proudly, held out her hands.

THE END

Choose from Thousands of 1stWorldLibrary Classics By

A. M. Barnard	Booth Tarkington	Edward Everett Hale
Ada Leverson	Boyd Cable	Edward J. O'Biren
Adolphus William Ward	Bram Stoker	Edward S. Ellis
Aesop	C. Collodi	Edwin L. Arnold
Agatha Christie	C. E. Orr	Eleanor Atkins
Alexander Aaronsohn	C. M. Ingleby	Eleanor Hallowell Abbott
Alexander Kielland	Carolyn Wells	Eliot Gregory
Alexandre Dumas	Catherine Parr Traill	Elizabeth Gaskell
Alfred Gatty	Charles A. Eastman	Elizabeth McCracken
Alfred Ollivant	Charles Amory Beach	Elizabeth Von Arnim
Alice Duer Miller	Charles Dickens	Ellem Key
Alice Turner Curtis	Charles Dudley Warner	Emerson Hough
Alice Dunbar	Charles Farrar Browne	Emilie F. Carlen
Allen Chapman	Charles Ives	Emily Bronte
Alleyne Ireland	Charles Kingsley	Emily Dickinson
Ambrose Bierce	Charles Klein	Enid Bagnold
Amelia E. Barr	Charles Hanson Towne	Enilor Macartney Lane
Amory H. Bradford	Charles Lathrop Pack	Erasmus W. Jones
Andrew Lang	Charles Romyn Dake	Ernie Howard Pie
Andrew McFarland Davis	Charles Whibley	Ethel May Dell
Andy Adams	Charles Willing Beale	Ethel Turner
Angela Brazil	Charlotte M. Braeme	Ethel Watts Mumford
Anna Alice Chapin	Charlotte M. Yonge	Eugene Sue
Anna Sewell	Charlotte Perkins Stetson	Eugenie Foa
Annie Besant	Clair W. Hayes	Eugene Wood
Annie Hamilton Donnell	Clarence Day Jr.	Eustace Hale Ball
Annie Payson Call	Clarence E. Mulford	Evelyn Everett-green
Annie Roe Carr	Clemence Housman	Everard Cotes
Annonaymous	Confucius	F. H. Cheley
Anton Chekhov	Coningsby Dawson	F. J. Cross
Archibald Lee Fletcher	Cornelis DeWitt Wilcox	F. Marion Crawford
Arnold Bennett	Cyril Burleigh	Fannie E. Newberry
Arthur C. Benson	D. H. Lawrence	Federick Austin Ogg
Arthur Conan Doyle	Daniel Defoe	Ferdinand Ossendowski
Arthur M. Winfield	David Garnett	Fergus Hume
Arthur Ransome	Dinah Craik	Florence A. Kilpatrick
Arthur Schnitzler	Don Carlos Janes	Fremont B. Deering
Arthur Train	Donald Keyhoe	Francis Bacon
Atticus	Dorothy Kilner	Francis Darwin
B.H. Baden-Powell	Dougan Clark	Frances Hodgson Burnett
B. M. Bower	Douglas Fairbanks	Frances Parkinson Keyes
B. C. Chatterjee	E. Nesbit	Frank Gee Patchin
Baroness Emmuska Orczy	E. P. Roe	Frank Harris
Baroness Orczy	E. Phillips Oppenheim	Frank Jewett Mather
Basil King	E. S. Brooks	Frank L. Packard
Bayard Taylor	Earl Barnes	Frank V. Webster
Ben Macomber	Edgar Rice Burroughs	Frederic Stewart Isham
Bertha Muzzy Bower	Edith Van Dyne	Frederick Trevor Hill
Bjornstjerne Bjornson	Edith Wharton	Frederick Winslow Taylor

Friedrich Kerst
Friedrich Nietzsche
Fyodor Dostoyevsky
G.A. Henty
G.K. Chesterton
Gabrielle E. Jackson
Garrett P. Serviss
Gaston Leroux
George A. Warren
George Ade
Geroge Bernard Shaw
George Cary Eggleston
George Durston
George Ebers
George Eliot
George Gissing
George MacDonald
George Meredith
George Orwell
George Sylvester Viereck
George Tucker
George W. Cable
George Wharton James
Gertrude Atherton
Gordon Casserly
Grace E. King
Grace Gallatin
Grace Greenwood
Grant Allen
Guillermo A. Sherwell
Gulielma Zollinger
Gustav Flaubert
H. A. Cody
H. B. Irving
H.C. Bailey
H. G. Wells
H. H. Munro
H. Irving Hancock
H. R. Naylor
H. Rider Haggard
H. W. C. Davis
Haldeman Julius
Hall Caine
Hamilton Wright Mabie
Hans Christian Andersen
Harold Avery
Harold McGrath
Harriet Beecher Stowe
Harry Castlemon
Harry Coghill
Harry Houidini

Hayden Carruth
Helent Hunt Jackson
Helen Nicolay
Hendrik Conscience
Hendy David Thoreau
Henri Barbusse
Henrik Ibsen
Henry Adams
Henry Ford
Henry Frost
Henry James
Henry Jones Ford
Henry Seton Merriman
Henry W Longfellow
Herbert A. Giles
Herbert Carter
Herbert N. Casson
Herman Hesse
Hildegard G. Frey
Homer
Honore De Balzac
Horace B. Day
Horace Walpole
Horatio Alger Jr.
Howard Pyle
Howard R. Garis
Hugh Lofting
Hugh Walpole
Humphry Ward
Ian Maclaren
Inez Haynes Gillmore
Irving Bacheller
Isabel Cecilia Williams
Isabel Hornibrook
Israel Abrahams
Ivan Turgenev
J.G.Austin
J. Henri Fabre
J. M. Barrie
J. M. Walsh
J. Macdonald Oxley
J. R. Miller
J. S. Fletcher
J. S. Knowles
J. Storer Clouston
J. W. Duffield
Jack London
Jacob Abbott
James Allen
James Andrews
James Baldwin

James Branch Cabell
James DeMille
James Joyce
James Lane Allen
James Lane Allen
James Oliver Curwood
James Oppenheim
James Otis
James R. Driscoll
Jane Abbott
Jane Austen
Jane L. Stewart
Janet Aldridge
Jens Peter Jacobsen
Jerome K. Jerome
Jessie Graham Flower
John Buchan
John Burroughs
John Cournos
John F. Kennedy
John Gay
John Glasworthy
John Habberton
John Joy Bell
John Kendrick Bangs
John Milton
John Philip Sousa
John Taintor Foote
Jonas Lauritz Idemil Lie
Jonathan Swift
Joseph A. Altsheler
Joseph Carey
Joseph Conrad
Joseph E. Badger Jr
Joseph Hergesheimer
Joseph Jacobs
Jules Vernes
Julian Hawthrone
Julie A Lippmann
Justin Huntly McCarthy
Kakuzo Okakura
Karle Wilson Baker
Kate Chopin
Kenneth Grahame
Kenneth McGaffey
Kate Langley Bosher
Kate Langley Bosher
Katherine Cecil Thurston
Katherine Stokes
L. A. Abbot
L. T. Meade

L. Frank Baum
Latta Griswold
Laura Dent Crane
Laura Lee Hope
Laurence Housman
Lawrence Beasley
Leo Tolstoy
Leonid Andreyev
Lewis Carroll
Lewis Sperry Chafer
Lilian Bell
Lloyd Osbourne
Louis Hughes
Louis Joseph Vance
Louis Tracy
Louisa May Alcott
Lucy Fitch Perkins
Lucy Maud Montgomery
Luther Benson
Lydia Miller Middleton
Lyndon Orr
M. Corvus
M. H. Adams
Margaret E. Sangster
Margret Howth
Margaret Vandercook
Margaret W. Hungerford
Margret Penrose
Maria Edgeworth
Maria Thompson Daviess
Mariano Azuela
Marion Polk Angellotti
Mark Overton
Mark Twain
Mary Austin
Mary Catherine Crowley
Mary Cole
Mary Hastings Bradley
Mary Roberts Rinehart
Mary Rowlandson
M. Wollstonecraft Shelley
Maud Lindsay
Max Beerbohm
Myra Kelly
Nathaniel Hawthrone
Nicolo Machiavelli
O. F. Walton
Oscar Wilde

Owen Johnson
P.G. Wodehouse
Paul and Mabel Thorne
Paul G. Tomlinson
Paul Severing
Percy Brebner
Percy Keese Fitzhugh
Peter B. Kyne
Plato
Quincy Allen
R. Derby Holmes
R. L. Stevenson
R. S. Ball
Rabindranath Tagore
Rahul Alvares
Ralph Bonehill
Ralph Henry Barbour
Ralph Victor
Ralph Waldo Emmerson
Rene Descartes
Ray Cummings
Rex Beach
Rex E. Beach
Richard Harding Davis
Richard Jefferies
Richard Le Gallienne
Robert Barr
Robert Frost
Robert Gordon Anderson
Robert L. Drake
Robert Lansing
Robert Lynd
Robert Michael Ballantyne
Robert W. Chambers
Rosa Nouchette Carey
Rudyard Kipling
Saint Augustine
Samuel B. Allison
Samuel Hopkins Adams
Sarah Bernhardt
Sarah C. Hallowell
Selma Lagerlof
Sherwood Anderson
Sigmund Freud
Standish O'Grady
Stanley Weyman
Stella Benson
Stella M. Francis

Stephen Crane
Stewart Edward White
Stijn Streuvels
Swami Abhedananda
Swami Parmananda
T. S. Ackland
T. S. Arthur
The Princess Der Ling
Thomas A. Janvier
Thomas A Kempis
Thomas Anderton
Thomas Bailey Aldrich
Thomas Bulfinch
Thomas De Quincey
Thomas Dixon
Thomas H. Huxley
Thomas Hardy
Thomas More
Thornton W. Burgess
U. S. Grant
Upton Sinclair
Valentine Williams
Various Authors
Vaughan Kester
Victor Appleton
Victor G. Durham
Victoria Cross
Virginia Woolf
Wadsworth Camp
Walter Camp
Walter Scott
Washington Irving
Wilbur Lawton
Wilkie Collins
Willa Cather
Willard F. Baker
William Dean Howells
William le Queux
W. Makepeace Thackeray
William W. Walter
William Shakespeare
Winston Churchill
Yei Theodora Ozaki
Yogi Ramacharaka
Young E. Allison
Zane Grey